UNRAVELING

UNRAVELING

KAREN LORD

DAW BOOKS, INC.

DONALD A. WOLLHEIM, FOUNDER

1745 Broadway, New York, NY 10019

ELIZABETH R. WOLLHEIM

SHEILA E. GILBERT

PUBLISHERS

www.dawbooks.com

First Printing, June 2019
1 2 3 4 5 6 7 8 9

DAW TRADEMARK REGISTERED
U.S. PAT. AND TM. OFF. AND FOREIGN COUNTRIES
—MARCA REGISTRADA
HECHO EN U.S.A.

PRINTED IN THE U.S.A.

For all who seek redemption.

BOOK I

NIGHTMARE

CHAPTER ONE

A chorus of tree frogs trilled in the damp, velvet darkness, wide awake and relentless as they spoke their authority over the nocturnal world. The village of Makendha slowly marked the hours to midnight with a quieting of laughter and argument, a dimming and darkening, and a staccato punctuation of ending sounds—the shutting of doors, the dropping of shoes, and the weighty hush of a house empty of talk but filled with dreaming.

One house kept vigil with a single glowing window. Behind the curtains of pale ivory gauze, gilded by the light of an oil lamp, an age-old scene was unfolding: a mother of the village sitting at the kitchen table, interrogating her adult son about his life, his loves, and his future. Because the mother was Paama, a woman known for quiet strength and infinite patience, the conversation was calm and loving rather than sharp and resentful. Because the son was Yao, also known as Chance, one of the undying who had become human more by accident than design, questions that involved love and the future were difficult to answer. Such is the lot of mortals who birth myth and legend in the midst of the mundane.

"At last you come to visit your old mother." Strong, patient, but not at all above a little emotional manipulation.

Chance, occasionally called Yao, smiled fondly. "I have been busy. You know that, Maa."

"Your trickster brother is the wanderer, not you. Why so vague about what you are doing? Who is she, this woman that you are working for?"

"I don't keep secrets from you, Maa; you know that. But sometimes things are simply incomplete."

She studied him in the lamplight. "I will try to understand. I know you have always been unique."

"Unique? You had two of us," Chance reminded her teasingly. "Two undying ones turned human for the privilege of being your sons."

Paama shook her head. "Silly boy. I would have to be very old and dotish to forget what your brother is, but you . . . you are something beyond even him."

A mother always knows her child. Chance did not dwell on those times when he had been a capricious otherworldly creature rather than a dutiful human son. And yet . . . there were days when he remembered as vividly as nightmare the moment when Patience, his elder and superior and as much a mother as an undying one could be, took him and unraveled his essence, all but unmaking him to make him human. Growing up Paama's son had been a long, slow awakening from near oblivion to deep self-knowledge. With Paama as his

mother and the Trickster as his brother, mortal life was not
hard—it was even sweet. And yet it felt like it wasn't enough.

Sometimes things are incomplete.

*The beginning of one person's tale may be for another a mid-
dle . . . or an end.*

*All these finished and unfinished tales, with neither krik nor krak
to bookend them, make a story and, more than a story, a history.*

Paama took up the teapot, poured for herself, and offered
with a gesture to refresh his half-full, cooling cup. He answered with a shake of the head and his hand over the rim. "I
must stay awake. I have somewhere to be later tonight."

"Vague again," his mother chided. "Don't act as if I don't
know you. Give me something. A name."

Chance pondered. He knew that his mother worried about
him, perhaps even more than she worried about his brother,
although she would never say so. She had the same concerns
as other ordinary parents. Was he happy? Was he prospering?
Was there someone to take care of him when she was gone?

"A name?" he mused. "Very well. Her name is Miranda."

It was three in the afternoon at the Crossing Bar, a watering
hole famed for its proximity to the Courts of Justice, and
Miranda Ecouvo was discovering, to her deep dismay, that
the day was not improving.

"Murder by numbers," said Khabir Lucknor, her boss.

"Playing doctor," countered Fernando Cavel, her colleague.

"Reverse hangman," Khabir riposted cheerfully.

They looked at her with anticipation, waiting for her to add to the game. She gave a blank stare in reply and drained her drink. Bad enough to be depressed without dealing with their dubious, macabre humor as well.

"Well," said Fernando, huffing the word out on a big breath to break the tense silence. "We all have our ways of dealing with the stress. Bartender? Another one of these right here." He leaned over, his body one long, skinny curve sheltering a neat arrangement of empty shot glasses, and waved a finger to get the man's attention.

"Smoke?" Khabir said hopefully, but Miranda stayed silent. "Another drink?" He was the opposite of Fernando—not fat, but slightly rounded with affluence. He had no favorite drink but kept to a varied range of mood-altering chemicals, used in moderation. He was the consummate professional. In time Fernando would match up to him.

"No," she said at last. "I should go."

Four hundred meters of twisting alleys and uneven cobblestones led from the Courts of Justice to that convenient drinking stop. Eight hundred and forty of straight avenue, broad sidewalks, and level flagstones went from there to Lucknor & Associates. It was an easy route for most. City professionals of a certain age learned how to be drunk at four in the afternoon and not look it. Miranda still lacked that skill, so she kept her head down and her steps brisk, hoping that would carry her the distance without mishap. She got safely to the main door of Lucknor & Associates, safely inside, and safely, if not steadily, up the curving stairs. Her steps slowed, but she kept her face stern and made it past the receptionist with only a nod. Once inside her office, she stumbled slightly while trying to reach for her chair but managed to sit with dignified grace. She took off her shoes, put her feet on her desk, and drank two cups of sweet lemongrass tea from her flask. Near her heels, near enough for her to kick if she merely straightened a knee, her briefcase lay where she had thrown it. She looked at it with increasing disgust as sobriety slowly returned.

She picked up the phone, dialed, and waited.

"Hello, Miranda. It's a little busy here." The words were rushed, distracted. In the background, a recorded voice spoke in a charming professional lilt. "Like many ancient walled settlements on the continental coast, the City has a history that dates back to—"

"I wish *I* were an ancient walled settlement," Miranda said. "All that bombardment and danger in the past, nothing but serene meditation in the present, and only a little crumbling at the edges to look forward to in the future."

"Are you drunk?" the live voice asked in a low, suspicious murmur, clearly trying not to be overheard.

"I have been drinking with Fernando and Khabir," Miranda replied with dignified precision. "The case is over."

There was a pause during which Miranda thought she could hear the sound of a long, sympathetic exhalation.

"I'll get home early, put some soup on."

"Thanks, Kieran," Miranda said, trying not to weep at the expected kindness. She swallowed and hung up quickly. Three quick breaths, and she had the composure for another call, this one internal.

"Lucknor here." *His* speech remained unslurred, but then again, he had the experience.

"Khabir?"

"Yes, m'dear?"

"I'm going home." On another day she would have asked.

"Yes," Khabir replied simply. "I believe I am too."

"Call Fernando's wife. He's still drinking at the bar. He shouldn't drive."

"I'll take him home." That was fine. Khabir had a chauffeur, befitting his station as head of the firm.

When the call ended, she sat for a while, gazing blank-faced at the briefcase. She muttered:

"All roads lead to the city at sunrise.
All roads lead from the city at sunset.
And I, who live in the heart of the city,
must suffer teeming days and lonely nights,
surfeited and starved on humanity."

It was terrible how tired she was, how much in need of a good bawling cry she was. And there was still the report to write. She dragged herself up and gathered herself for the day's last bit of professional pretense: the walk home.

The City could be beautiful at twilight, when the sky was still bright with gold and purple but the sea and land were dark and the sounding waves invisible as you went along the boardwalk. But early morning was lovely too, because the sun was still low and golden and kind, and you could lean carefully over the rope railings and look at the old cannons poking out of their recesses, thick-painted against the salt spray, never to fire again. When it was high tide, the waves smacked hard enough that you might have a good excuse for a salt-wet face when you straightened up. That was half the journey, the boardwalk.

The rest was less picturesque and consisted mainly of dodging traffic in the most tangled and congested thoroughfares of the City. Worse, it required alertness, an alertness that Miranda might feign but did not have. She wavered for a moment on the sidewalk, dashed to a central island between two lanes, and waited. It was the usual zoo: big omnibuses; nimbly buzzing scooters steered by risk-embracing students; small, fast cars driven by impatient young men; and large luxury cars with chauffeurs in front and sleek, comfortable bosses in the back. All were departing, as was expected of those who were not Freemen of the City, a privilege that neither wealth nor fame could buy. Miranda felt a wave of unwarranted pride for the accident of birth that had led to her ownership of the little town house overlooking the bay, not quite at the heart of the City but close enough.

A space appeared in the line of traffic. Miranda began to step out, and in that moment she saw something so shocking that a pulse of adrenaline overrode the remaining blur of alcohol, sharpened her awareness and immobilized her completely.

A woman appeared at her left hand. She was wearing the same clothes as Miranda, which was bad enough, and the same face, which was unconscionable. The strange twin smiled at her—a quick, reassuring smile—and then, while Miranda stood frozen in disbelief, she ran deliberately into the path of an oncoming omnibus.

I t was midnight in Makendha, and two figures were in conversation near the well. This was a common enough scene except for the time of night and the nature of the individuals. They were similar enough in size to stand comfortably side by side, but after that all resemblance ended. One mimicked humanity in both attitude and attire, but his ordinary white cotton tunic and trousers, so like a peasant farmer's, contrasted with his fantastical bluish purple skin. The other made no effort to appear human at all, remaining a blur of wings and eyes spinning through a multidimensional topography accessible only to immortals and theoretical physicists.

"We are sure you understand why we called you in to handle this situation," said the angel. "It is the question of the human element in conjunction with the undying element. You are reputed to be an expert."

The undying one, son of Paama, who sometimes allowed himself to be called Chance, looked uncomfortable. "Awkward. Very awkward. I would prefer if you dealt with it at your level, but I suppose you have your reasons."

"Yes," said the angel. "We do."

It could have been a rebuke, a reassurance, or simply a mild joke. It was not only the tone that was ambiguous; the double meaning inherent in the angelic plural added another layer of intent and interpretation. Chance found that some angels, particularly those who were closer to the human world, accepted the limits of communication and enjoyed being inscrutable. Still, being inscrutable to *him*, given his far greater capacity for understanding, was something of a nose tweak.

"Uriel will take over from us," the angel continued. "It is their department, after all. Furthermore, they are a little easier on mortal eyes. And—just a warning—watch out for the Other Side. They are unusually invested in this. We think they are intrigued."

A rare expression of worry crossed Chance's face. "You do not expect me to—"

"No, not at all. Only be aware. Be careful. It can be hard to tell us apart. You know what it can be like among the undying ones. We are not so different from you."

Chance gave them a disbelieving look.

"It is only a difference in scope," the angel explained.

They flashed, fluttered, and vanished abruptly, having said all that was needed. Chance raised his eyebrows in instinctive surprise. Farewells were such a human habit, but one to which he had grown too accustomed. He shook off his feeling of foreboding and concentrated on the details of his duty, a trick that required him to focus all of his attention on a point in the present so that the probabilities would emerge clearly. What he saw made him smile. He understood why the angel had been so teasingly secretive.

"Is it that sort of time already?" he mused, the human idiom rolling off the tip of his tongue as easily as a line from childhood memory or a phrase from a future assured.

He knew where to go; the old sense of duty was like a

compass, taking him to the opportune point in the paisley-patterned tapestry of space and time, avoiding that straight thread that was his human life. The City was his destination, a place well known to him in its incarnations as war fortress, pirate refuge, and living museum. He emerged beside an intersection that was tangled in a writhing snarl of human and mechanical travel trails. No one noted him, but he was alert, searching for a figure that would be so familiar.

There she was! *Miranda!*

CHAPTER TWO

Chance lacked any tendency toward volatile emotion in his present frame, but there was enough in him to feel as if his breath should catch or his heart should skip. He shook off the somatic memory and moved forward, keeping his eyes fixed on her as she stood waiting at the crossing, her shoulders tense with the weight of her briefcase and other matters, her head moving stiffly as she glanced nervously from left to right to assess the traffic.

Best to stay unseen, grab her, and take her away; there would be time for explanations afterward. He stood behind her, prepared to gently encircle her—

Her head snapped around in shock; not his fault, he had not even touched her yet. Someone had come up beside them while he had been intent on approaching her, someone whose features gave him a similar shock. He had to choose quickly, and so he seized the one who was in front of him, catching her as she turned away from her double, cowering, closing her eyes and putting her fists over her ears. Chance had no time to see what became of the other. He was too busy tearing open the fabric behind him and dragging them both down into the colorless, half-lit environment of between-worlds. It was a clumsy transition, but he had been too startled for his usual elegance. Instead of screaming, Miranda craned her neck back to look at him with dazed, reproachful confusion as they fell through cloud.

Chance tried his best to look harmless and apologetic. "I'm sorry. I just do as I'm told. This won't hurt at all, but it takes a little time."

Miranda gasped and gave a faint, incredulous whisper. "I know you . . ."

"Of course you do." He smiled, put a finger to his lips, and let her go.

She screamed and fell faster, eddies of mist trailing from her limbs as she snatched and kicked out. He paused to close the breach, then followed her into daylight, blue sky and green grass. Miranda lay on her back where she had fallen, still winded and wheezing from the sudden impact, but he knew she was unharmed. Nothing could hurt her in this place.

He sat next to her and began to talk quickly. "That was amazing! I've never seen that before. I didn't even know humans *could* do that. *I* can't."

"What?" Miranda replied weakly.

"Being truly, actually beside yourself. That's nearly impossible. Even I can't be two places at the same time. I don't suppose you know how you did it?"

Miranda's expression slowly transformed from bemusement to horror. Very likely, Chance thought with sympathy, she was absorbing the possibility that she had gone mad.

"No!"

"Of course, of course," he said soothingly. "I don't mean to babble, but you see, I was told to pick you up and bring you back, and I didn't expect to see two of you. I hope I got the right one—ah, yes."

He motioned to her right hand, which was gripping the briefcase as if it were her sole anchor to reality.

"There it is. That's what we need."

He got up, extending his hand to her. She cautiously took it and let him help her to her feet.

"You'll probably be more comfortable if you have a name to call me. Chance will do. Naturally you'll have some questions. I'll lead you to the answers, if you'll allow me."

Miranda looked around. They were standing on a hill overlooking a landscape of half-tamed country with irregular fields and woods, and somewhere out of sight there was the sound of water running. There were dragonflies and butterflies about, birds in the sky, and grazing animals in the distance. There was no evidence of roads, buildings, or anything constructed by human hands. Chance had made it a very peaceful setting— purposely so—and he felt a little bit of triumph when he saw her shoulders relax.

"Do I have a choice?" she asked him, her tone whimsical rather than sarcastic. A good sign.

He smiled. "Always."

They walked uphill in silence for a while. Eventually he pointed ahead to a large figure seated beneath a sheltering pavilion. The form appeared human-shaped even to his eyes, but the strangely diminished surroundings betrayed the fact that it was at least four times larger than the norm. A fierce, androgynous beauty marked the nonhuman face that, though strong, showed no emotion, neither joy nor sorrow. The bronze-and-gold skin glowed with near-painful intensity, as did the bright white cloud of hair and the white cloth that wrapped about the waist and poured over a shoulder with a fall that was smoother than silk, heavier than wool. The surrounding air sizzled and shimmered with a variety of colors, the light fracturing and fragmenting against some unseen border and giving the impression of overhanging wings, wings of stained glass come alive.

Chance held Miranda's right hand firmly in case she bolted, but she continued to walk forward, though with a dazed and disbelieving expression. At last the angel turned and looked at her, and she fell to her knees with an inarticulate gasp of terror and awe.

Chance tried to hold her up, distressed at her reaction, and chided the angel. "Can't you be a little gentler, Uriel? She's already had a lot to take in."

Uriel spoke mildly, as if to compensate for their overwhelming appearance. "Stand up, Miranda."

It did not help. Shivering, overcome, Miranda was not even able to look up. Uriel sighed, then gently clasped Miranda's left arm between two huge fingers and a massive thumb. With a gentle tug, they set her on her feet. Miranda briefly grasped one of the fingers as it withdrew and stared in wonder at her hand, tiny like a newborn's wrapped around a parent's finger.

"Your briefcase," said the angel. "Don't let go of it."

The oddly pragmatic request woke Miranda from her

daze, and she looked instead at the brown leather, scratched and worn, that represented her own familiar world in this strange place.

"I . . . I won't," she managed to answer. "But, why—"

The angel interrupted her, anticipating. "You are here because we are detaining a man on the path to immortality."

Miranda shook her head, perplexed, and Chance smiled, understanding her puzzlement. Like a triple echo, the words *have detained* and *will detain* vibrated through the statement.

"All that he is and all that he has done is within that briefcase," Uriel continued.

Miranda understood at last and frowned. "But then why didn't you stop him?" she asked.

"That *was*/is/*will be* your task, and his." Uriel inclined their head to Chance, who bowed in acknowledgment. "We are here only to observe."

"And to impress upon us the seriousness of the task," Chance added dryly.

"And that," agreed Uriel, calm as ever.

"What do I have to do?" Miranda asked. Her expression was somewhere between wonder and worry at the unexpected assignment.

Chance took hold of her hand again—whether to reassure her or himself, he was not sure. "You already know what to do. You've done this many times with your clients, but this time, you'll be the client."

She raised an eyebrow. "You're going to psychoanalyze me?"

"With your help." Then Chance looked at Uriel. "I'll take her down to the mazes. Will you stand watch for us?"

"Always," said the angel.

Chance seized Miranda's other hand. "We could walk, but if you close your eyes for just a moment—that's it. See? Here we are."

"Here" was a wide, green valley containing a number of strange features. There was indeed a maze of high hedges, but there was also a flat, circular labyrinth of red brick on a cream-white limestone base. A deep, moss-green pool was situated to one side, a thicket of twisted trees on the other.

"I know it appears a little confusing," Chance said, "but I thought you'd like to pick out a maze for yourself."

"What's the maze to be used for?" Miranda asked, squinting in the bright, hot light that radiated from all directions.

"To calm your mind, help it to focus . . . that sort of thing."

"Then the pool won't work. I can't swim. And those woods look like a fairy tale gone mad."

Chance gave a small sigh, a slight slump of the shoulders. Miranda must have noticed out of the corner of her eye, because she immediately amended her brisk tone. "But . . . um . . . the red brick thing's very pretty. I like that. And the hedges."

He smiled. "Thanks."

She smiled back and asked, "You made them, didn't you?"

He nodded and gestured out over the valley a second time. "Is that better?"

She looked again and blinked. There was the stone labyrinth, larger, spiraling to the center, and the hedge maze behind it, taller and sprawling. There was no sign of the pool or the thicket. "You . . . you really *did* make them, didn't you."

"I made all of this, actually," Chance said without a hint of a boast.

"Chance . . . what *are* you? You're not an angel."

The inevitable question had come, but that did not make the answering any easier. "No, I'm not one of the beings you refer to as angels. I'm . . . hmm. I suppose you might think of me as an elemental."

"Fire, water, earth, and air?" she listed, tilting her head doubtfully.

"Not quite. More physics, less alchemy."

"Oh, well, if you're going to invoke the gods of quantum—" she started to say with manic cheerfulness.

"Miranda," he interrupted gently, "I made plenty of time for us, but we'll have to begin at some point."

"I talk when I'm nervous," she said, her teeth clenched, almost but not quite controlling a tremor at the corner of her mouth.

"I noticed. Now, walk and talk." He gestured toward the stone labyrinth, courteous but firm.

She approached it with clear trepidation. "How does it work?"

"Step on, start walking, say something," Chance said. He tried to make his tone reassuringly everyday as he sat cross-legged on the grass with his chin propped on his fist and his elbow on his knee.

She sucked in a deep breath, trotted the last few steps to the edge of the labyrinth, and set her foot on the first of the red bricks. Nothing. She glanced at him, and he nodded her on. She brought her other foot forward, saying inanely, "My name is Mir—"

"My name is Dr. Miranda Ecouvo. I'd like to help you."

Chance went with her. He knew his presence would trigger a telltale sense of déjà vu, impossible to avoid when the subject was not so much remembering as reliving an experience. He watched as it affected her; she closed her eyes for a moment and shook her head as if shaking away dizziness.

"No. No nononono more doctors." The woman's thin whisper was more a chant than a stammer, but it had a robotic sound to it that suggested, along with the repetitive, jerky rocking, that something in her mechanism was broken.

"I'm not that kind of doctor," said Miranda.

"You're shivering," noted the woman spitefully.

"It's colder than I'm used to," Miranda replied calmly.

The woman unfolded suddenly from her crouch at the edge of the pool and slid into the water. She swam one quick length with smooth, confident grace while Miranda watched her carefully.

"You have to keep moving," she called out as she reached the other end. Then, without warning, she went straight down, deep underwater. Miranda tugged her goggles over her eyes and slowly immersed herself, keeping a hand on the tiled edge, until she could see her client's slow, acrobatic ballet. They came up for air at the same time.

"Why do you want to help me?" the woman demanded. She was strengthened by the water, her limbs under control once more as she lay back, fanning her hands like fluttering gills and glaring at Miranda. "This city hates foreigners. You should throw me out with the trash like you do all the rest."

"You're not . . . quite like the rest," Miranda said between gasps. "You have something to say, something a jury might like to hear." She clutched the side and pulled off her goggles to see the woman's expression.

"You can't swim," the woman observed. "You're afraid of the water."

"Well, *you're* comfortable in it," Miranda noted.

The woman did a leisurely backstroke to Miranda's side of the pool, ending up with her back to the tiles, her arms along the edge, one hand nearly touching Miranda. She didn't meet Miranda's eyes, and the old tremor echoed briefly in a convulsive twitch of her shoulders.

"So, what kind of doctor are you?"

"The kind that separates memory from nightmare," Miranda replied. Her voice sounded suddenly strange, as if it were being pulled into the emptiness of a wide-open space instead of echoing off the tiles of an indoor pool.

"Good," said Chance, smiling at her, sitting cross-legged in the center of the labyrinth. "I can see you've got the hang of it already."

CHAPTER THREE

"So," said Chance, "I've been going over your case notes, and to be honest, they're a bit depressing."

He had taken the contents of the briefcase and spread the files in a circle around him. Miranda kept standing, still looking somewhat disoriented after revisiting that too-recent memory.

"That's an understatement," she murmured.

"The Mermaid," he began, gently touching a file. "Galina Arnaud. Danil Skalnis. Niko Tsavian. Xandre Lacalle."

His flitting fingers paused over the last file. They both spontaneously observed a moment of silent respect.

"Depressing, but they're very good notes," he continued, lifting his tone to a more cheerful register. "Very thorough, almost intuitive. The intuitive aspect, by the way, is what the other maze is for."

"This maze is memory, so the other must be nightmare," she surmised.

Chance's face screwed up in frustration. He wagged his head from side to side, in the throes of mental pain as he struggled to express his thought. "Not nightmare. It doesn't have to be nightmare. But your mind does have ways of working things out below the surface of your conscious thoughts. Would you like to try it out?"

"I'm a bit scared," she confessed. Her tone was light, and she even smiled, but her eyes looked a little lost.

"Don't worry," he told her. "It's not like you can die here or anything. Not with the angel of the dead watching over you."

"I forgot that's who he was." A half-suppressed shiver made her voice tremble.

The correction rose automatically to his lips. "Not *he. They.* Not singular nor masculine nor feminine, the angels. And *was* is entirely the wrong word to use with an angel, given their sense of time."

"So all that *was/is/will be* really means something? You have a similar sense, don't you? You told me you'd made time for us, and you read all my notes when I was away for only minutes."

He laughed. "I suppose I could claim to have a similar sense if it weren't for the fact that my memory of the future is as poor as my memory of the past. Angels—now, they're at another level. For them, all choices that are made can be seen as clearly as this present moment. I can see what people may choose, but I can't see what people have chosen, are choosing, and will choose."

"I don't understand."

Chance bowed his head and grimaced. For some topics, talking to humans could be as challenging as talking to angels. "It's hard to explain when you can't voice the angelic tense. I see probabilities, not realities. The probability is the 'may choose'; the reality is the choice that only a human can make, the choice that contributes to the shape of creation."

He grew pensive for a moment. "That is why there can be no redemption for angels. They see so clearly, you see, that there's no excuse. But fortunately, there's redemption for humans . . . and even for such as I, who can see so very broadly but not at all clearly."

"You sound sad," she said, both puzzlement and sympathy in her voice.

"I was just thinking . . . time can be wasted even when it doesn't go in only one direction. I still regret the time I wasted when I was . . . when I was learning how to become myself. And speaking of which," he continued, giving her a sharp look, "I've given you a long enough diversion to settle your nerves. Are you ready for the second maze?"

"Not yet," she admitted.

A recent memory of grounding and peace gentled Chance's voice. "Perhaps this will help."

The green grass between them was suddenly empty of folders and papers, and the space was now occupied by two small bowls and a fat, round pot with a steaming spout. He took the pot and poured slowly, trying not to laugh at Miranda's dazed blink, and cheerfully singsonged his mother's traditional chant, a staple of his childhood. "Sit, sit. Take something hot into your belly and relax your legs for a moment."

Miranda obediently sat and accepted a cup from him, her face blankly bemused. She sniffed the steam skeptically and carefully sipped. Chance knew what she was doing. She was verifying the world, testing her senses and welcoming the mundanity of the slight burn of hot liquid, the bitter tingling of ginger grass and spice, and the happy hum of sweet honey. A few seconds passed, and then she sighed and smiled, disarmed of all suspicion. "Delicious."

"Thank you. I blended it myself. It's my mother's favorite." He was expecting the startled look, and she did not disappoint. Even better, she was still smiling. He smiled in answer—not directly at her, which might have been too much, but at the hand holding her already half-emptied cup.

See, I am not so strange after all.

She drank two cups, and Chance one, and after that a few more moments passed in easeful silence. Miranda's eyes were closed, and she did not notice when Chance waved the teapot and cups aside and returned the files to the space between them. When she opened her eyes and saw the change, her face fell.

"Are you ready?" he asked.

"Can I try this one again first?"

Chance shrugged, carefully neutral. "I'll meet you on the outside." It was not quite a lie. He was not yet ready to tell her that he could walk with her without her knowledge, seeing her life, reading her mind.

She started back on the spiral path, silent of chatter at last, just one confused thought riding the surge of déjà vu.

I never did find out that woman's name.

Names.

Names are important.

"You're . . . Karen," Miranda said, looking with wide-eyed anxiety at the two-meter-tall, red-haired, foreign young male. "Karen . . . Michael . . . Mair."

"Yes, that's me, Kieran, your new tenant," he said. His cheerful expression soon faltered under Miranda's silent, intense scrutiny. "Um . . . that's all right, isn't it?"

"One moment," Miranda said. "Please don't go away." She shut the door gently in his face and went quickly back into the living room, where a woman sat before a low table bearing two cups of herbal tea and a sheaf of papers.

"Priya," Miranda began in a tone of reproach. "That was my new tenant at the door."

Priya blinked in surprise at the tone and the information. She opened her mouth to ask the natural question, but Miranda continued, still with that curious note of mild censure.

"In the short time that I spoke to my tenant, I realized a few things. First of all, I admit that the next time I ask you to do me a favor, I should probably be a little more detailed than, 'I'm a busy woman; find me a tenant.' Second, when you told me, 'Your new tenant, Karen, will be coming by this afternoon,' a gendered pronoun might have added some important information to that statement."

"Ohhh," said Priya, finally understanding. She burst out in a howl of laughter.

Miranda sighed, leaned against the wall, and waited. Finally the storm of hilarity subsided into a fit of sniggering and Priya was able to talk again, her voice shaky with incipient chuckles.

"Let's look at the positive side of this. What did your last two tenants have in common?"

"They were female?" said Miranda sarcastically.

"And . . . ?"

Miranda scowled. "They were certifiably, dramatically insane," she muttered in defeat.

"Exactly! Now, I can personally vouch for Mr. Mair. He is a nice, normal, balanced young man who works as a tour guide—not an actor, not a model, not a performer of any description. Wouldn't it be refreshing to have a tenant who didn't create extra work for you when you got home?"

Miranda recalled the mania, the cutting, the screaming fights with transient lovers. And that had been just one tenant. The other had been worse—strange noises filtering up through the floor (her alternative music compositions), loud arguments with herself (rehearsing her lyrics), and a nasty, cloying tendency to attach herself to the nearest human ear and pour forth all the details of her angst-filled life without so much as a *hello, how are you* for a preamble.

Miranda quietly thanked Priya and returned to the front door. "So sorry about the delay. Would you like to come in and sign the contract?"

The young Mr. Mair looked a little anxious at first, but she settled him in a chair, fetched him a cup of tea and a plate of sweetmeats, and smiled innocently over her own cup of tea as he scrawled his signature and added his full name below it in clear, legible block capitals. Priya placed her stamp on the papers, her lips pressed together with a resolute sobriety that was somewhat marred by the occasional twitch.

"Here's the key for downstairs," Miranda said, handing it to him. "Welcome to city living."

Long after, when he had become more of a friend than a

tenant, she finally told him about the confusion his name had occasioned.

"Names are important," said Chance.

"What?" Miranda asked, looking wistful and disoriented.

"Names are very important. I used to laugh at how humans use names, but I was very foolish. Humans can make the act of naming powerful, even dangerous."

He tapped a page from her notes. "This woman—she had no name."

"We called her the Mermaid. She was so comfortable in the water."

"It would be a great help if I could find out her name."

Miranda frowned. "It would help me as well, but she never told us, and we never found out. She was a transient, part of the City's flourishing underground. No records, no relatives, no trace."

Chance glanced down for a moment, looking at the end of the red brick path where she stood. Then he looked over his shoulder at the hedges, now closer than ever. Her journey out from the center had brought her to the opposite side of the labyrinth.

She pursed her lips mutinously but soon wilted. "All right," she said.

No sensation would accompany this maze. It was a purely mental journey, something Chance could observe without moving from his place. Miranda stepped forward. Her next inhalation was shaky and constricted. The hedges were tall and close, tall enough to dim the interior to twilight and close enough to trigger the slightly smothered breathing of imminent claustrophobia.

"All right," she whispered, and went in.

It was the forensic lab; she recognized it easily. The chief pathologist stood with his back to her, dressed in the usual white coat with gloves, boots, skullcap, mask, and goggles. He took up a bone-cutting saw and bent over the corpse on the stainless steel slab before him.

"I know this nightmare," Miranda said. "It doesn't signify anything more than first-year jitters in the criminology course."

Just then, the corpse shuddered and shifted, unexpectedly unfurling a large fishy tail. "You can't hurt me. I'm a mermaid," she protested bitterly to the pathologist.

"Mermaids don't drown," he noted absently. "Please lie back. I have to prepare the site for grafting."

"Chance!" Miranda yelled. "I don't want to do this!"

"The legs are ready," sang a new voice behind her.

Miranda whirled around. In real life, the pathologist's assistant was a short, middle-aged, motherly woman. In the nightmare, the person standing in the doorway with two severed legs clasped in his arms was most definitely not her.

The saw whirred to life, and the corpse began to shriek. Miranda screwed her eyes shut, clapped her hands over her ears, and screamed louder. Something hit her in the face, scratched and scraped over her skin, fluttered and twisted in her hair like the wings and claws of a bat or a bird. She thrashed out in panic.

"Dead end," Chance said.

The horrible noises stopped like a radio switching off. Miranda opened her eyes, panting, and saw that she'd been wrestling with a wall of twiggy foliage. She turned around.

"Dead end," Chance repeated quietly, seeing that she had awakened fully. "Let's go outside. I have to think about this some more."

He showed her the way out, an arch positioned right behind them over the traces of Miranda's steps. Miranda stumbled out and immediately lay flat on the warm grass, her lips pressed tight, while Chance sat calmly nearby, rearranging the notes and spreading them out.

"The Mermaid, as you called her, was found without feet, victim of an untidy amputation that resulted in further complications and the loss of both legs above the knee." He kept his tone carefully dispassionate as he listened to Miranda's breathing become slower and more even. "A few days after your initial meetings with her, she was found in the hospital pool, drowned."

"She should never have been left unsupervised," said Miranda, dragging her hand over her eyes and forehead. "Look, Chance, I'm a bit confused. Why are you going through my notes again? We know who did it. He was tried and convicted, and he'll suffer the penalty. If we're supposed to 'detain him on the path to immortality,' please tell me what that entails, because if we can just twist time, go into the past, and get this bastard before he has a chance to hurt anyone, I'd like to do it now."

There was a profound silence. Miranda sat up and stared at Chance, who kept his gaze on the papers before him. "And now you're going to tell me time doesn't work that way," she said.

"It doesn't, but that's not the point," he mumbled. "I don't want to lie to you, Miranda . . . like you lied to that woman."

"What?"

"You told her you could help her," Chance reminded her. "Is it really your job to help people? Or is it your job to get at the truth? What does a forensic therapist really do?"

He glared at her until she understood that he was expecting an answer to the question. She took a defensive, pedantic tone. "Witnesses of traumatic events can be unreliable. It's the job of a forensic therapist to separate memory from nightmare. That sometimes means helping a victim who can't or won't speak to articulate what really happened to them. But it can also mean stopping a hysterical plaintiff from turning their inner psychoses into a witch hunt of innocents."

She paused. "I didn't lie to her. I *was* going to help her— perhaps not with therapy, but with justice. There's a kind of healing in that too."

"If she had lived, what would have happened to her?" Chance asked, a deliberate softness to his tone.

Miranda shrugged. "I don't know." It was an obvious lie, so she followed up quickly with the truth. "Deported, probably."

"And deported means . . . ?"

"It means set outside the City gates and barred from future entry, as you well know," Miranda snapped. "The City has always had walls, one way or another. We have plenty of workers and visitors to look after without—"

"Don't get angry at me, Miranda," Chance said mildly. "I just want to make you think. Who was the man in your nightmare, the pathologist's assistant?"

She grew even angrier. "You know who it was! Walther Grey, the killer, the Butcher of the City!"

"Is he a Freeman of the City?"

"No, a worker, a tenant. Not an owner of any property."

"The City protects its own, doesn't it?"

"Yes, I suppose, but . . . Oh please, Chance, what's your point?"

"My point is. . . ." He paused for a sigh and began again. "My *hypothesis* is that someone killed the Mermaid, drowned her in that pool, and it was not Walther Grey. Miranda, have you . . . has anyone imagined that the murderer might be a Freeman?"

CHAPTER FOUR

Miranda gave him an incredulous look. "You do admit that he killed all the others?"

"Well, of course; that's utterly clear from the evidence you have. But there's something different about this case that you must understand. I have been reliably informed—by the angel of the dead, no less—that the last seven victims were not supposed to have died when they did, and Grey may not have been the only person involved."

"How do you know she didn't kill herself? She could have just . . . stopped, let herself go under . . ."

"We know suicides, Miranda. The Mermaid wasn't a suicide. The resonance, the *tension* of intentionality that attends a suicide was nowhere about her passing."

Miranda pressed her hands together firmly, trying to keep them from shaking. Was it nerves? Was she feeling chilled? "Seven victims. You chose five files from my briefcase. Who are the others?"

Chance stared at her. "There's also Galina's child. Missing, and no body found—but you're cold. We shouldn't talk about this so soon after your nightmare."

She giggled. "Angels and elementals and mind mazes. How can I trust any of this to be real?" By now her teeth were chattering. "Why am I shivering?" she asked herself, her voice high and tremulous.

Chance looked up at the tall hedges of the maze, his brows creased in vexation. "Let's get you away from this." He held Miranda's wrist gently. "Please, Miranda, keep trusting me."

She gazed up at him. Her eyes begged him to be a dream, to confirm his impossibility by evaporating or turning into the kind of surreal, laughable creature that can arise from bad digestion and vivid imagination. The unmistakable reality of the angel was fading, and her human defenses against mystery were beginning to fight back. Chance realized they could not communicate while she remained in this condition. Even the powers of his special tea blend would not be enough.

Sleep was not possible in the world he had made, but rest was. He guided Miranda to where the grass was thickset and soft, gently pushed her to sit down, and took her mind into a wakeful dream that smoothed the worry from her face and drained the tension from her limbs. She sighed, already looking through him to some calmer vision, and slowly settled herself down into the curled-up posture of a napping child.

"You should have anticipated this. She was too calm."

Chance spun around, surprised to be surprised in his own backyard. When he saw who it was, he could only grimace. *"You."*

His brother grinned at him. "Just keeping it in the family. You *do* need help, don't you?"

The Trickster used the same appearance as his human body in places where there was no need to do so, a measure of how much human life had changed him. Medium height, stocky, and broad-faced, he kept hints of his former spider shape in the bristling hairiness of his arms and the twinkling glitter of his black eyes. Instead of simple cotton, he wore a white linen wrap around his waist—too long for an acolyte, too short for a chief. The hem was embroidered with a light dashing of gold thread, like the meandering trail of a vine.

Chance shrugged. "It wouldn't hurt. You might be able to go where I can't."

The Trickster glanced once at Miranda's faintly smiling face, nodded as if reassured, and raised a finger, about to tear open a door. "Let's go see this Mermaid, then."

They went like hounds questing for a scent, tasting Miranda's memory as the starting point for their trail but spending no longer than a flicker of a second, more than enough time for the Trickster to perceive the Mermaid's signature vibration in reality. It was an advantage to have shared the same womb, for Chance knew the Trickster like he knew himself, and they had learned to dance together in and out of times and places with the ease of ink curling through water. The topography of time and place subtly guided the interwoven journeys of the undying to create tapestries far more elaborate than the straight-cut lines of human lives. But limits did exist, and not every path was open to them. Chance saw in an instant that the road to the time of the murder was closed to them; the Trickster saw the same, and together they flashed back to another location that sang deep with portent.

The narrow back alleys of the City, made to admit nothing wider than a rider on horseback or a hand-drawn cart, were further choked with clusters of tumbled debris. They looked like haphazard piles of organic matter in the yellow light of the streetlamps; they were not. They were shelters, tiny lean-tos made of discarded material from roofs and fences and crates. The inhabitants must have had some warning, however brief, of what was to come, for they had taken themselves and what scanty goods they kept in that place to a safer spot. Thus it was that the driver of a small streetsweeper buggy, buzzing and trundling through at the strange and silent hour of four in the morning, was able to pass with an extra-large shovel attachment and a conscience that, though not completely easy, would at least not bear the burden of murder or maiming.

"There she is," said the Trickster with a jerk of his chin.

The driver could not have seen the smear of blood that trailed behind him, but perhaps he had a good nose to pick out the scent of blood amid the other strong odors of rotting produce, unwashed humanity, and decaying vermin. Or perhaps he had already learned the soft but distinctive strike of machine against live flesh, but either way it was to him that the Mermaid owed her life. Chance and the Trickster watched dispassionately, well used to strange and gory sights, as the man stopped the sweeper and pulled apart a mound of refuse to discover the woman. He ripped his own tunic to shreds and tried to stem the terrible flow of blood, shouting for help as he did so.

The brothers closely examined those who responded to

the call. Some ran to make themselves useful; some gawked on the periphery; still others looked on briefly, then fled the ugly sight. One old woman touched her heart, forehead, and lips nervously in a gesture invoking protection. There was a babel of voices at the core of the growing crowd and a murmur at the edges.

The Trickster twitched, breaking his focus on the tableau, and cocked his head inquiringly at his brother. "Do you realize how close we came to arriving at the time of the attack?"

"Someone's blocking us," Chance agreed. "Or at least me. I told you, you might be able to go where I can't. Try now."

The Trickster blinked and concentrated, but soon shook his head in frustration. "Definite interference. There's more to it than just you, then." His face brightened. "Well! This is a challenge! Just like old times, hmm?"

"Except," Chance said soberly, "that in these new times, we care a little bit more when humans die needlessly. Being human ourselves and all."

"Oh, no," said the Trickster, ignoring his brother's attempt to dampen his levity. "I don't care unless they happen to be humans I know."

Chance glared at him. The Trickster shrugged. "A lot of humans think the same way I do, Chance. You're too tenderhearted—always have been. You mustn't let things get to you. Now, where next?"

Chance closed his eyes as if reading something inside his head. "There's something in Miranda's nightmare that matches something I found in the case notes. This amputation was hastily done, but not inexpertly so, which explains why the

Mermaid was able to survive. It makes me think that the initial intent was *not* to kill but simply to take the required limbs."

"Building a body out of spare parts?" The Trickster laughed without humor. "How unoriginal."

Chance ignored him. "So it's possible that at some point, for whatever reason, someone issued instructions to add a ritual component to the attacks."

"*Someone* being the person you think was pulling the strings on Walther Grey."

Chance nodded. "Remember all the faces here. There has to be some common denominator. I wouldn't be surprised if we found there was at least one person who knew all the victims whose name is *not* Walther Grey."

His voice slowed and grew pensive; he frowned. Someone was standing at the crossroads where the back alley intersected with the road. His copper hair stood out among the blacks and browns, and his pale face shone as he came out slightly from the lee of an overhanging balcony that looked onto the main street. A gas lamp at the balcony's corner had been illuminated by the house's owners, their curiosity having overcome their caution, and it poured soft light over him. Chance assessed him. Legal, since he braved open light with the authorities soon to come. Inquisitive, as his attire indicated that he was on his way to work—or from it—and had stopped to see what the crowd meant. Compassionate, if the expression on his face was genuine. And utterly familiar.

"Someone you know?" murmured the Trickster.

"Maybe," Chance said, still in that slow, pensive tone. "Let's sniff out his path."

They followed him forward and back: forward to his early shift on one of the harbor's floating museums, back to his small apartment in a town house basement and hours spent in innocent sleep.

"I understand your interest in this fellow," remarked the Trickster as he detected Miranda's path coiling thickly in and out of the main door of the town house. "But remember, it's a small city at night with most of the legal workforce gone. It's not that surprising that he would have passed there, given his usual route and all."

"Fair enough," Chance admitted. "We need another trail, then. I think we should check the chief pathologist at the main forensic lab. He knew Walther Grey."

"Did he?" asked the Trickster, idly scuffing his heels on Miranda's welcome mat as he gazed out at the view. "You know, you can see the harbor from here, even the ship that young man works on. Very picturesque. I should become an artist."

"The chief pathologist taught Grey," continued Chance, ignoring the digression with the ease of years' experience. "Just one name among many on a very large class list, and Grey didn't finish the course, but still, it's a connection."

"Tell me exactly what you're looking for," the Trickster said. "If you're being barred from going to the important times and places, what do you hope to find?"

"All I need is to find the human who's involved." Chance paused, sighed. "The angels think this isn't finished. They're expecting another death."

"And after that? Is there a monster at the end of this chase, some shambling creature of human ritual and undying malice?"

"Impossible—though that's never stopped people from trying."

The Trickster frowned and shook his head, dissatisfied by Chance's answers.

They took in Miranda's path again, the feel of her thread through time and space, and looked for the nearest node. They found one, brief but sufficient. She picked up a report from the chief pathologist's office, and he greeted her casually on his way out to lunch. With his height and his high, domed head fringed with graying hair, he resembled one of the marble statues outside the Citadel Hall, the very stamp of the ancestral elders, with a full, curving mouth framed by deep creases that could be either stern or laughing depending on how he pursed his lips. He nodded to his secretary and hailed his waiting chauffeur with an absentminded courtesy. He was a noble of the professional class, and he bore himself accordingly.

His luncheon meeting was with another of that same class, a man of similar height and bearing whose thick, wavy hair proclaimed him to be of some origin other than the City's most common lineage. He stood, and they clasped hands carefully, observing the correct grip and movement, for they were brothers of a fraternity.

"Doctor Boadu."

"Professor Malveaux."

Dr. Boadu waved the professor back to his chair, a simple act of offered permission that indicated he was, in some minute sense, the senior of the two. "We should have done this a long time ago. How many years have we worked together on Club projects?"

"Three. Four. I don't recall. But don't feel a way. There are plenty of opportunities for food and fellowship at the Club. The fact that you wanted to meet somewhere else tells me this isn't Club business."

The lines on Dr. Boadu's face laughed in appreciation of the swift, blunt reasoning. He did not answer immediately but took up a menu and turned the conversation to the various dishes available.

Chance took the opportunity to whisper to the Trickster as they stood silently and invisibly observing. "The Club they're speaking of is the foremost professional fraternity of the City. If Professor Malveaux has been a member for four years, it means that he only recently obtained Freeman status."

"I figured as much," said the Trickster. He paused and then asked, "Shall I look inside his mind?"

Chance winced. "That old trick? I'm not sure Maa would approve. It's too much like interference."

His brother regarded him with eyebrows raised. "You had fewer scruples when last I worked with you."

"Yes," Chance acknowledged. "And look where it got me. We observe; we do not invade, intrude, or possess. We must tread lightly with this one. It touches our human lives too closely."

That last bit silenced the Trickster. Of the two of them, he was the one more closely connected to the City, and the small fact that he had not yet passed through its gates did not release him from the burden of caution.

The conversation at the table turned from the trivial to the significant.

"So, tell me more about the work you do with the City Shelter," said Dr. Boadu.

The professor shrugged. "I've already told the Club most of the details. We house a few, usually people who are waiting for their status to be regularized. City bureaucracy is horrendous." He paused to acknowledge the pathologist's nod of agreement with a small smile. "And we feed a lot more—mainly people on the streets whose status is a little more gray and unknown. We don't ask questions. A lot of children pass through. Children are always hungry."

"But how did *you* come to be involved in the shelter?"

"Oh!" The professor seemed surprised, as if this kind of question rarely came his way. "Well, I wasn't always a Freeman, and people would often come to me asking for help with forms and documents. I began to realize that there were some other simple problems to be solved. A shower and clean clothes for an interview doesn't sound like much, does it? But those things are difficult to come by when you haven't got money for the most basic guesthouse room."

"There are plenty of hostels just outside the City," Dr. Boadu protested mildly.

"Priced out of the range of most non-Freemen, I'm afraid. And then there are things like getting documents printed, accessing libraries." He paused and drank from his glass of ice water, slowing and cooling the pace of the conversation. "Things Freemen take for granted." Professor Malveaux spoke the final phrase in a detached manner, without censure, but Dr. Boadu bit his lip and looked saddened.

"I've been in pathology for a long time," he said. "My experience with these people has not been the best. I usually see them on my table, victims of crime, industrial accidents, or simple neglect. Some suicides too. I've become inured. It's not good."

Chance saw a fleeting hardness set the professor's ordinarily genial face into a grimmer mold, but then the moment passed and his features relaxed once more into an expression that seemed like compassion.

"Anyway, last week was the last straw for me. That boy . . ."

The professor inhaled and breathed out a slow, sorrowful sigh. "I did not know him. I'm ashamed to say that I did not know him, or if I did, I do not remember him."

Dr. Boadu smiled. "You can't expect to be everywhere, Malveaux. You do a lot as it is."

"It's never enough." Professor Malveaux shrugged.

"Well, I've decided to do something practical with my guilt. I want to make a personal donation to the shelter, and I also plan to recommend to the Club that we take it on as one of our permanent charitable concerns." Dr. Boadu was already fumbling in his pocket; he withdrew a neatly folded rectangle of paper and passed it to his colleague.

Professor Malveaux looked as if he wanted to slip the paper discreetly into his own pocket, but curiosity prevailed. He cracked open the check slightly and glanced at the number in the currency box. His eyes widened. "That's a lot of guilt."

Dr. Boadu frowned to himself, looking down at the table. "He could have been saved if someone had gotten to him in time."

"How did he die?" asked the professor in a tired, unwilling tone.

"Like a thief of old, washed up on the harbor rocks with both hands cut off and his blood drained out," the pathologist said, his voice cautiously soft as he glanced sidewise at nearby diners.

The professor appeared to swallow, and his breathing hitched for a moment. "He was a thief?"

Dr. Boadu looked at him, baffled. "A notorious pickpocket, according to the police. Look, we're going to set this aside for just a while and have an enjoyable meal. You look like you're going to pass out. I keep forgetting I mustn't tell people the gory details of my work."

The professor nodded weakly. He looked very strange; a bloodless undertone grayed his skin. Dr. Boadu immediately began to chat about light matters, keeping a keen, professional eye on the other man.

The Trickster turned away from them and faced his brother. "The hands."

"The boy was killed eight days before the Mermaid was drowned," Chance confirmed. "The body must have been almost complete."

A look of extreme distaste twisted the Trickster's face, as if he were perceiving a terrible, painful untruth that had no inherent humor to redeem it. "Like you said, that doesn't work. It's a folk tale that doesn't mean what they think it means. It can't work."

"Someone thought it did, or was encouraged to think so."

The Trickster turned away again. "That's a very sick joke."

Chance gazed at him, unexpected affection distracting him from the puzzle at hand. "Of course. If you didn't think that, you wouldn't be here now."

A name in the conversation at the table suddenly snagged their attention. That name was "Walther Grey."

". . . he's a success story, in a way. He's managed to adjust better than many who went through post-conflict deprogramming," said Professor Malveaux.

"I had no idea," Dr. Boadu said. He looked slightly queasy. "But why didn't he finish my course?"

Professor Malveaux paused and spoke carefully, his eyes once again shadowed as they had been when speaking of the dead boy. "I think it may have been a little too close to his experiences during the war. I advised him to try a more theoretical field of study, so he took up philosophy."

"Sensible," said Dr. Boadu, and from the expressions on both their faces, it was once more time to find another topic of conversation.

"They suspected something," murmured the Trickster.

"Perhaps," Chance agreed, thinking of the pathologist's reports. "But they didn't have proof yet."

Exasperation edged the Trickster's reply. "Nor do we, since you insist on doing this the hard way. Come. Let's try another trail."

Invisible to any mortal eye, black ink and indigo dye bled swiftly through the labyrinthine whorls of time's tapestry, leaving the professor and the pathologist to their lunch.

CHAPTER FIVE

"What more can the pathologist tell us about the boy?" mused the Trickster.

"I've already read all his reports," Chance said.

"No, I mean, maybe he's encountered someone else connected to the death."

Wordlessly Chance invited him to lead the way. The Trickster moved back to an earlier time, taking as his guide the professor's comments about the Club. After a bit of meandering, he managed to land them somewhere meaningful, some type of holiday celebration at the shelter, where Club members mingled with shelter staff, denizens, and visitors in an excess of magnanimous hospitality concentrated on that one day of the year. The regulars were bemused and reticent, the newcomers were overly cheerful, and everyone compensated for the awkwardness by showering attention on the children.

Dr. Boadu stood between a bored-looking young woman in a staff tunic who was holding a tray of assorted sweet biscuits and a rotund man dressed in a sloppy, casual fashion that suggested he had neither boss nor spouse to advise him on his wardrobe choices. He was holding forth like a stage performer while Dr. Boadu slowly made his choices from the tray with fussy precision.

"What is it to be a starving artist? It is to have a small stomach and a big heart, to say 'Fuck you' to your patron and write for yourself, then eat satisfaction because that's the only meal you can afford. It's to live shamelessly for the time and space to write, and then one day, one day, a single, ridiculous, half-baked idea takes off and captures the attention of a crazy world, and you ride that star and eat and grow fat and write with nostalgia about the starving days that are no more."

"Well, Julian, that explains where the small stomach went," said Dr. Boadu, eyeing the man's paunch. "But what happened to the big heart and writing for yourself?"

"Oh!" Julian went silent after that small syllable, but his smile was sly.

There was more of the cynical than the sly in Dr. Boadu's smile. "So it *is* true. You write under a pseudonym as well?"

"Perhaps. Perhaps my pseudonymous self is the figure you see here, portrayed by an actor whose only writing skill is the signing of autographs. Perhaps the real author is somewhere in his own broad land, feeding both his stomach and his heart. You'll never know, will you."

He turned at last to the staff worker, who had been trying to look as if she could not hear a thing. "Don't be fooled. I *might* be an actor. I wasn't always this size, you know. I was young and fit and witty, and the readers loved me. Now I'm old and fat and witty, and the readers still love me. It's a good life."

Dr. Boadu's cynicism grew, the woman's boredom increased, and Julian looked around for more diversion. He took a gingerbread man from the tray and held it out invitingly as he beckoned a child closer for a conspiratorial whisper.

"It's kinder to eat them headfirst. Severs the nerves in the neck. A painless death."

The child gave him an anxious look and ran off, the gingerbread man firmly gripped in his hand.

"Julian, you are far more sinister in person than your books would suggest," Dr. Boadu said wryly, but his eyes followed the silent child with puzzled concern. He leaned toward the woman before she could move on with her tray and asked quietly, "Whose child is that?"

The volunteer paused, eyes scanning the crowd. "That's his mother over there," she said finally, indicating a thin woman with a narrow, unsmiling face.

Dr. Boadu frowned; then his eyes widened, and he turned away quickly.

"You know her?" asked Julian shrewdly. "Old girlfriend?"

The pathologist looked around nervously, exasperated by the indelicate comment, but fortunately the woman with the tray had made her escape and moved too far away to overhear. "Her husband was a murder victim."

Julian made a moue of distaste. "Is everything in your life about work? Aren't there any other pathologists in the City? Tell me now, because the idea that someday *I* could be on a slab with you slicing up my innards makes me want to move far, far away."

"Unless you plan to get murdered, I don't think you have

to worry," Dr. Boadu replied, but he said it absently rather than with sarcasm, still staring surreptitiously at the woman and the boy. "Why is that child so quiet?"

Julian's eyes narrowed with professional malice. "Wait here. I'll go find out."

Shocked, but too slow in his reaction, the pathologist watched helplessly as Julian walked straight to the child's mother. Afraid he would be caught staring, he retreated and nudged himself between a wall and a large potted plant near the end of the buffet table. In an effort to appear occupied, he grimly began to fill his plate with savory hors d'oeuvres.

"What a marvelous fellow," the Trickster murmured to Chance as they looked at Julian settling himself in a chair beside the woman. "He could be one of the Lesser Lords of Misrule. A man like that is never comfortable unless others are uncomfortable. His sort is useful to me. They make it their business to know everything scandalous and tell it abroad. No need to rifle through minds with them around."

Julian soon came wandering back, a sly smile on his face. The expression in his eyes, however, did not quite match the smile, as if there were some things that even he preferred not to hear. He went to where Dr. Boadu's overfull plate sat on the table and began to pick from it without asking.

"Well?" asked Dr. Boadu, reluctant to gossip but interested in spite of himself.

Julian swallowed and reached for a napkin. "Her son, who is called Lukas, has not only lost a father. He has also lost a friend who I believe may also have ended up on your slab with his innards on display."

The Trickster and Chance turned in an instant to fix their attention on Lukas.

"Follow him?" asked the Trickster.

"Definitely. Perhaps we can get closer to his friend's murder than the Mermaid's."

They went over to the small boy. He was seven or eight, all beautiful bones and large, long-lashed eyes. He looked like what humans thought angels looked like, not least because of the hollow sadness in his gaze, which gave him an otherworldly air. He shivered and looked around nervously, as if he knew himself to be observed.

Chance felt pity but did not voice it. He was distracted by a strange feeling, an inability to grasp hold of the information he needed. "Do you see it?" he asked his brother at last, frustrated.

"Yes," said the Trickster. "And I can see that *you* can't. I'll have to go alone."

"Meet me at my place when you're done. I'm going to check on Miranda," Chance said, his words clipped and irritated.

The petulance he felt expressed itself as a spiteful precision as he sliced open a door and dropped into his own world with a far greater adroitness than his previous scrambling entrance with Miranda. At the sight of her, still dreaming and at rest, his vexation leached away.

He sat beside her and woke her with a soft nudge. She frowned slightly, the bemused, disgruntled frown of a small child wakened too early, turned to look at him, and stared.

"Better?" he asked gently.

She blinked slowly and gave a weak smile. "Well, you're still here, so I suppose I have no choice but to adjust."

He smiled back but did not hesitate. He had too many questions that he wanted answered. "Are you willing to walk the mazes again?"

"If I must. If it helps."

"Miranda, believe me, there are many things that I cannot do, and some things I can only do with the assistance of mortals. I am grateful for your help."

She stood up and considered the landscape. "How do I handle the nightmare maze? What did I do wrong that made me run into a dead end?"

"You did nothing wrong. A dead end means something you don't yet understand or can't face." He said it in a neutral tone, careful not to upset her again.

She glanced down at him, then started to walk toward the maze. Startled, he scrambled up and followed her.

"I'm going in again," she insisted, striding with determination.

"Of course you are," he said gently, "but last time you went in fearful. This time you're going in angry. There may be some effects."

She turned on him fiercely. "Then *you* go in with me. Hold my hand, or whatever is necessary."

Chance blinked, startled into stillness. He slowly nodded. "I can do that."

He held out a hand to her. She took it as carefully as she had touched the angel's finger, and that new reserve to her movements told him that she was now fully aware of the otherworldliness in him that she had chosen to overlook before.

She even squeezed it slightly, as if testing the strength of the illusion of bones and sinew beneath the indigo skin.

She exhaled and closed her eyes. "Go ahead. Lead me."

He led her in.

First there was darkness, then the sound of laughter in a boy's voice, harsh and loud and self-conscious, as if laughing to prove his amusement to someone else. They walked toward that sound, and the light grew to show a rough trestle table, darkly lit with the kind of light that would come from a lantern hanging high above. Seated at the table on low benches on opposite sides were Walther Grey and a boy with no face.

No face. No mouth to be laughing with. No features at all, only a smooth golden blur in the amber light. The only characteristics that mattered were the thin wrists, and the bare upper body with its ribs outstanding like the keys of a macabre xylophone under semitranslucent skin, slightly sliding with each breath.

Walther Grey was not laughing either. He stared at and maybe through the boy with a small, fixed smile that meant nothing.

The laughter faded into the background, a murmur of conversation began and grew louder, and louder yet was the sound of footsteps approaching. It was Kieran, wearing an expression of kindly distraction, bearing a platter with a bowl of steaming soup. He set it before the faceless boy, between those thin wrists, and went away again.

The boy did not move, but the bowl did. A shadowy figure reached down shadowy hands and took the soup away. The boy still did not move, and neither did Walther Grey, though his smile grew sardonic.

Kieran returned swiftly, harried and concerned now, and placed another bowl filled with soup in the same place as before. He had barely disappeared before it met the same end as the first, carried off by shadow into shadow. The murmur and chatter had the disconcerting normality of a cocktail party hum, and the vague background surged and shifted with the turgid ennui of a crowd of people assembled to elegantly waste time.

The boy's hungry ribs breathed, and that was all.

Kieran brought bowl after bowl with greater and greater haste; the boy did not move, but his mouthless, noseless breathing became panting; and Walther Grey smiled and grinned and finally erupted into laughter—the laughter of a boy who is in pain and trying to hide it.

The boy leaped up onto the bench, lunged over the table, and snatched at something around Walther Grey's neck. Grey's laughter turned to a groan of sick fear. He clutched the two thin wrists easily with one hand; the other hand rose, wielding a cleaver . . .

"No!" yelled Miranda.

The cool green light of the maze's deep interior pushed back the nightmare. Miranda was breathing in shallow, rapid gasps, her face hidden in the rough, rustic cotton of Chance's shirt.

"Why did the boy have no face?" he asked her gently.

She swallowed. "I looked at the pathologist's report, but I couldn't bear to look at the pictures."

He was silent. He let her grip the fabric of his shirt with angry fists, understanding very well that the anger was not for him.

At last she burst out, "I think he might have been one of the street children that Kieran feeds sometimes. They come to the basement door. I pretend not to notice. I was afraid I might recognize him."

She cried for a short while. Chance stood still and tried to organize his thoughts, to separate what she had dreamed and what he had included from his own store of disjointed images. The trestle table was, now that he thought about it, exactly like the one that had been in the shelter under a festive table-cloth and a buffet of seasonal excess. The golden light was the light of the streetlamp in the alley where the Mermaid had been attacked. The idea of Grey punishing the boy for attempted theft came from the pathologist's remarks. Or did it?

"Miranda, I know that Walther Grey never bothered to explain his reasons for the murders. But tell me, did he at any point complain about someone trying to take something from him?"

She stepped away from him, hands at her sides and head down. She shook her head. Even though her face was wet with tears, he noted that she looked reasonably calm and not yet desperate to leave the high-hedged closeness of the maze. Likely she had needed to cry about this for a long time. He patted her shoulder in reassurance.

"Is this really helping?" she asked quietly.

He gave her a small smile. "I think I understand what you're asking. You're not *that* afraid of walking the mazes.

Perhaps what you need is to find out who's really responsible for the boy's death. I think we're making some progress."

He took her hand again and led her out of the maze. When they turned the last corner to the entrance, there was the Trickster standing outside, perhaps one meter from the threshold, with his back to them and his face to the labyrinth.

"A friend," Chance murmured quickly to Miranda as they came out into the full light.

The Trickster turned around.

"Are you sure?" Miranda whispered.

The Trickster looked furious. He ignored Miranda and stared at Chance with a look that was ice, edge, deep contempt, and strangest of all, worry.

"What happened?" Chance demanded.

The Trickster gave an odd grimace. "Well, Chance, why don't you tell me? You were there."

"What?" Chance was so startled that his world actually flickered, the light dimming, then flaring, the edges of objects blurring, then reforming their lines with painful precision.

Miranda stepped away from both of them, staring wide-eyed at the scene.

The Trickster advanced on him. "You—were—there! I saw you! I *spoke* to you! You were in the middle of it!"

"Did I do anything . . . ?" Chance trailed off. Whether it had been his future or his past, he could not remember it, but he remembered an era when he was so full of a weary hatred against humankind that the idea of killing had not been that far from his mind.

The Trickster saw the panicked look and took pity on him.

"You weren't utterly vile, but if I could estimate from what I know of your lovely character and its development, I'd say that you were in the early period of your cerulean phase."

Chance breathed again. Amazing how the somatic reflexes owned one after a time of being human, even when in a form for which oxygen was irrelevant.

"Well, tell me what happened. Tell me what I did," he insisted.

With a small shake of the head and a rueful smile, the Trickster raised his hands defensively. "Not me. Besides, there's no need." He stood aside and made a mocking flourish. "Time to walk your own labyrinth."

"Oh, please—" Chance began, but the Trickster cut him off.

"I didn't see everything. We need your full memory of the event, not my fractured retelling of it. Besides"—he looked at Miranda, and his features softened for the first time—"besides, it will give me a moment to get acquainted with this lovely lady."

Miranda looked startled. Chance raised his eyes heavenward. "Very well, I'll walk the labyrinth. Don't say anything you shouldn't, and don't shock her. I'm responsible for her here, and Uriel will also be watching you."

"I'm not worried about Uriel," said the Trickster, but the way his voice hushed when he spoke the name betrayed him.

"I feel as if I know you too," said Miranda in a soft, uncertain tone.

"You certainly will." The Trickster grinned, recovering full irreverence.

Chance frowned, too preoccupied to rebuke his brother.

"Can we hurry up and get this out of the way? I'm dying of curiosity, metaphorically speaking."

There was a moment, just a mere second, when it looked as if a flash of satisfaction crossed Miranda's face to see him standing on the first few bricks of the labyrinth. He couldn't blame her, but at the same time, she had no idea what this was like for a being like him. It was akin to a memory of dying, of stagnation. It was taking a fair bit of his courage to walk smoothly ahead with an apparent lack of concern. He tried to motivate himself. He was only going where he had already gone before. There was nothing to fret about; this was simply an exercise in traveling the same thread twice.

And what happens when all the threads of the tapestry have been traveled? Do you then go over them again and again in an attempt to relive the best parts? Because nothing will be like that first experience. Nothing.

Chance walked on.

CHAPTER SIX

His emotions were layered in this strange state. At one level there was the sulky, smoldering anger of a person forced to perform an unwanted duty; at another level there was a lighter, somewhat sorrowful acceptance born of the wisdom of hindsight. He whirled into a darkness of night and close walls and low ceilings, hovered and sat cross-legged with remembered elegance, then raised his head to see who had been so foolhardy as to summon him.

Two boys crouched before him around a low, fat candle with a sheltered flame, their poses suggesting that they had not yet decided whether to stay or flee. The smaller, younger boy, barely recognizable in the shadows, was Lukas, and Chance suspected that the other boy bore a name that would soon feature in a pathologist's report. He froze them in place with a glare.

"You bring me to this miserable hovel. You do not speak the right words or present the required offering. Explain yourselves."

The older boy pulled himself together in a show of bravado. "You have to obey this!" he protested, holding up a coin-like amulet on a leather thong. The metal circle was inscribed with a coiling symbol that showed a path with neither beginning nor end, but half of it was obscured by a dark smear. It was still smoking from being passed through the flame.

Chance's lips curled in a mockery of humor while his eyes narrowed in calculation. "Where did you get that?"

"It belonged to my grandmother. She met one of your kind, and they gave her this." The boy was bolder now. He spoke with authority.

"I see," said Chance. "And she knows that you have it? She gave it to you?"

The boy opened his mouth, faltered, and said nothing. No doubt he had been warned not to lie to whomever the amulet brought. "I stole it," he admitted. "I stole it from my father, who never gave me anything. But his mother, she was kind to me sometimes, when my father's wife couldn't see. She's old now. She hasn't remembered me for more than a year."

Chance leaned forward slightly, frowning. "Stealing another's rewards is a risky thing, as foolish as taking on another's debts. You still have time. Return the amulet."

"Please, Xandre!" Lukas squeaked, breaking his silence at last. "We should do as he says!"

Xandre turned on Lukas, his face changed in an instant from fear to contempt. "He is the one who has to do as we say! Do you *want* your father's murderer to walk free?"

"What's this about a murder?" Chance interjected. "I don't

kill people. If you know anything about the amulet, you know that."

"No," Xandre breathed. "You don't get to kill him. I do. You just have to help me get close."

It was hard going through that emotion again, the mingled pity and disgust that filled him both then and now as he looked at the boy's fanatical face. "What makes you so eager to kill his father's murderer? Who appointed you his avenger?"

The boy stared at him as if trying to impress him with his steadfastness of purpose. "He's killed others—people I knew, people who helped me. And he'll kill again."

Chance pondered. He hated amulets, but occasionally there were instances when humans did some favor that deserved compensation. Of course, the idea was that they would use their reward to benefit, not harm. Where did killing a murderer fall on the scale of good to evil? Particularly a murderer who might kill again? And did this boy really have the strength of mind to do it?

"Show me the man," Chance said.

Xandre led the way to a landing at the back of a town house, then three stories up a narrow stone staircase that ended far below in the suck and slap of waves at high tide. The three looked in through a window at the small, cluttered lodgings where a man lay sleeping on a narrow bed, barechested in the heat. Chance stared at him—not because he looked harmless nor yet because he seemed familiar in that odd way that hinted at future rather than past acquaintance, but because of what he wore around his neck.

Chance smiled again with that humorless smile. "I'll make you a bargain," he murmured in Xandre's ear. "Don't kill him. That thing around his neck—get it for me, and I will make sure he never troubles anyone again."

The boy's eyes were wide and terrified as he finally began to grasp that he was dealing with something he did not understand. "The window grille is bolted," he whispered, his breath coming shallow and fast.

Chance laid a gentle hand on the boy's shoulder, gradually increasing the pressure to something less friendly as he moved behind him and said, "Should that stop a thief of your experience? But here—iron *does* rust, and it's a shame that the landlord won't do the proper maintenance."

There was a dull chime, the sound of metal unleashed from a point of stress, and the grille sagged very slightly.

Seizing both shoulders, he turned the boy to face him. "Breathe easy," he said softly and not at all kindly. "He'll hear you coming."

Shivering, Xandre went in through the window, too distracted to notice that somewhere amid all the touching and turning about, he had lost his spent talisman. Chance watched him go, absently crushing in his fist the amulet that had summoned him there. When his hand opened again, an insubstantial dust floated out and was quickly taken by the wind. Lukas was a weeping, trembling heap of fear in the far corner of the landing. Chance gave him a brief, direct look, wondering if he would have to prevent him from crying out at the wrong moment. Lukas eyed him and tried to crawl farther back.

A shout rang out from inside, then a muffled scream, and

both of them turned. Lukas had of course reacted to the sound, but Chance had been jolted by a less human stimulus, the sudden sensation that one of his own kind had just torn open a passageway in spacetime. He rushed to pass into the room—and found himself blocked, blocked as solidly as if a wall had been placed before him, a wall that even the undying could not pierce. Silently he railed, sending static crackling into the night like stunted lightning as he fruitlessly tried with all his knowledge and skill to break through.

Then it happened, as he had somehow known it would from the moment he began this duty. Xandre came through the open window, thrown like a kitten in a sack, his arms bound in deep red tendrils that began to fade as soon as Chance perceived them. The boy cleared the narrow landing and began the long tumble down. Now his arms were free, and as his limp body spun, they flung out dark, liquid tendrils of their own that carried a rich, choking scent to rival the sea-salted air.

Chance grabbed Lukas and dived off the landing, knowing without seeing that the murderer and whatever it was that had aided him were coming out to see their work. His hand smothered Lukas's face so that even the shock of hitting cold water did not elicit more than a short gasp. Then he remembered his limitations.

"Swim, boy," he growled, releasing Lukas to the mildly surging water. "I cannot help you any further. You must choose for yourself. Swim or die."

Softly crying, Lukas did as he was told. Chance flashed to dry land in a single step and stood watching, invisible, until the small shaking figure clambered up the big rocks lining the coast road and started stumbling homeward. He gave a thought to following Lukas, then wondered if it would be any good to see if Xandre had survived. Before he could decide between the two, another tearing sensation sent a crackle through him. He whirled around and stared into the murk, already furious at whomever this intruder might be.

"Chance? Is that you?"

He tilted his head and peered more closely, considering. "Do I know you?"

An ordinary figure, very human-looking but with an otherworldly glitter about the eyes, stepped forward out of the darkness and into the amber circle cast by a streetlamp. "You might. You will."

Chance pondered that and risked stepping a little closer to examine the shadow carried by this undying one. It was unfamiliar in a way that was disconcerting, as if the undying one had actually transformed himself into some other being rather than merely crafting a facsimile. As to whether the substance below the shadow was familiar, Chance could no longer say. The entire event was beginning to ring so loudly of déjà vu that he couldn't even trust himself to know which direction he was facing.

"I was watching earlier from the edges," the stranger continued. "How did you come here? What duty did you have?"

"Amulet," Chance spat. "And not even wielded by the right person. I'm not responsible. I gave him plenty of options, and he chose the worst ones."

The stranger smiled a bitter smile and looked keenly at him.

"Not a lie, but not the truth. He would not have gone for that other amulet if you hadn't put the possibility into his head."

"We shouldn't allow amulets at all," Chance hissed in anger, livid at being seen through so quickly. "That one left back there will do some damage yet. I'm not responsible. I've done what I can within my limits."

The stranger shrugged. "For now. I must get back. There's nothing more to see here."

"Wait," he began, but the stranger slipped away before Chance could ask any more questions.

Dizzied and sickened by the doubling, echoing vibration of the place, Chance ripped open an exit rift and left with more haste than skill. He stumbled into the center of the labyrinth, fell to his knees, and retched. Hands rested on his shoulders, tentatively concerned.

"Give him a minute," he heard the Trickster say.

He was grateful, not only to Miranda for the human concern she showed but to his brother as well. The Trickster held the made-world steady as Chance collected himself, a gesture as good as physical support would be to a creature of flesh and blood. Slowly he raised his head.

"Well," said the Trickster.

"Well indeed," replied Chance. "I think I know where we must go next."

He turned to look at Miranda. She was still touching him lightly with bewilderment in her eyes that he could be capable of showing such weakness. "I have to leave for a moment. Literally a moment, for you. Wait on us. You'll be safe here."

"Where could I go?" she answered, spreading her hands

wide but tempering the helplessness of the gesture with a shaky smile.

The Trickster helped him to his feet. Chance thought for a moment, his resurrected memories swirling, settling, and organizing themselves. Then he looked at his brother, a look that held all the information they needed. Quietly they flashed out from the center of the labyrinth.

As far as twilight years went, she had fared well. Her daughter-in-law was loyal to family, and family was marriage as well as blood, so even after her sons were long dead and their children scattered in fortune from obscure poverty to indifferent affluence, she had the good luck to be housed and fed and cared for in the tenement of a Freeman. The infirmities of age were her only afflictions, and she eased them as best she could—sitting by the window for the warm sun and the fresh breeze, looking out at the sea to soothe her tired, clouded vision with its cool, deep blues, and humming to herself as recent memories faded and old ones took their places with a strength that was more than mere nostalgia.

When Chance and the Trickster appeared beside her, she did not startle or scream.

The Trickster leaned in to whisper to Chance. "She's completely senile. She can't help us."

"Oh, yes, she can. She will."

The Trickster frowned at him. "Don't overreach yourself. Will Uriel permit this?"

"Uriel can stop me if it's not permitted," Chance said harshly, and he realized as he spoke that he truly meant it. Taking the time to ponder the ethics of each move was exhausting him, and it was a respite to be able to place at least one responsibility on the shoulders of a superior.

He set a hand on the old woman's chair and pulled her out of the room and into his own world. Miranda, who was still sitting in the center of the labyrinth going over some files from her briefcase, jumped back nervously and scattered pages as the chair legs scraped along an edge of the spiraling, brick-faced path, then dug into soft grass and stopped.

"Ahhhh!" the old woman gasped, fully awake at last. "I can *see* you."

"Not as well as I would like. Not as well as you should. Not nearly well enough," Chance said grimly. He gripped her thin wrist, uncaring and ungentle in his desire that she should know the reality of him.

She reared back as if trying to escape, the bleared eyes wide with recognition and fear. "After all these years, you appear! They said the amulet would give me protection and help, but because of it my boy is dead!"

"You should have kept a better lock on your possessions." Perhaps he was doing this too soon after walking that memory, for the old bitterness and hatred seethed with fresh familiarity. "Don't blame me for the boy's death. Tell me about the amulet."

"Which one?"

Chance let her go. He dropped down to sit cross-legged

before her, rested his hands calmly on the cool grass, and re-peated in a slow, measured tone, "Which one?"

"There was the one that was given to me in payment. Then there was the one that was made some time after—but not by me!" she added with fear and haste.

"What do you know about the making of amulets?" asked the Trickster, coming to stand next to Chance.

"N-nothing, I swear!"

The Trickster's eyes flashed wide with fury. "Don't think you can lie to a trickster. You were given the first one, and instead of setting it aside until the day of need, you let curiosity eat at you. Didn't you?"

She began to cry. "If you knew all this, why didn't you stop me when I was young? Why did you wait to torture me now I am old? Why did you let my boy die?"

"We don't 'stop' anything, and we don't 'let' anything," said Chance dispassionately. "But you already know that."

They waited in silence. They had time. She eventually stopped crying. Miranda watched from a distance, her expression appalled and helpless all at once.

"Tell us where your curiosity led. Tell us what you learned about us," the Trickster said, calmer now, but as cold as Chance.

She drew a shaky breath and looked into the distance, seeking a long-ago memory.

"There are three ways for the undying ones to enter the mortal world," she began. "They may take the shadow of an animal or borrow the shadow of a human, or they may make their own shape from matter and illusion. These two ways are temporary, and the undying must eventually return to their formless existence.

"There is a third way. I—I don't know the third way. It is a way for the undying to become immortal—"

"That makes no sense. Undying means the same thing as immortal," Miranda interrupted.

"It does not," Chance said. "We have a limited existence. We are tied to this scroll of space and time like an ant constrained to trace patterns on the same tapestry, always walking the same path in the same manner, never passing the hem. To be truly immortal, one *must* die, and thus go beyond all boundaries."

His eyes met his brother's gaze, and they shared a somber look. That was the theory as they knew it, but what it actually entailed in practice was something neither of them knew.

"An amulet can tie an undying one to a human," Chance continued. "It takes at least two people to make an amulet— one undying and one mortal, and no other may be made by them thereafter. You would never have been able to make another one like yours, but someone learned enough of the craft of making from you. Who?"

"I know nothing more," the old woman insisted.

Chance nodded with a spreading fury that lacked a proper target. He stood up and once more set a hand on the chair. "Then back you go."

She startled him by clutching his hand. "Don't send me back," she begged. "To think clearly again, to understand who and what I am—don't take that away from me. I'm sorry I was careless. Please don't punish me."

He shook her off, infuriated by her plea. "Age is not a punishment. It is merely the passage of time, and it is not my duty to prevent it happening."

"Be still," murmured the Trickster as she started to cry again. "You won't remember this. It will cause you no grief. It need cause you no grief now. Be still."

Miranda got to her feet. Her arms were wrapped around herself in an attempt at self-comfort, and her face was troubled. She bit her lip as if she dared not speak. Chance tried to ignore her, but he could not ignore the sensation of mild shame that filled him when he saw her expression. He nodded to the Trickster, and they went off again to return the old woman to the sunny window, the breezes, and the ever-changing blues of the sea.

Later, as they journeyed back to Miranda, the Trickster broke the pensive silence and asked the expected question. He communicated with his brother as undying to undying, not face to human face, demanding a detail and depth of answer that no mere language would have been able to convey.

"You of all people, allowing yourself to be tied to an amulet! How did that happen? Do you even remember?"

Chance was prepared. He had asked that question of himself, delved beneath the years of his human life, the multitudinous strata of each turn and passage in his undying experience, until at last he had found the moment. With that knowledge, he wordlessly proffered an invitation to his twin, a plea for silent witness and sympathy.

Come and see.

The earliest times of his awareness as undying echoed the similar journey he had taken in his human adolescence. The universe was a delight and a distraction, to play was to learn, and to learn was to risk both fear and joyful surprise. Wilderness was home and adventure at once—the breadth of the savannah, the densely teeming forest, the vastness of deep ocean—each with its range of large, small, complex, and simple intelligences. In shadow, with shadow, Chance grew quickly in skill. But the edges of human habitation soon enticed him, especially the laughter of children.

In every country, old wives' wisdom warned children to keep away from otherworldly creatures lest they be stolen. Most never needed such a warning, as they encountered only the danger of flesh and bone. A few who *did* need the warning were not fortunate enough to receive it.

And then there were those who knew, who had been told but did not care, who chose to seize both fear and joyful surprise together.

"She told me her name," Chance said to the Trickster, and then his past drank them up—Chance to run the route, and the Trickster to observe, just as before.

Six houses nestled in the crook of a curving hill; green crops and rich soil patchworked the terraced land on either side of a brook that ran from hilltop to horizon; and a copse stretched half the length of the hill's gentlest slope, close enough for thirsty roots to tap the watercourse. Throughout the settlement, adults and older children busied themselves with the day's duties. Amid such industry, it was easy to be overlooked when one was old enough for some independence but not yet old enough for some work.

A small child stood at the edge of the trees and spoke with the casual courage of a princess in her own lands. "My name is Joy, and my age is four years and seven months," she declared.

The shy shapeshifter in the woods considered her for a moment, and in answer attempted its first human face. Joy squealed her delight as the dappled light and shadow became a girl of her own age, her perfect companion, and lured her in. As they played, light and shadow became so common to her that she lost track of time completely, and it was only when they came close to where the full sun touched the grass that she heard the voices and wandered out into daylight.

Surrounded by her family, bombarded with sobs and shouted questions, Joy discovered that she had been missing not for a mere afternoon but for an entire year.

"I don't understand. I didn't understand," said Chance then and now.

"Ohh," the Trickster said, too moved to stay silent. "You do not/did not yet understand how time works for us, my friend."

Chance looked at him with all the pain and confusion of the young undying and the pain and knowledge of his mature being. "I'll try/I tried to make it right."

And thus the Trickster saw Chance return to a young woman named Joy, of whom it was said that she had spent a year with the fairies. Much grown, he had come to make amends, but by then she too was older and had grown rooted in a linear time and a stable place. Still, she let herself be persuaded to accept the silver coin and the couplet he gave her in payment for a long lost year.

Blood on the silver, silver in the flame,
Come to my aid when I call your name.

"You meant well," the Trickster reassured him as they departed.

"Is that ever enough?" Chance replied.

CHAPTER SEVEN

When they returned to the edge of the labyrinth, Miranda glanced at them but said nothing. She quickly repacked the briefcase except for a single file, which she held firmly before her. There was a look of determined neutrality on her face. She still stood in the center of the labyrinth, but now she clung to that center as if the path were a barrier or border that would keep her safe.

"I have to talk to you," she said, looking at Chance. Her gaze drifted uncertainly to the Trickster, then focused on Chance once more.

He shook his head in impatience, anticipating trouble from the tone of her voice. "We don't have time for—"

"You told me you always have time," she interrupted. "Listen to me. I—I didn't like how you treated that woman."

Eyes narrowing, Chance angled his head to one side and examined her. He knew the expression would make him look like his old inhuman self rather than the friendlier version who had brought Miranda to his strange new world and reassured her. He wanted her to remember that other Chance and what he was capable of.

"*You* tell *me* that?" he said sharply. "*You* get at truth any way you have to. Isn't that so?"

"Yes," she admitted reluctantly. "But . . . it isn't right when I do it either."

"'Right,'" Chance repeated flatly. "I don't think you know enough about anything to be able to talk about 'right' just yet."

"I want to come with you," she said, raising her voice.

"What?" said the Trickster, startled at last.

Miranda raised her hands to Chance. "I saw him. When you walked the labyrinth, Ajit showed me what you were seeing."

Chance gave his brother a startled look, surprised on two counts: that Miranda had experienced the memory, and that the Trickster had given Miranda his human name.

"I hated myself," she continued. "I tried so hard not to see that boy's face when I was working on the case, and then when I actually saw him die, I couldn't even . . . I didn't feel the way I thought I would, the way I should have. I hated him. I hated his foolish attitude and his foolish choices, and I wanted him to hurry up and die since it was going to happen anyway. And I hated myself for feeling that way. He was just a boy. I thought I'd cry if I saw what he looked like. I thought I'd care."

Tears ran down her face. She lifted her chin and steadied her voice as she raised the file in her hand. "I've been reading, trying to find connections. There are three other victims who might have known the old woman . . ."

"Go on," Chance said.

"Xandre knew Niko Tsavian, Lukas's father, and he mentioned that the murderer had killed people who'd helped him. I think he meant Danil Skalnis, the man who died just before Tsavian, and Galina Arnaud, who was the next to be attacked after the Mermaid and the first one to die. Skalnis and Arnaud were known to volunteer occasionally at the shelter Xandre visited."

She took a breath. "And at some point you're going to have to tell me the other names in your significant seven. There's Galina's baby, but he's listed as missing. No body was found. And that still only makes six."

Chance nodded absently, ignoring her concluding words. "That makes sense. We'll look for where their threads intersect and see who else is there."

"First we'll use Lukas again," the Trickster said. "He'll be able to lead us straight to his father."

"So you'll let me come with you?" she asked.

"Why would you want to?" the Trickster asked in genuine astonishment. "Are you hoping to *force* yourself to care?"

Miranda shook her head and confessed, "I don't know."

"You can't come," said Chance. "There's no point. Besides, it's not safe to have you roaming about in a time and place where you're not supposed to be. You might be seen."

"I could hold her at the edge," said the Trickster, his eyes alight with a troublemaker's innate curiosity. "Or, better yet, give her a little of your power so she can open a window for herself."

"No," said Chance, frowning at him. "I know you love to experiment, but no."

A quiet echoing whisper meant only for him came from the

Trickster's sly-smiling, motionless lips. *She might be able to see things that we can't.*

Chance hesitated. *That might not be advisable,* he answered, also in silence.

We'll take her memory anyway, won't we? Come on. You had a sense of adventure once. Where did it go?

"Very well," Chance said, speaking for Miranda to hear. "And *you're* responsible for her, understand? Keep on the edges, and don't get in my way."

The Trickster smiled and moved instantly and invisibly to stand behind Miranda. He wrapped his arms around her, shocking a gasp from her. "I'll keep her safe and sound," he crooned with an impudent wink.

Paying him any further mind would only encourage him, so Chance simply opened a door and left, trusting them to follow instructions. His brother would charm when he wished and tease as he liked, and there was never any stopping him. He doubted Miranda could be scared off at this point; she was determined to solve the puzzle.

Chance found Lukas easily; the boy's thread still hummed strongly from the previous encounter. Finding Lukas's father was much harder. It was not that the boy lacked for intersection points with his father—rather the opposite. Grief had touched them all with a poignancy that made it difficult to identify which encounters were truly significant and which were merely sentimental. Deciding at last on a reasonably meaningful node, Chance focused on an ordinary scene: a small backyard in the middle of a row of squat, working-class town houses overshadowed by the rear view of a complex of taller City Administration buildings.

Lukas was playing football on a tiny patch of grass with two older children. His father was playing dominoes with a group of men on the back patio. Three women sat near the door in what appeared to be the kitchen, their enjoyment clear from their conversation, wine-drinking, and loud laughter. The men concentrated on their game, occasionally punctuating the general chatter with the explosive sound of tile slammed against wood.

"Annnnd, that's me done," said one with a final victorious crash of his last domino. He reached for a small black board propped up against the patio rails and ceremoniously chalked himself a stripe. "Ravi: three, Sherwyd: one, Niko: one, and Latky: nil."

Ravi laughed loudly and unkindly in the way good friends do at each other, his double chins flattening out against his broad chest as he crouched over to reposition the scoreboard. There was a clacking and sliding as everyone tipped over the dominoes and pushed them toward Sherwyd to mix and deal out again.

"Niko, you're not doing too bad for a novice," Ravi said, clasping his fingers over his belly and looking at the tall, skinny man who was watching the tiles as they spun under Sherwyd's hands. "You should come out more often."

Niko shrugged. His eyes were shadowed as if he had had little sleep for some time. "You know what my work schedule is like, Ravi."

Latky, who had responded to Ravi's mocking laughter

with a sidelong glance and a curl of his lip, arranged his features in a friendlier set as he addressed Niko. "Your son's enjoying himself. Why didn't you bring Marinel?"

"She said she wanted me and Lukas both out of the house so she could get some proper cleaning done," Niko murmured, gathering up his allotment of dominoes as Sherwyd shot them to him one by one across the table. "I wasn't going to complain about that."

The other men laughed, again loudly and unkindly.

"Niko, there are *maids*, and there are *wives*." Sherwyd nodded to one of the women inside the house, presumably his own spouse, who was leaning back with her wineglass tilted dangerously as she laughed at a friend's words. "Please try not to confuse the two."

"I played it safe. I married a maid," said Ravi, deadpan.

Niko was unfazed by their ribbing. He appreciated that whether his wife cleaned house or didn't clean house, they would mock him either way.

"At least she have sense to send Lukas with you, make sure you come straight home," said Latky shrewdly.

"Me, fool around? Marinel find out and leave me one time, so."

"You don't want her to leave you. You keep her like an old suit you hope might fit you again at some point in the future," Sherwyd said with a callousness that suggested he knew Niko better than the other two.

"Oh, God, no," Niko groaned, forcing a smile. "It ain't so bad. I just . . . well, I got a lot of work, you know? Two jobs holding down, barely any spare time. But now is the time to make money so we can be comfortable when we retire. Plenty of time to get reacquainted then. Empty house, with Lukas grown up and gone. Hire a maid for the cleaning and all." He laughed a little more naturally.

Latky's face returned to what appeared to be his default expression—a curl of the lip and a sideways glance—but this time it held not contempt but pity. "Danil missing in action today?" he asked their host.

Sherwyd was pondering his hand and answered absently, not noticing, as Chance did, the touch of maliciousness in the other man's tone. "He said he couldn't make it. Double-booked."

"Once he's not cleaning house too," Latky remarked, sparking another round of chuckles at Niko's expense.

The laughter faded suddenly; the Trickster had tapped Chance on the shoulder and shaken his focus. He carefully removed himself from the scene and found himself in a bizarre made-world. It appeared that the Trickster had taken him very seriously after all, for he had created an ordinary sitting room for Miranda with a comfortable chair facing a large window. There was even a long, low table for her to spread out the papers from her briefcase, which she had done. She was leaning forward in the chair, flipping a pen between her fingers, engrossed in some matter.

"What?" Chance asked his brother irritably.

"Danil. Sounds familiar. One of our victims, yes?" said the Trickster.

"We'll get to him soon enough. Don't we want to see how close we can get to Niko's death?"

"No," said Miranda, eyes fixed on the papers before her.

Chance raised an eyebrow. "Oh?"

"Not necessary. All the details are here, and I understand you're not interested in evidence that leads to Walther Grey. You're looking for the person who's directing him, using him like a tool. Showing up at every death scene isn't the most efficient way to find that out."

She looked up at him, partly puzzled, partly annoyed. "If you can do this, simply go to whatever part of whoever's life, why don't you simply look at Grey's life and find some evidence there?"

The Trickster beamed at his brother with a fake, ferocious smile. "Yes, Chance. Why *don't* we simply do that? After all, that would be the sensible thing to do if we were looking for some *human* influence."

Chance glared at him. This was not a conversation he wanted to have. "There are . . . other aspects to these murders, Miranda. I think you may not have fully understood what you saw when I walked the labyrinth and what you heard when we spoke to the old woman."

Miranda tapped her pen impatiently against the papers on the table. "It's all here, Chance. We always knew we were dealing with some kind of myth-related ritual. We've heard the legend about making a whole body out of parts and calling a *djiena*, an undying one, to ensoul it. That's what the amulet was made for, right?"

Chance was silent.

"Right?" she pressed, her tone uncertain.

The Trickster took pity on both of them. "The legend *is*

just a legend, Miranda. It wouldn't work. It doesn't stop people from trying, apparently, but there's no way we could animate a collection of dead limbs and organs. It's impossible."

She looked down, slightly relieved. "Then there's something else you're not telling me, and I think it has to do with the fact that you didn't say we'd *go* to Niko's death, you said we'd see *how close* we could get to it. Why is that?"

Chance spoke quickly, but not too quickly, and told the part of the truth that would serve him best. "Sometimes we can't get to a place and time if another one of us gets there first."

"And that's what's been happening?" she asked.

"Yes," said the Trickster.

"Do you know who, or why—"

"Yes," said the Trickster abruptly, eyeing Chance. "At least, we have an idea."

Chance said nothing. The malfeasance of the undying was not an easy topic at the best of times; a vague sense of uncertainty and shame made him speechless. Miranda waited, tapping her pen on the table and observing the tension between them.

"All right," she said eventually. "While you two hold onto *your* idea, which, I take it, deals with things beyond mortal ken, I'll share *mine.* I'd like to look in on Marinel. I think it would be very interesting to see—or see if we *can* see—the last time she spoke to her husband."

The Trickster smiled a broad, triumphant, I-told-you-so smile at Chance. "I agree. Why don't you take us there, Miranda?"

"I'm not—" Chance began, anticipating the Trickster's request.

"Just a little," the Trickster coaxed. "And you've done it before, so there's precedent."

"Done what?" asked Miranda anxiously.

"Shared power," Chance clarified, glaring at his brother. "But I didn't do it willingly, and even a small part of my power is still too complex for a human to wield properly." He looked away in defeat from the Trickster's persistent smile. "I'll help you. You just think about who you want to see and where and when you want to see them."

Miranda raised her eyebrows, but she nodded and closed her eyes. Chance looked on with surprised approval as she flicked through memories of the case much as one would run fingers over the physical tabs of a row of hanging files. She tagged every glimpse and mention of Marinel Tsavian and of her husband, Niko. Then she narrowed the selection, jettisoning those of Marinel after her husband's death, and focused on events after the mutilations began.

"What am I doing? How does this help?" she murmured, concentrating.

Chance leaned closer to her ear so that he too could speak in a low voice. "Can you feel anything? A certain similarity? Your senses might interpret it as a sound, a flavor, or a shading of a particular hue. What do you find in all of these scenes?"

"A smell of jasmine," said Miranda in a distant voice that sounded almost sad. "Jasmine and old sandalwood."

"Good," he breathed, careful not to disturb her semi-trance. "Now, leave the case files, leave what you know, and move outward. There's a whole universe before you, but somewhere in it there's the scent of jasmine and sandalwood. Find it, follow it to where it grows stronger."

"I'm afraid of what I'll see," Miranda whispered.

"Too late for that," murmured the Trickster. He raised his voice. "You said you wanted to care. So care, then!"

Miranda's eyes flashed open, and she stared at him with challenge and fury. Chance shot him a quelling look, then turned his back on him, intent on Miranda. "What do you see? Can you find her? Show us."

Miranda's attempt fluttered for a moment, unsure of its direction, but then it took strength from her surge of determination and anger. The scene outside the window, which had stalled on the football game in the backyard, fragmented and reassembled itself into a darker picture: indoors, nighttime, the warm glow of flame under glass in a lamp. There were two people sitting at a table in the room: Niko and Marinel. Niko was crying, not the silent tears of the kind men will admit to, but the gulping, desperate sobs of a small boy. Marinel's face was the face of the woman Chance had seen with Lukas at the shelter, though full-fleshed and unshadowed by grief. She turned slightly away from her husband in irritation as he broke down, and her eyes were half-closed in contempt.

"It doesn't matter, Niko," she said. "I am still leaving."

CHAPTER EIGHT

"All I've done," Niko cried, "everything I've done has been for you and Lukas."

Marinel stared at the wall and replied in a monotone. "I am raising our son by myself as it is. You can still provide money for his support. Nothing will change. You already give us your money instead of your time. Nothing will change."

"Just a few more months," he begged. He was water poured out, a beaten and empty man. To hear him was to cringe in shame and pity. "Just long enough to finish the project. Then I'll be back to one job. We can go back to the way it was before."

"*Was* there a before?" she asked with sudden sharpness. "I don't recall. It feels like it's been this way forever."

She made a small sound of frustration and disgust. Her eyes never looked at him, and her face turned even farther from him. Her coldness seemed to hurt him more than screams and tears and loud words of anguish; at least those would have hinted that she still needed him.

"Danil—" he began bitterly, but she cut him off in an instant.

"*Don't* say his name. Don't dirty it with your insinuating tone and your hatred and your—please, *don't!*"

He laughed—or perhaps it was a sob—astounded at her forceful defense of her lover, as if *he* were the one who had suffered injury and had to be protected from more harm.

"My son," he said, gathering himself together and speaking more calmly. "You'll let me see him?"

"If you can find the time," she said. "If this is what it takes for you to notice him, I should have made this decision a long time ago."

He looked down helplessly. Once or twice he opened his mouth as if hoping words would emerge that could change everything miraculously, but each time he closed his mouth and shook his head as a fresh look of pain and disbelief seared through his clouded gaze.

"I hate this," Miranda whispered.

The Trickster glanced at her, his expression curious, not kind. "Does this help?"

The room shifted. The group of witnesses changed from eavesdroppers at a window to a small front-row audience in a theater. Miranda inhaled sharply and gripped the arms of her seat, tears spilling from her eyes.

"There," said the Trickster, looking at the figures on the stage, looking away from her face. "Suspend your belief. They are only players, and the action is in the past. It's the future that concerns us now."

"Don't be so hard on her," said Chance softly. "She does

this every day, you know. Perhaps not as directly as this, but enough to have to distance herself or go mad. You've been human for long enough to know that."

A small smile quirked the Trickster's lips. "Of course I know the effects. Haven't you noticed a significant increase in my own personal store of eccentricity? I think you had the right idea, going through so many years of your life in self-imposed, blissful ignorance."

"Shhh," said Miranda, still weeping but still intent on the drama before them.

"I'll leave," said Niko suddenly. "I'll take a post on a ship. It's hard work, but it's a lot of money in a short time. We'll take some time apart and discuss this when I get back."

"Nothing will change," Marinel began wearily.

He rushed on. "You should stay here till I get back. Don't upset Lukas's life. Not yet. At the very least, it will give us a chance to do things properly, calmly. Without haste. Without regret." His voice was strengthening. He spoke as if he knew this was the one tactic that could work: when prevention fails, delay.

She shrugged, but she did not say no. His breathing relaxed and quieted at this small scrap of hope. She got up and left the room, but he stayed at the table, breathing slowly and with increasing deliberation. Only the look of naked shock that remained in his eyes spoke of the blow to his soul.

"Curtain," whispered the Trickster, and he let a fabric-like ripple erase the scene before them. "Good, Miranda—very good for a beginner—but that wasn't the last time they spoke. That was the context, if you will. Are you ready for the final act?"

Miranda coughed and cleared her throat. She had dried her face, and though her expression was still focused, it was peaceful. She had started to come to terms with what she was doing and how she was doing it. Her voice, however, was still rough with tears. "Yes. That's the point of all this."

The Trickster looked at Chance and nodded. Chance sighed quietly and murmured to Miranda. "As before, jasmine and sandalwood."

Miranda's eyes were already closed in concentration. "And tears," she said softly.

In many respects, Niko and Marinel were perfectly suited to each other, for when they argued again, each took on the tone and mannerisms of the other from the first confrontation. He was supercilious and cold, refusing to make eye contact when they met in the street. She was shaken and humiliated, trying every gesture and tone to reach him, crawling in the dust of his footsteps. He kept walking along the road away from her, ignoring her words. When he opened the door of the town house they had shared, she jumped forward and stood braced over the threshold as if afraid he would bar her from entering, but he merely pushed past her. His entire attitude was an implicit insult as he started to take off his muddy overshoes without even bothering to see whether or not she was coming in.

She shut the door quickly behind her and stretched out her hands toward him.

"Please! I have nowhere to go. They think I had something to do with it."

"You mean you didn't?" he asked casually, hanging up his rain jacket by the door. "I wonder why they'd think that, then?"

"I'm so scared, Niko. I'm scared for myself, and I'm scared for Lukas too. Whatever it is, what if it comes for him next? You *do* want to protect your own son, don't you? You *must*."

He gave her a glance out of the corner of his eye, paused long enough to see her shoulders slump in despair, then shrugged. "Then leave him with me. You know I'll take care of him. But you—you can take care of yourself."

She gave a soft sob, and at the sound of it he broke suddenly, his face going from coldness to fury. "You heard me! Bring him here. I don't want you in my life ever again. I want my son!"

She collapsed slowly, gradually huddling to the floor, where she knelt and moaned and rocked. He looked at her in disgust, raising his fist reflexively, but he struck the wall instead. Tearing his jacket from the hook, he flung the door open with enough force to make it thump loudly against the wall, then slammed it closed again with equally brutal impact, shutting himself out of the house and into an early, cloudy twilight with a pale gray drizzle. He paused on the doorstep, one point of tension and turmoil in a peaceful, neutral scene, his chest heaving and his entire body shaking.

His breathing calmed, and he pulled on the jacket slowly, but he still shook. He turned toward the docks and walked the familiar road, now obscured and eerie in the misty rain.

"This is it," Miranda whispered. "That's the jacket he was wearing when they found the body, and that was when she claimed she saw him last. This is the day he died."

Chance exchanged a startled glance with his brother above Miranda's head.

"Keep on," the Trickster breathed, too fascinated to remember his usual cynical nonchalance. "See how far we can get with this one."

It was bad luck, perhaps, that Niko was so distraught, because he took to the narrower alleys of the City in his desperation to avoid the few people who were out in the clammy, unpleasant weather. He turned up his hood and walked on in a dream as the pale gray became dark gray and the streetlights came on. Their light illuminated the fine droplets close by but failed to penetrate deeper, and Niko was soon walking from island to island of reality, disappearing from their sight each time he entered the shadowed space between lamps.

It took him some time to notice the footsteps with his hood up and the rain falling on it with a light sibilance. Nor did Niko call out when he did notice. The man did not look dangerous. He held no weapon. He merely ambled slowly along the road, head down and shoulders hunched under his raincoat, and stopped a few meters before he reached Niko.

"Niko Tsavian?" he inquired. "Former supply master on the merchant ship *Winter Sun*?"

Niko paused, turned slightly, and squinted through the drizzle. "Yes. Who wants me?"

"We do."

It was too quick for him to cry out. The slender knife went

straight up and into his chest with such suddenness that all he could manage was a choked moan, then a long, low sigh as he slowly sagged. Walther Grey held him as he fell and calmly dragged him to the shelter of a small cul-de-sac, where he laid him down gently on the wet paving stones. He tugged loose the knife from Niko's chest, wiped it thoroughly on the dying man's wet jacket, and tucked it into his own raincoat. From another pocket he took out a scalpel and held it aloft in gloved hands, pondering the first cut.

"Only a touch."

The voice did not belong to Grey. It was more than sound; it echoed in flesh and bone and made the skin prickle with the passage of subtle lightning. Chance stiffened, noting without a glance that his brother had also gone very still and that Miranda was looking at them both, sensing the tension and puzzled by it. Couldn't she see it? Couldn't she see that formless figure, that undying one, standing on the edge of human reality, observing the slaughter with a casualness that suggested this was an old trick?

"I can do it," Grey replied, trembling in irritation and fear.

"You are too careless. A touch is enough. I will do the rest."

Grey cut through outer and inner garments until Niko's bleeding torso was bare. He carefully lowered the tip of the blade, traced a shallow line over the sternum, and drew back. The bone cracked with a shocking sound like wood breaking. The ribs opened out like the leaves of a book, gaping red but strangely scant of flow, as if the blood vessels refused to acknowledge their severing. The shadow leaned forward at last with an eager hand, grasping the heart and folding it smaller and smaller into his fist until it was consumed, or absorbed, by his own substance.

Miranda, seeing at last, cried out. The tension increased a hundredfold, lightning gone from subtle to sharp. The entity on the edge wavered, blurred in disbelief, and then hardened with menace.

We have been seen. Chance and the Trickster discarded their human appearances and knit themselves into a protective cocoon around Miranda. The made-room, the theater for her viewing convenience, vanished. Chance could feel Miranda screaming within him. He ignored her and held even more tightly to his brother, ensuring that neither seam nor crack could be found in the shield that protected Miranda from annihilation. The rogue undying one, furious at being found, hit them like a hurricane, tearing at their combined fabric with desperate strength and malicious intent.

Chance could not think to decide where to go; he was far too occupied in keeping the barrier intact. Once he had bragged about not working with subordinates, but now he wished with all his will that he had someone to call on, someone besides his brother. To give him credit, the Trickster was fully present and putting all his effort into holding the shield, but even that might not be enough. Neither dared to unravel himself long enough to attack, and defense was a waiting game that they could not win. Part of him, a very small part that was not engaged in the struggle, felt angry and ashamed that he had brought Miranda into this after all his promises that nothing could hurt her. He wondered whether Uriel knew what was happening and, if they did, whether they would intervene. It was not something to count on, for being a passive guard in an undying made-world was different from participating in a real-world fight. Interference was not a thing the angels undertook lightly.

Fortunately, the Trickster thought faster. "Patience," he shouted. *"Patience!"*

The hurricane stopped. The two brothers did not move at first, too stunned by the sudden calm to relax. The only sound was Miranda's panicked, panting gasps, the sound of a claustrophobic in the middle of her worst nightmare. Chance and the Trickster untangled from each other and reassembled in human guises on either side of Miranda. She lay curled like a child on the floor. A woman with silver hair came forward to comfort her with a gentle hand on her shoulder and a low hum of words.

I wish you two would pay attention when I tell you things, she said to Chance and the Trickster, but that was spoken in silence so that the soothing murmurs to Miranda could continue without interruption.

"How *can* we when you don't tell us everything?" the Trickster replied, annoyed that he had been the one to break and call on her.

Chance said nothing. He was too relieved to be troubled by such mild chastisement. He looked around instead to reassure himself that they were safe. They were in an open space with a ceiling invisibly lost in ever-increasing light and a horizon that continued to extend the longer he looked at it. The floor was mundane earth, smooth and close-packed like a lake bed that had slowly dried out and weathered under a gentle breeze. Somehow, in spite of the vastness, when he stopped trying to guess at the boundaries and looked toward the center again, he felt the comfortable closeness of a small room surrounding him.

"I told you not to take her out of your world. Why do you think I asked Uriel to help us?" Patience said. Her face was relaxed, her tone almost offhand. Chance stared at her, but her attention was almost entirely on Miranda. She crouched closer, put her arms around Miranda's silent, shivering form, and rocked back and forth. Chance began to reach toward Miranda, awkward in his guilt and shame.

There was a blurring of vision, a subtle shift as if a too-heavy foot had shaken reality, and Uriel stood before them, casting a massive shadow that was slashed with light and color. The angel did not look angry—yet—but the tension in the air was frightening. Both Chance and the Trickster stopped short, speechless.

"You should not have brought her outside," the angel said.

"It was only for a moment. A blink of an eye. She was never in the world, just on the edges," the Trickster tried to explain.

"You took her from our protection. There is nothing we can do for her now." The angel turned away from them, and there was a sighing and drawing up of the very fabric of the place as it warped under the strain of their leaving.

"No, wait!" Chance shouted. "Please, you promised your help! We still need you!"

The angel refused to turn around as they stated with finality, "You brought her out. He has the feel of her thread now. There is nothing that can be done. We did what we said we would do. We can do no more."

They became one with the overwhelming light at the horizon and disappeared.

"Well," said Patience sadly, "that's that. I will have to step in after all. Now that you have the trail, you can go find him. I'll take care of Miranda."

"Who was that undying one? You already know—why don't you tell us? Why send us to waste time chasing him down?" The Trickster sounded angry, but Chance knew he was still scared.

Patience looked up at him, and her smile was strangely sorrowful. "You of all people should know that I cannot pick and choose when it comes to which of my children I can help. I have decided to allow free will, and I am holding to that decision, as much suffering as it may cause me from time to time."

She looked down at Miranda again with pain and regret. "Now go, before he causes more disruption."

Chance went on one knee before Patience and touched Miranda's arm lightly. His gaze fixed on Patience. "I am sorry."

Patience bowed her head in acknowledgment, and her grieved expression eased somewhat, but she only repeated softly, "Go."

Chance stood and turned to the Trickster. In silence they agreed on their destination, and in silence they vanished.

CHAPTER NINE

"You are far too calm about this," the Trickster snarled.

They had come to the edge of the village at a time of usual quiet: midnight. The river ran nearby; the scant flow of dry season was so muted as to be nearly inaudible under the shrill, incessant chirping of frogs and crickets.

"You know me better than to say that," Chance murmured. "Nothing wrong with pausing to think for a moment instead of running amok."

The Trickster paced a short track up and down the bank while Chance stood silent, head slightly bowed and arms folded, expressionless in the dark. Finally the pacing steps slowed and stopped.

"Chance, what will happen to us when we die—as humans?" His tone was unusually subdued.

"I don't know," Chance admitted. "Perhaps when the ending of the mortal thread is complete, we will go back to being purely undying and not this betwixt and between."

"Perhaps we will simply cease to exist," the Trickster countered, a nasty edge to his voice. "A full and final death."

"So? When all the paths have been walked, all the threads traveled—some twice and thrice over—that which I call 'I' will eventually fragment and dissolve, and my essence will return to whence it came. The journey will be complete, the tapestry finished. It is not a death, but it is still an end." His words turned poetic with a singing cadence that nonetheless sounded very somber.

The Trickster shook his head with a wry smile, recognizing the ritual chant in Chance's words. "Do you *really* trust Patience to know everything, much less tell us what she knows?"

Chance sighed. "I cannot even trust the angels to do that. *Why me?* I asked the one who summoned me, and they gave me a nonanswer about my being an expert on human and undying interactions. And when I saw it was Miranda—"

The Trickster chuckled. "Yes, I thought that was amusing. That's when I suspected Patience was involved. She likes counterpoint patterning. She's very good at it."

"Amusing, you say. Perhaps not. Perhaps I've been mistaken about everything. You know what the real problem is."

"Yes." The Trickster began pacing again, but more meditatively. "The fact that you cannot approach this undying one suggests that you share the same essence."

Startled and angry, Chance glared at his brother for daring to voice such a thing. "What do you mean? You haven't been able to approach him either. You couldn't get close to the time of the murders."

"Of course, he's done his best to hide his presence from other undying," said the Trickster, speaking in a gentler voice. "That's not what I'm referring to. When we joined to protect

Miranda and he attacked us, the shock was formidable, but it was all sound and rage and buffeting—except when he tried to rip me apart. *I* felt that. But Chance, he wasn't able to touch any part of the shield that was *you*."

Chance unfolded his arms slowly and raised his head so that his gaze went to the horizon of trees silhouetted against starlight. He had been fragmented only once, just before he became human, during his earlier era of arrogance and rebellion. To punish him, Patience had bled off a portion of his power and transferred it to a Stick. He remembered what it had been like to lay hands on that Stick while he was still barred from taking back his power. A storm of light, ice, and gales had been unleashed as reality struggled to reconcile two separate embodiments of a single being.

Somewhere in the midst of his fight with their adversary, he had sensed a similar storm.

"He is not me!" he insisted harshly.

The Trickster sighed. "No, he is not you. But I'm guessing that he *is* made of your undying essence."

Another pang of memory went through Chance. No, not once—twice. Twice he had been unmade. When at last he had returned to Patience for judgment, she had proposed a unique solution. He shivered, recalling the sensation as Patience had peeled and unwound his very being from him, like stripping bark from a tree, preparing the tender core of his soul for rebirth into humanity. "Patience," he said softly. "What has she done?"

The Trickster's eyes glittered in the starlight, wide with shock. "All the time we were growing up as Paama's sons, hiding from the world of the undying for our various crimes, I thought you were pretending to forget. I thought you made yourself small, weak, and dormant for the same reason I did, so as not to attract attention, but she really *did* pare you down."

Chance veered away from considering the unthinkable and focused on his initial question. "Why me? I believed I was sent to effect a change. Now I wonder if I am simply the canary in the mine, a way to detect what cannot be seen."

"Canary in the mine or bait in a trap," the Trickster amended.

Chance nodded slowly. "If he *is* of my essence . . . this changes everything, even what we imagine to be real."

"What has already happened might . . . unhappen?" mused the Trickster.

"Balanced probabilities, unformed realities, waiting for a critical choice to be made and witnessed. A rare occurrence and a challenge to resolve, but not unprecedented."

"Ah," said the Trickster, his eyes filled with awe and fear and anticipation. "One of *those* situations. I should have guessed."

"I should have known. Tell me, since we were born, have you been able to touch any new threads in the far future, any threads more than one hundred years hence that we have *not* already traveled in pure undying form?"

"I have not," the Trickster acknowledged. "It has all been past-work since we became human. Why is that?"

"It makes a kind of sense," Chance said, forcing himself to sound more upbeat. "Humans can't see into their future, and we are temporarily human."

"It also makes a kind of sense if who we are comes to an end when we die as humans," the Trickster said grimly.

"There's that," Chance replied, no longer upbeat.

There was a long silence.

"What do we do?" asked the Trickster at last.

Chance shook his head. "We go forward. We have to find the human who made a deal with this undying one and discover which death will be the turning point. I was told that one of the deaths is significant. It could be the last thing needed to complete the deal."

"And that death could be mine, or yours," said the Trickster.

Chance did not reply, already scanning the files in his memory for the next step to take. They had to go; their respite was over. Never before had time seemed so scant or so precious.

"We're going hunting," the Trickster sang gleefully.

Chance glared at him. "Please, focus. And while I am glad you're enjoying this, please consider for a moment that I might *not* be and have some respect."

"We all have our coping mechanisms, dear brother," murmured the Trickster with a sudden serious twist to his mouth.

Chance nodded in sympathy.

"What do you think Miranda is doing right now?" the Trickster asked almost wistfully.

"Being safe," Chance said brusquely.

He stooped, picked up a twig, and traced slow, careful spirals into the fine, dry soil of the riverbank. "We're going hunting," he confirmed, his expression strong, peaceful, and adamant. "But there is more than one way to hunt."

The Trickster stepped closer, leaning in to watch Chance's patterning. "Bait in a trap."

"Better than wild chasing at this stage." Chance twiddled

his small stick, sat back on his heels like a small boy waiting to pitch marbles or an elder contemplating his next move at warri.

"To what purpose? We are not fooled by rituals, remember?"

"No, but we are drawn to them. I will craft such a labyrinth out of their images of him that he *will* be caught like a foolish flame between many mirrors." Chance snapped the twig and stood. "I will need more space."

The Trickster tilted his head, a growing light in his eyes that was part admiration, part excitement. "I almost forgot how powerful you are. In fact, I thought you had forgotten too."

Chance curled a finger and spoke mid-transition. "I'm not sure either of us fully understands what power is."

They came in darkness to an open land that felt vast, cold, and dry. Stars sparkled with an aggressive fire, unmuted in the clear night sky. Chance knew the terrain well. It was the Great Desert south of the City, a place that boasted some small human presence near the coast and around the scant springs and wells that by some happy geological accident tapped the rich reservoirs of the grasslands on its western border. The rest was waterless, a dead land with neither witness nor impediment to strange happenings.

Chance settled his feet firmly and began.

Light puffs of air trailed chill along the back of his neck. The wind picked up, turning this way and that, flinging up the fine sand to sting his ankles. A small dust devil, gleaming faintly with reflected starlight, coalesced near his right hand. He sent it out with a twitch of a forefinger. More funnels were appearing, each dipping a toe into the smoothly rippling desert and carving a shallow path. They drew more than sand in their wakes; it felt like the tug of a trawling net.

"Fine control," said the Trickster as the little spinners split and multiplied, chasing all over the landscape in a coordinated flurry.

"Thank you," Chance replied, his voice distant as he concentrated. "I believe this should be large enough."

The Trickster stepped back slightly, as if trying to escape from the increasing pull. "Do you need me for this?"

Chance said nothing, quietly choreographed the wind and sand, and waited for the real question. The wind sang and the sand hissed, but the Trickster did not speak until the wind died down and the sand was placed exactly where it should be. Only then did he try again.

"I cannot walk this one with you."

"I wouldn't ask it of you," Chance replied, "but I hoped you might at least remain as an observer. You know me better than anyone. Whatever emerges from this labyrinth, you will know how to deal with it."

It was a rare occasion to find the Trickster without a smile, whether of glee, bitterness, sarcasm, or mischief, but his face was drained of expression while he contemplated. Eventually he nodded briskly. "I can still be useful. Wait."

He walked a little farther away from the border of the labyrinth and sat down cross-legged on the bare sand, the gilt-threaded hem of his white wrap glinting in the light as it pressed taut against his legs like a bandage or a strip of winding sheet. Resting his hands on his knees, he bent his head and shut his eyes.

Chance watched closely.

A dark gray haze burned off the Trickster's body like steam from a hot road in rainy season. More liquid than smoke, it coiled out with a motion that warned of sentience and independent power. He raised his hands and began to weave and braid the black gossamer before him. His eyes remained closed, but his face was intent with an inward gaze as the web grew dense, thick and wide, billowing up and out like a sail.

"That should be enough," he whispered, resting his hands on his knees once more. "Come closer."

Chance did not know what to expect, and yet he went forward and stood below the canopy that now hid the stars. The web settled over him like a collapsing tent and brushed his skin with a vibrant thrill that was at once terrifying and familiar. He did not fight it as it sank into him with caution, maintaining a distance that was skin-deep from his own quintessence yet swaddling him completely.

"What is this ?" he asked, not daring to guess.

"A partial shadow. He won't expect you to be able to touch him, but now, with my covering, you can."

"Clever," Chance said. "And generous. Thank you." He frowned, suddenly comprehending the Trickster's unusual stillness. "But . . . you have weakened yourself."

The Trickster tried to shrug but only managed to twitch a shoulder briefly. "I wouldn't have been much good in a fight anyway."

"Then at least go where you can be protected. Go to Patience. She can look after you and keep Miranda safe at the same time."

"I think I will do just that," came the quiet reply. "I can think of a few other ways to make myself useful. Good hunting, brother."

Chance flexed his fingers within his new skin, almost wanting an excuse to linger, but he did not indulge himself. He nodded a farewell to the Trickster and turned away to enter the labyrinth.

BOOK II

MEMORY

CHAPTER TEN

"Why me?" Miranda whispered.

After Chance and the Trickster had departed, she had become still and quiet, like a child wearied by crying. Now, pulling awkwardly away from Patience, she stood up and surveyed her surroundings, turning fully to see all around and above her. Somehow, in all her scrutiny, she managed to avoid looking directly at the strange woman who had been consoling her.

"Where is Chance now?" she asked.

Patience pressed her lips together. It might have been an almost human gesture of caution. It might have meant nothing. Even if she was of the same ilk as Chance and the Trickster, she was far less readable.

"I want to go home," Miranda snapped. "I don't care who you are or what happened just now. I want to go home."

Patience remained seated on the floor, her hands folded in her lap, her gaze lowered. "You cannot. He is looking for you."

Miranda's anger gave way to confusion. "Chance is looking for me?"

"Not Chance. Another whom you did not see and have not met. Not yet. Not ever, if I can help it."

Miranda spun around in helpless fury, but there was nothing to throw, no walls to hit or kick. She was reduced to clenching empty fists, stamping and shouting. "Let me go home!"

"I do not advise it," Patience said soberly. "Your past and your future are now changing significantly. You cannot go until they have been resolved. It would be like walking on quicksand—perilous and likely to take you in a direction that you do not intend."

"Don't say that! How dare you say that? That's not possible!" Miranda fidgeted, rubbing her fingers together, trying to persuade herself of her own reality by mere touch.

Patience waited, and eventually Miranda grew still once more, her gaze lowered in resignation.

Miranda raised her head and looked steadily at Patience. "There's no need for this. Stop it now. Let me go back."

"No," said Patience. "Nothing can hurt you here. As for elsewhere . . . I cannot be held responsible."

Miranda kept silent. She sat on the floor and stared down again, grimly swallowing back tears. For a long time, the hall was quiet.

Head still bowed, Miranda spoke slowly. "You want something from me." She looked up and glared at Patience.

Patience did not meet her eyes. "Yes. Something I cannot ask."

Miranda began to laugh. "You're not even trying. You won't tell me what's going on. You won't even look at me. What am

I supposed to say? Do you want me to give you permission to ask? You want me to say I trust you?"

"I do not want you to trust me," Patience said harshly. "I do not want you to like me or fear me or pay me any mind whatsoever. I want your decision on this matter to have nothing to do with me."

"All right," said Miranda, standing up shakily. "I'll ask, then. What do I have to do to get back home?"

"That is the wrong question," said Patience, her voice soft with regret. Her face was ageless, and only her silver hair hinted at an elder's status, and yet between the gentle voice and the serene, resigned look of sorrow, she seemed very like a mother, and Miranda her rebellious child.

"What do you need me to do?" The words came unwillingly.

Patience looked at Miranda, meeting her eyes at last. "I will need your help to put an end to the undying one who is looking for you."

"Why?"

"I am too close to him, too much akin. He can sense my presence and be gone in an instant. I know where he will be, but I cannot approach him without his knowledge. I would need a disguise."

"There are three ways for an undying one to enter the mortal world," Miranda recited. "They can make their own shape, but they can also borrow the shadow of a human. Is that what you want from me? To steal my likeness?"

"No," Patience said softly.

Miranda swallowed, breathed deeply, and continued, "The

third way—the old woman who made the amulet wouldn't speak of it. Is that what you want from me?"

"Something like that, but not as permanent," Patience replied.

Miranda mulled over the words as if trying and failing to convince herself that they were reassuring. "Explain," she said finally.

"An undying one may be willingly hosted by a human, but over time they will bleed into each other, and fuse their spirits together. Then, when the time comes for the human to die, the undying nature will take over."

"What does that mean?"

Patience smiled as she tried to find words adequate for human understanding. "It is rarely attempted for good reason. The human may become undying. The undying may become human. Melded together, both may or may not become immortal. It is a gamble. I do not know if the two elements are meant to combine in that manner."

"Uriel told us that our task was to detain a man on the path to immortality."

Patience lifted up her palms in a gesture of helplessness. "The angels know more than I do, but a path is not the same thing as a destination."

"This . . . hosting. Will it hurt?"

"The hosting, no. The leaving . . ." Patience trailed off, her eyes growing troubled. "It is not a trivial matter for an undying one to be hosted by a human. It is an operation of some depth and entanglement. A grave shock is required to sever the connection."

"What kind of shock?"

"You would have to die."

Miranda's face drained of all emotion. "But . . . but you said at that point the undying nature would take over," she mumbled.

"If the time of hosting is short, it should be possible for me to leave."

Miranda pressed the heel of her hand over her brow. "So you're asking me to die for you."

"That may happen, but perhaps someone will manage to resuscitate you in time."

Miranda dropped her hand and looked at her with tired eyes. "After all that, would death be preferable?"

"It might be, and yet . . . and yet surviving at any cost might be precisely what I need you to do."

Miranda brought both hands up and pushed them firmly against her eyelids. "Nice choices you have for me. Death, or worse than death."

"This is why I tell you: do not trust me."

"You have a problem, then. If I can't trust you, how will you get me to help you?"

"I will show you. Then you can choose." Patience spoke with certainty; she had finally come to the desired point of the conversation.

"Show me what?"

"Your future. *A* future. A very likely one. Possibly the only one that will lead to the outcomes we desire. You and Chance will detain a man on the path to immortality, I will correct a personal error, and you will go home."

The atmosphere shifted. Miranda turned quickly, her breath suddenly shallow. To her right, where there had once been featureless ground, was a large white stone labyrinth patterned in the dark soil.

"That's not like the one Chance had me walk," she whispered.

"No. That was the past. This is the future. You may suffer some déjà vu if you decide to live it again."

"Are you trying to trick me?" Miranda asked, still whispering. "These are only illusions."

Patience shook her head. "Once you walk that labyrinth, you will *know*. It is the only way."

Miranda had already abandoned disbelief; now even fear was leaving her. She had been told the worst; now she was accepting it. She looked at the labyrinth again, or rather she focused on the white stone that marked the start of the path. She stared at it, and gradually her face and body relaxed.

"Very well," said Miranda quietly. "Let's go."

She stepped forward onto the first stone.

The Trickster, silent witness throughout, took the opportunity to show himself. He coughed apologetically.

"Ajit," said Patience, looking at him with the expected lack of surprise and an unexpected amount of tolerance. "Chance has started the work?"

The Trickster nodded. Patience was not omniscient—she merely knew him too well—but she could still awe him into good behavior and serious speech. "I couldn't stay to help him, but perhaps I could help Miranda?"

Patience almost smiled. "She's perfectly safe."

"She . . ." The Trickster hesitated. "She is," he acknowledged, "but she will not know that. May I go with her?"

She regarded him silently for a moment. "It is a very large labyrinth."

"As large as only you can manage," he agreed. "I understand what that means. I'll keep my head on. I will remember that it's not real."

"You must not expect to be able to change anything. I am obliged to show her the worst case so that her choice, when she makes it, shall be fully informed."

"Yes . . . an interesting choice. You prepare in advance?"

Patience chuckled at his folly. "I prepare in the moment, every moment, wherever it may fall in time."

"Of course. Being human has made my thinking lazy. But I do wonder, in my small, limited way, what you are really expecting to get out of this."

"I know you have been guessing at that for a very long time," Patience replied. "Now, will you walk the labyrinth, or will you keep talking in the hope that I might say something that will satisfy your curiosity?"

He laughed. "I'll walk. I'll walk and wonder and keep an eye on my friend Miranda. You're a cruel mother, Patience."

"Because I expect my children to grow up?" she countered. "Go take care of her."

He approached the first stone, stopped, and breathed deeply. He was afraid. What Patience called "safe" was not always comfortable. A cruel mother indeed—she had sent him to be human, and being human had taught him new ways to fear— but he trusted her with every tiny scrap and sliver of innocence that remained in the depths of his jaded Trickster soul. And at last, as always, his curiosity triumphed over his fear. He took a step into the labyrinth and let go.

CHAPTER ELEVEN

"Miranda?"

He kept his voice gentle. He knew she was awake. Already the labyrinth had shaped her, putting her body in a hospital bed, broken and still, immobilized like a trapped insect in a web, held in a complicated tension of supports, restraints, and dangling counterweights. Already her mind had shaped *him*, making him into a doctor, white coat and all. He fingered his stethoscope and wished he had the heart to laugh.

Her eyes were barely open. A soft noise, too faint and voiceless to be a moan, came from her lips. Absently, still intent on watching her face, he took up a fresh damp cloth from a small basin on a nearby trolley. He touched it gently to her mouth so the moisture could seep slowly into her parched skin and noted her injuries. Scrapes and deep-blooming bruises were clearly visible, and he could also sense the fractures and fault lines of pain that traced her skull—brow, cheekbone, chin, teeth, and jaw. But those were murmurs, a soft hum of woodwinds under the loud, sharp brass of cutting, digging, crunching pain that blared out from her lower back and hips.

A long spasm of pain squeezed her eyes closed, squeezed her entire body tight in a vise of trembling muscles. He put aside the cloth, hesitated, and placed his hand near her on the bed, unsure whether his touch would comfort her or add to her pain. When the spasm was over, she opened her eyes and looked directly at him. For a moment he could not tell whether there was awareness in that look, but then she brushed a finger against his hand. She tried to speak and wept instead, two scant tears that barely tipped over the corners of her eyelids. That made up his mind. It might be cheating, but he could not bear to see her suffer.

"Come with me for a while." He held out his other hand and showed her a large spider sitting on his palm, one of the hairy-legged desert varieties that allegedly made good pets. He leaned over and deposited it just below her sternum, smiling at the growing confusion and anger in her eyes. Outrage became slow realization as she detected the pull on her consciousness. When it was over, her eyes were left half-closed, empty of understanding and too close to the look of death for comfort. But the spider's eyes now glittered with interest.

"This isn't a real spider," Miranda said. She raised a foreleg and examined it curiously.

"No. It's a shadow. I made it for you," replied the Trickster. He scooped her up and took two quick steps away from the bed and her barely tenanted body, far enough to back slightly off the labyrinth path and into a side bubble of his own making.

"Where are you taking me?" she asked, but mildly, as if unconcerned about anything beyond the blissful absence of pain.

"Here," said the Trickster, raising the flat of his hand like a pedestal and showing her a pastoral scene, green fields rising and falling in low hills and shallow valleys. "Not Chance's world, but very like it. I thought you might like to be in a familiar place."

He sat, put his back against the broad bole of a tree, drew his feet up, and placed Miranda carefully on one bent knee. To his surprise, the stethoscope was still around his neck, bouncing against his hand as he settled himself. He pulled it off, coiled it up, and threw it away into the distance. "So, how are you holding up?"

"What a question!" chirped Miranda. "I don't know what's happened to me. I don't even know if I'm alive or dead from one moment to the next. For now, I'm glad the pain is gone."

The Trickster nodded firmly. "Yes. We owe you that at least, for a time." He paused, gazing at her. "You do have to go back, but I'll come again, you know," he said, answering her unspoken question.

"But not yet?" she asked quickly.

"No. Not yet. Enjoy the shadow. Test it out."

"He can't find me here, can he? That thing that attacked us?"

The Trickster shook his head. "He's occupied. Chance is keeping an eye on him for us."

The spider eyes looked at him suspiciously, but she left it alone. It was obvious that she did not want to know.

"Show me how to spin a web," she demanded.

He laughed at her.

"Show me how to spin a labyrinth."

He stopped laughing. "Why do you want to do that?"

"I'm walking a labyrinth right now, aren't I? That's the way the undying get humans to travel through time. Maybe if I spin one myself, I can go where *I* want."

He kept careful control of his expression as he tried to assess whether she had returned to full rationality or whether she was still dazed by the memory of pain and drugs. "If you want to leave the labyrinth, all you have to do is tell Patience your decision."

Miranda scuttled down from his knee, across his lap, and onto the back of his hand, her legs busy with nervousness. "My decision—"

"Yes. If this is too much, you don't have to do it. You can stop. Say you want it to stop. She can't force you to do what she wants. She won't." He stopped himself before he began to sound pathetic in his pleading.

"No," Miranda agreed. "But she did seem to think this was the only way to be fair, to show me why I should help her without my having to trust her word."

He grimaced. "That's Patience for you. She loves the *idea* of free will."

Miranda fell silent again. The Trickster watched her, his hand flexing slightly under her.

"I can't show you how to make a labyrinth," he said at last. "You're too human for that. But I *can* show you how to weave a fence to hold back the pain."

She looked up, all gem-bright eyes and eagerly twitching limbs. "Show me. Show me now."

Weaving was like labyrinth-walking in some ways. It took the mind to a place of narrow focus, shutting out the distractions that pulled the consciousness every which way. He took as long as was needed for her to learn the movements of body and mind to craft a cocoon as strong as a hospital narcotic. He also remarked that she would need to practice when she returned in order to convert the spider leg movements to human finger movements.

"But it's all in the mind, really," he reassured her.

He continued to talk, distracting her, avoiding difficult topics and choosing to act as if their only concern was weaving and weaving well. Her return to the hospital was swift, like a sleight of hand, a very smooth and professional transition between worlds as if he too had improved his concentration after the weaving exercise. He put her on the linen-swaddled heap in the bed, his cupped hand restricting her vision, and sensed her consciousness trickle back where it belonged, running along tributary nerves already blissfully numbed by a fresh dose of painkillers.

"Will I see you again?" she asked.

He hesitated. This was, after all, her journey and not his. "Eventually. I can't be sure when. Would you like me to bring you a shadow again?"

"Yes . . . well, no . . . not the spider," she mumbled slowly. "It feels like I'm missing four legs now. I don't like it. Maybe no shadow at all. I don't know. I'm tired."

He touched her hand briefly, took up the small shadow, and drew back until the room faded to gray fog. Years as a human had not yet taken from him the ability to see in multiple ways, and so even as he stood aside, he could see the true Miranda more clearly, her eyes closed and body upright, walking slowly on the broad stones of the labyrinth with the concentration of a high-wire artist.

He looked away and caught Patience observing him watching Miranda.

"You never do things singly," he mused. "There is more to this than Miranda's permission. What *are* you doing?"

"You should ask," Patience scoffed gently. "I have seen you weave a web so threadbare that you had to go back and fill in the gaps before you could hope to catch anything."

"And what are you hoping to catch? Or should I say whom?"

He did not expect a direct answer, and Patience did not disappoint. "It would be good if Miranda were to find out who is truly responsible for the murders in the City."

"You're giving us that much reality within the labyrinth?" he said, astounded. "I mean—"

"I understand what you mean. Reality is, after all, relative, but yes, I am giving you enough information to be able to uncover the truth. My own hands are somewhat tied, but a little natural curiosity from a trickster may be overlooked."

Hands tied. The Trickster did not question her further. He had long ago discovered that Patience had a strange regard for some unknown set of rules—rules that did not at all apply to the small powers at his junior level. Part of him did not wish to know, and so he moved on to another question. "I assume I can take appropriate action depending on what I find?"

She smiled at him, a little sadly but with great affection. "I am counting on it."

He blinked, fighting a surge of unexpected and complex emotion. For a moment she had sounded just like his mother— his human mother, Paama. It was the tone of mingled pride and exasperation that had been a common feature of his teenage years. Then he shook himself free of sentimentality. If he started thinking of Patience in human maternal terms, there was no telling what he might let her get away with. Instead he nodded curtly and turned back into the flow of the labyrinth.

Miranda lay half-asleep in the hospital bed. He had traveled days ahead, he was sure of it. The bruises had begun to heal, and the traction apparatus looked less complicated. Imperiously impatient, he did not wait for her to wake up but quickly called up a shadow, wrapped a hand around her wrist, and pulled her sharply out of her body, her room, and her dreams. She snarled and began to struggle.

"Don't waste my sleep time," she complained. "Real sleep is a rare and precious thing for me now. Why don't you come around when I'm staring at the ceiling and the nurse has that stupid radio drama on that makes me want to murder her with a bedpan?"

The Trickster raised his eyebrows at her, pausing in the passage between-worlds to look at her properly in the dim light of moonglow mist. "Did the pain barrier not work?" he asked her mildly.

"Pain is only one of my problems, can't you understand that? I'm tied down to that bed, literally, but I'm not really quarreling about that because if I tried to move I'd probably put a bone splinter through my intestines or something." She stopped, frowned, and tried to look at her hands. "Wait a minute. What shape am I in now?"

"Oh. I've made you into a desert cat, the miniature breed. So, you're telling me you're bored?" He moved on, drawing them both out of the cloud and into a new landscape of overcast sky and grassed-over sand dunes.

"I'm worse than bored. I feel like a boxed-up doll."

"And yet still eloquent," murmured the Trickster.

"Don't laugh at me. I'm *this* close to calling Patience."

"Why don't you?"

She started to snap, paused, and huffed at herself instead. "I suppose I want to *know*."

It was such a trickster's answer that he could not hold back his laughter. It was difficult to take her pique seriously. Out of convenience, he had made her new shadow kitten-small and able to fit in the palm of his hand. She made an attempt to slap him, which turned into a playful-looking bat at his wrist. "Stop laughing at me! Why are *you* here?"

"I'm here because I know exactly how you feel," said the Trickster soothingly. "I too have gone in the blink of an eye from talking to Patience to waking up in a body I couldn't control."

He bent and put her on the ground, then sprawled out comfortably, flat on his back, tilting slightly up the low-rising side of a dune. He twiddled his bare toes, laced his fingers behind his head, and let out a sigh of contentment.

"What do you mean?" she asked, padding up the scraggly grass of the dune to the level of his ear.

He turned his head and smirked at her. "Bored enough to be curious now?"

She swiped at his nose, claws out.

"Fine," he said, flinching out of range. "The next shadow I bring for you will be a tortoise." He softened the threat with a smile. "So, you want to know how I became the human named Ajit?"

She scoffed at him. "You were never human."

"Oh, but I was. I am. Patience set it up for both Chance and me, but like you, I didn't quite trust her, so I kept my wits about me." He sighed. "That's something I don't recommend. There are good reasons humans forget what it is like to be small, helpless, and incontinent."

Her claws retracted. "Do you mean it? You were born as a human? But I thought—"

"You thought there were only three ways for the undying to enter the mortal world. Ordinarily, yes. Chance and I were special cases, variants of the third way. Rather than shadowing existing human lives, we were born with human bodies and grew and developed independently like normal human children."

"Not normal," Miranda said. "How could you be normal, knowing what you had once been?"

The Trickster laughed shortly. "Chance had the advantage over me there. He kept himself half-aware, half-asleep. *He* trusted Patience. Or perhaps he didn't, but he felt he could handle himself, even in a limited form." He frowned slightly. "Maybe he even wanted to lose himself in forgetting."

"If you were born human, but you're here now as undying, where is your human self?" Miranda snagged the white linen he wore with her claws and tugged, not maliciously but experimentally, confirming that he was solid.

The Trickster shrugged. "Relative to the time you would be recovering in the hospital, I'm working with my father in another town and talking about going to study law and investigative processes. Relative to here and now—well, I *am* here and now. Bilocation is possible, but risky. It's better to move with all your probabilities at once instead of spreading yourself too thin."

"That undying one who attacked us—why is he using Walther Grey to kill people instead of just being born like you were?"

The Trickster closed his eyes, pondering. "I can't explain it. I barely understand the theory of how amulets work. I know a lot depends on human choice. I also know that there are some events—both those in the past and those yet to come by human reckoning—that are already completed, and others that are waiting for a choice to be made. Change or thwart those choices, and you change the world—past and future."

"There is no way I am going to understand that, is there?" She wagged her head in tired defeat. "Let me try another question. What do you think will happen to you when you die . . . as a human?"

The Trickster fell silent and turned his head slightly to look away at the distant, unreal horizon. Mercifully, she waited and did not press him.

"I don't know," he admitted. "Perhaps I will go back to this." He indicated his shape, undying but humanlike, with a sweep of his hand. "Perhaps I will simply cease to be myself. We do not die, but we do have an end—when all the paths that we can trace have been traced, we fragment and dissolve and return to our source." His voice grew stronger, chanting the final words in recitation of some half-forgotten litany.

"But what about what happens to humans when they die? Might that not happen to you?"

"I don't know," he repeated. "I don't know what happens when you die. We've never been able to follow where you go."

He looked down at her and quirked an amused eyebrow at her obvious disappointment. "We are neither all-powerful nor all-knowing. I thought you had realized that by now."

He looked away, pensive once more, and tried again. "The undying are not meant to be immortal, but humans—now, they *can* be. So, theoretically, the first step to immortality would be to become human."

"And the second step?" Miranda prompted as he paused.

"Change fate. Make an important choice. Create a completely new destiny." He spoke without conviction, listing hypotheses, not facts.

Choice. He noticed that she flinched as he spoke the word.

"Did Chance bring me out of the world to solve my own murder?" She spoke lightly, but the question retained a terrible weight.

The Trickster sincerely did not know, and the novelty of the situation tickled him; he let his lips twitch and his eyes crinkle. "I think that's the wrong question, but I'm sure we're making progress."

CHAPTER TWELVE

"It's not that I *mean* to be cryptic," he said apologetically as he rubbed at the fresh scratches on his wrist and put himself a safe distance from her short but rapid reach. "You see, this has never happened before. We're all a bit baffled. Well, except for Patience, probably, but as you've noticed, she prefers not to interfere. She'll only tell you what you've already guessed for yourself."

"All my guesses are pretty grim right now," Miranda hissed, "at least as far as *my* life is concerned. If I'm meant to die, why can't I die quickly? What's the point of all this suffering? And if I'm meant to survive this, how can you claim I'm dead?"

"I never said you were dead," the Trickster exclaimed, shocked into genuine compassion by her distress. "Just that there was a probability that you might die."

"I don't understand all this talk of probability," she said. "Did I die? Was it an accident? A murder? Do I have a choice of any kind?"

"I don't *know!*" the Trickster shouted. "That's what I'm

trying to tell you! The past is fluid. The future is fluid. The only thing you can be sure of is now. I don't know what choice you're supposed to make!"

"Patience told me she might need me to survive at any cost. Does that mean anything?"

"'Might'?" spat the Trickster with cynicism. "There's no certainty in 'might.'"

"What does she want me to see? What does she want me to know before I can decide?"

His face cleared, and his expression became intent. "Better. Let's discuss what we *can* find out. What we still need to know is the name of the man who's willing to arrange multiple murders to live forever, or at least live indefinitely as an undying one. I think that's your task."

Miranda looked unhappy and wearied at his words. "I'm strapped to a hospital bed. I'm broken. How can I do that now if I couldn't manage it when I was free to go where, when, and how I pleased?"

He tapped a finger to his head. "Haven't you learned anything from us? It's all up here, Miranda. No more scouting around, no more searching for clues. It's time to *think*. We got what we wanted: the trace of that undying one so *we* could hunt him down. Hunting humans? That's a human's job. *Your* job. Find him, Miranda. After that you can decide whether or not you're meant to live or die, but don't leave this task unfinished."

"I don't even have my briefcase anymore," she sulked. "I left in a hurry, remember?"

"Leave that to me," he said, "but don't let that stop you. Like I said, everything you need is already in your head." He

felt a growing uneasiness as he spoke, the discomfort of someone powerful knocking on his made-world. "You must go," he
added hastily. "I've kept you too long. Remember what I've
taught you."

The small cat faded as Miranda returned naturally to the
stronger pull of the reality made by Patience.

"What is it?" he snapped at the invisible presence. "Check-
ing up on me? Don't you believe I can manage this?"

His mind stretched like rubber, warping every sense and
perception to the point of nausea, and then he was on his
hands and knees on the ground—splayed out like a spider, in
truth—facing Patience in her roofless chamber. She sat comfortably on her heels, considering a small, translucent marble
between her fingers.

She offered it to him. "You would not have been able to
keep her there much longer. The doctors are reducing the
painkillers, and she is becoming more lucid."

He took his world from her hand and crushed the thin
boundary, absorbing its essence easily into his skin. "Chance
did it when she was lucid."

She did not answer him. She would not bother to repeat
the obvious, that he did not have his brother's degree of power.

Then it hit him. "Wait a minute. What doctors? What
painkillers? This is all your crafting, not reality!"

"Ah," she said, shifting her feet to one side with a graceful
lean and twist, her face and poise showing both amusement
and gentle mockery, "you admit that you were beginning to
forget what is real?"

He took her cue and settled himself on the hard ground

before he answered. "It's a very big labyrinth, as you said. I wouldn't be surprised if you had a bit of reality leaking in. Is it true, my Lady, that out of all of us, you are the only one who can see the parallel lines?"

She leaned forward and traced a net crisscross in the dust. "Lines? Or orphaned threads, cut and trailing from the main fabric?"

The Trickster shook his head, disbelieving. "Who has the power to cut a thread?"

"*We* do, when we travel in unexpected places." She slashed a hand across her net, cutting not mere threads but the knots where warp and weft combined. "I will help you."

The last was said abruptly. The Trickster blinked, wondering what he had missed.

She clarified. "I'll help you catch the murderer. Miranda cannot find him, not in a labyrinth that is, for the most part, not real."

"And once we have him, then what?" he asked eagerly. "Do we crush the amulet, yank the binding cord, and reel in the undying on the other end?"

"*You* will not. That one would destroy you, as he almost did before you called my name. Chance can deal with him. It was very good, what you did for your brother. It may make all the difference."

She leaned forward and touched a hand to his cheek. Substance and strength flowed to him from that contact, restoring a little of what he had given away, but she drew back too quickly, leaving him once more blinking in confusion.

"Go back to Miranda before she begins to think you were only a dream."

He turned to the labyrinth, randomly chose a nearby loop in the path, and stepped in.

Miranda had walked far ahead. Within the labyrinth, as expected, medical staff weaned her off the painkillers, and her thinking sharpened until she began to doubt, then deny. She made herself forget seeing the Trickster, imagined that the entire mad encounter with angels and undying ones and murder victims had been some kind of hallucination induced by the blow to her head, the stress of the accident, and the cocktail of narcotics she'd been given. Certainly it must have been a coping mechanism dreamed up by her brain to deal with the mental trauma of an upsetting case followed immediately by the physical trauma of a near-fatal accident. There was enough to worry about without adding insanity to her troubles.

"My family . . ." she said, speaking clearly for the first time.

The young doctor who had been examining her chart looked alarmed at the unexpected conversation. "Your employer contacted them, but we haven't allowed visitors—"

"My tenant . . . my house . . ." These were not idle concerns. There were strict laws about City residency. If Miranda's house stayed unoccupied by a Freeman for more than three months, it could be placed on the auction list and she would lose her landed status.

"I'll speak to your employer. He's handling all your affairs."

Miranda felt somewhat easier. Khabir was a good lawyer and a good friend. He had the sense to identify what needed to be done and the wherewithal to do it.

Her focus shifted to more pressing matters, like the small victory of the first spoonful of soup she was allowed and being measured like a piece of furniture for an intricate brace that would allow her to move the uninjured parts of her body while keeping the broken bits immobile. Relatives came to visit at last, an awkward and emotional time made worse because they had to travel so far to reach the City and could not stay long. How could she blame them? Her uncle worked hard with his small construction business, but he wasn't rich in time or money. Her aunt, the most comforting person out of all of them and the one Miranda most wished would stay, was devoted to him. Her mother . . . she knew from the start that her mother would not come.

"She's very upset," Aunt Silvie said quietly and briefly.

An understatement. She had been upset when Miranda had inherited the property and Freeman status of a paternal great-aunt and left to go to the City. She was ever contemptuous of the City, calling it an outpost of a long-dead empire whose denizens clung to outdated forms and traditions out of a misguided desire for identity. Miranda saw her inheritance as a chance for a new adventure; her mother viewed it as an encumbrance and a betrayal of principle. More pragmatically, she believed the place was so dangerous and crime-ridden that it would only be a matter of time before she was sent news of Miranda's death.

Miranda wondered if her mother had decided to imagine her dead from then on as self-protection. Of course she would not come.

The visit brought one unexpected and mixed blessing: her cousin Fae.

"She's staying on to help you," said Uncle Omado with a cheerful voice and anxious eyes, trying so hard to be positive for her. "She's always wanted to experience a bit of City life."

Miranda loved him for making the job of companion and nursemaid sound like a favor and not a burden. She was not particularly close to Fae, having moved away from home when her cousin was still a girl at school, so when she saw her again—a very young woman with wild hair, untidy dress, and dreamy gaze turned inward—she had doubts. It was out of her hands, however. Her boss, her relatives, and her tenant had had some kind of grand consultation, and Fae was installed in the town house as temporary caretaker.

The next visitor was Khabir. He chuckled softly, but his eyes were concerned as he looked down at Miranda. "I wish you wouldn't do this to me, Miranda. The office is going to fall apart without you."

"Nonsense, but I appreciate the sentiment." She hesitated and looked around at her private hospital room. "Tell me, Khabir, can I afford this?"

"Between your tenant's rent and your work compensation, you can. Don't worry," he said with a smile.

She felt a strange emotion. The way he was standing, the tilt of his head, even the kind tone and worried eyes—they all reminded her of her uncle. It felt odd, being semi-adopted and taken care of by her boss.

Eventually regular visits were permitted, and Fae and Khabir shaped her days. Fae was the background noise, reading aloud on request from books and newspapers, a distant, almost uncaring distraction that was pure relaxation in comparison to the friends who made a point of seeing Miranda yet could not hide how unsettled they were by her injuries. Khabir was made of stronger stuff. He was the highlight, coming to her in the lunch hour or at the end of the day, sharing mundane office gossip or giving a brief mention of the latest cases. *He's keeping me up-to-date*, Miranda realized. *As if I'll be back someday*. It was a happy thought.

She began to read for herself, preferring news to novels. Large broadsheets draped over her bed table as she squinted at the print from an awkward angle and turned pages with fingers that still lacked strength but at least had full feeling and control. Fae came, conscientious as ever, to read aloud at Miranda's request. Otherwise she sat quietly and wrote in her journal or stared out of the window with her usual dreamy gaze.

Weeks passed, then months, and as Miranda squeezed her fists and flexed her arms and slowly regained strength and solidity, she began to look forward to the hard days of learning to walk again. She realized she was counting down, however quietly, to the time when she could once more be at home or at the office, back to her routine life.

She said nothing out loud of her hopes. The doctors still

looked distant and answered her questions with vaguely soothing remarks or brusque avoidance.

One day near the end of three months, Khabir turned up
with something familiar in his hand.

"My briefcase," said Miranda, eyeing the unusually bat-
tered item with curiosity. "Where has it been?"

Khabir was almost smug in his satisfaction. "A young man
called Ajit returned it to me yesterday. His father's a tracker,
and he says they found this in some streetcomber's store."
Khabir pronounced "streetcomber" in a tone that heavily in-
sinuated "thief." "Still locked, still filled with papers. Pity it
took so long to get back here. I spent ages replacing all the
court documents after your accident. I thought they were
gone for good."

Miranda reached out her hands, and he let her hold it half-
tilted on her bed table. Some memories had been lost, some
memories were false, but she still recalled the lock code.

He laughed at her eagerness. "You must really be bored to
want to look at those old papers again."

She raised one shoulder in the best shrug her body could
manage. "It was quite a case. You said so yourself."

Khabir shivered, or perhaps he was shaking off a fleeting
flashback. "Never seen anything like it, before or since. But it
would make a good play, don't you think? Perhaps there's a
reason these old papers turned up after all."

Smiling in agreement, she unlatched and raised the flap.
She peered in, then stared, dumbfounded.

There was a hairy-legged spider perched on the edge of her case file.

"What?" said the Trickster. The voice was a tiny chitter, but it was unmistakably him. "I told you to leave the briefcase to me. Now get to work. You still have a task to do."

"Pardon?" said Khabir. "I didn't catch that."

Miranda flipped the briefcase shut, her eyes wide. "Nothing."

CHAPTER THIRTEEN

A spider in the house is easily ignored, even when it talks. The Trickster was both amused and peeved to discover that Miranda could only see him in his ordinary arachnid form and would then conveniently persuade herself that the voice she was hearing was in her own head. He kept to rafters and doorways, watched her steadily, and grew more amused. Now there was another active player in the game.

"Narrow doors. Steep steps. Small rooms," Khabir listed patiently.

"Yes, yes," Miranda acknowledged, her voice crisp with irritation. "I get it."

The country villa was beautiful, with all the comforts of the City contained within a high-walled enclosure. It was also well staffed. The Trickster had already seen a nurse, a driver, a cook, and a housekeeper.

"Busy streets," Khabir added.

"Are you done?" Miranda cried out, exasperated. "If I have to hear you tell me one more time why I can't go home—"

"You're not very good at this convalescence thing, are you?" he observed.

"I'm sorry. Thank you. I *am* grateful."

"Hush," said Khabir. "That's not what I meant, and you know it."

She fell silent.

He sat by the atrium's small central pond, trailing his fingers absently in the water for the fish to nibble, looking at her curiously. She was in a modified recliner, a grand antique couch fit for a desert queen but augmented with an arrangement of dense, sloping cushions that created the right position for her limbs and spine. The couch was broad enough and sturdy enough to support the heavy brace that held her emaciated body. It was also wide enough for her to spread papers and files within easy reach of her hand.

Khabir gave a small shake of the head and indicated the papers with a disdainful lift of his chin. "You don't have to do that."

She smiled, a rarity since the accident. "I've told you my theory. I only have to prove it."

"That's what I mean. You don't have to prove it. Grey has been convicted. The murders have stopped."

She tilted her head, scrutinizing his expression. "Tell me about my accident. How did it happen?"

"Miranda, what are you saying?" His voice was pitched low in warning. "Do you really think that had anything at all to do with the case?"

"No need for that. I haven't gone off the deep end yet. But

I'll tell you what might keep my mind occupied. There's at least a routine police report for my accident, am I right? Can you bring me a copy of it?"

He brought his hand out of the water, flicked droplets briskly from his fingertips, then got up and slowly walked toward her with a concerned frown. "Will it occupy you or distress you? Be honest."

"Honestly? Boredom drives me crazy, and something isn't right. Let me pick at it. If it looks like it's doing me harm, you can just take it away from me."

He stopped, stared down at her, and nodded slowly. "Fair enough."

"Khabir," Miranda said softly, "I really do appreciate everything you're doing for me. Let me work, even if it's make-work. I can keep my mind sharp at least."

"Fair enough," he repeated, giving her a resigned smile. He leaned over and pressed a gentle hand to her shoulder. "Be good. I'm going back to the office. I may have something for you when I return."

As Khabir passed under the arch of the atrium and into the foyer, the Trickster risked a whisper. "Ever the mother," he said, his words sly but admiring.

Khabir kept going as if he had heard nothing, but just as he opened the door to go outside, he turned back and looked directly at the spider. There was a moment of grotesque disorientation, as if the villa were being turned inside out, and then the Trickster found himself on the other side of a solitary doorway, vomited out of the labyrinth, once more in human shape. The villa had vanished, and the figure that had been Khabir was changed.

"Multiple human shadows. How do you do it?" the Trickster marveled.

Patience closed the door. "It has to be done. Everything in the labyrinth is me."

"Except for what goes in of its own free will," the Trickster guessed.

Patience gave him a silent nod of confirmation.

"But dear Patience, I have had so many doubts about you and your love of free will that your mastery of puppetry does not appease my concerns."

She sat down on the ground without grace, as if suddenly exhausted. "Shall I tell you how I achieved this high skill?"

The Trickster dropped down beside her. He choked back his yes, sensing that the knowledge would be both unpleasant and impossible to forget, but it was too late.

She leaned forward, demanding his full attention with an intent gaze. "Every path I dreaded to take, every weakness I rejected, even the joyous passions that threatened to overwhelm me—in sum, every part of me I could not control—I set apart from myself. I gave my wild selves their own incarnations and pushed them out to work their will in the space and time allotted to them. I have whittled myself down piece by piece, in pain and in bliss, until what remains is my core of iron, molten and compressed under the burden of all my ifs and maybes."

The Trickster had no answer but silence.

She straightened, taking away some of the force of her

presence, and spoke more gently. "I am sorry, my love, my self. We cannot escape responsibility for our decisions, even when we want to be persuaded that someone else is to blame for that final 'yes.' That is as true for you as it is for me. I know how free is the will that I gave you, and yet I am also responsible for your actions. How shall we live out this paradox?"

Unshadowed and true, she rose to her feet. "The world is my labyrinth, and everything in it is me, except for what enters of its own free will."

"Free will . . . ?" he began, uncertain of his own query.

"Free will is a game—only a game, but a necessary game. The greater my power, the more care I take to honor its rules."

She bowed her head. The Trickster was still unable to speak, but he had to make some effort to convey the awe and concern he felt for her. Crouched on the ground, he too bowed his head; he reached out his hands to her warm, dusty feet and touched them softly, like a small child reassuring himself of his mother's presence and attention.

"Go back to the labyrinth," was all she said, but the gentleness of her tone comforted him.

She was there ahead of him in the form of Nurse Benet, patiently guiding Miranda through some basic exercises and making pleasant conversation. As before, the Trickster settled his spider shadow into a corner and listened.

"And how was your day, Dr. Ecouvo? Lots of visitors this morning."

Miranda's reply was a polite, patient effort modulated by pain as she stretched her arms slowly up and out. "My work colleagues. They're very kind. They don't want me to feel . . ."

She huffed, partly a pause for breath, partly a laugh. ". . . bored and lonely."

Nurse Benet made a disapproving noise. "They brought work files for you."

"Just one small report. Keeps the brain working, just like you're doing with my body," Miranda countered.

"Well, I'm happy to hear that, because after a few more weeks of this, I think you'll be ready for physiotherapy at the hospital pool."

Miranda shivered under a cold flood of unwelcome memories.

The report proved to be a disappointment. The bus driver was a longstanding employee of a well-known company with no connection to the Walther Grey case. Miranda scanned the files from her briefcase, worried that she had forgotten something important, but it was all too familiar.

She was soon begging Khabir for more. "I need to see the summary report of the Grey case. Who drafted it?"

Khabir shifted uncomfortably in his chair. "It was done half by me and half by Fernando . . . and neither half very well. We were a bit distracted, obviously."

She felt suddenly teary at the thought of what it must have been like for them, but she controlled it and went on. "I'd still like to see it. It would help to see another perspective."

"On what?" Khabir's voice rose in uncharacteristic frustration. "I still don't know what you're looking for!"

"What *are* you looking for?" That was Fae, who was still spending silent, restful weekends with Miranda, immersed in all manner of reading and occasionally looking at Khabir with suspicion, as if she expected him to hand over a bill for board and lodging at any moment.

"I'm not sure," Miranda admitted. "I'm hoping to find some kind of evidence that there was someone else besides Grey involved in the murders."

Fae sat up. "You mean an accomplice?"

"More like a mastermind," Miranda replied. "Someone had to benefit from those particular people dying."

Remarkably, Fae put her book down. "A financial motive seems unlikely, as the victims were all foreigners and mostly lower income. It could still be blackmail, though—no need to assume all payments are made in money. There is also the possibility of a shared superstition being taken more seriously than we can imagine."

She paused and looked at their surprised expressions. "When you talk, I *do* pay attention, you know, even when you're not talking to me. It's an interesting case. I've been following it for some time."

"How do *you* know?" asked Khabir. "The newspapers didn't say that much about it."

"The newspapers are only interested in crimes against Freemen. They know their readership," Fae replied. As the only non-Freeman in the room, she had a right to be cynical. "Now, have you looked at the possibility that only a few of the murders are meaningful and the others are window dressing, so to speak?"

Miranda gave a small chuckle. "Yes. I *am* looking at only a few of the most recent murders as significant."

"Do you have a reason for that?" Fae asked. Khabir leaned forward, clearly interested in the answer.

Miranda opened her mouth, hesitated, and began to speak. "The ritualistic aspects only began in the later murders. Before that, the deaths were swift, silent, and clean. The attack on the Mermaid was the first attempt to take away limbs or organs. I'd like to know what changed."

"He became bolder—reckless, even. He began to take more time with each killing," suggested Khabir.

"Maybe," Miranda admitted. "And maybe there was some other purpose for the later murders."

"You're certain that all the murder victims—all those that you know about"—Fae corrected herself meticulously—"you're sure none of them were Freemen?"

Miranda nodded. "No Freemen, and quite a few were transient workers, which is why so many were connected to the City Shelter and also why there were so many murders before we caught Grey. People who are always coming and going aren't immediately missed when something happens to them."

"And it's not only the transients that people forget," added Khabir. "Some men keep their wives indoors, invisible. Those women can disappear very easily. 'Visiting her sister' is a common excuse."

Miranda thought for a while. "I wouldn't put Galina Arnaud in that group. Her husband, he wasn't a Freeman, but his family came from a nearby town, and he'd been a resident of the City for over a decade."

"She behaved like an old-world wife for some things,"

Khabir noted vaguely. "Look, we're trying to think about this like rational people. Grey was not a well man. It could be that he saw them all standing in the same room together, shoulder-to-shoulder, and decided there and then that he wanted them for hunting trophies."

"True," said Miranda despondently.

"Not necessarily," said Fae. "You've got Grey, but you don't believe he was acting alone." She turned to Khabir. "Miranda's trying to find the man who *directed* him. Maybe *that* man had a motive."

"You're asking us to restart the case from scratch," Khabir said to Fae, his stern voice contrasting with his amused expression.

"It could keep me busy, Khabir. It would make me happy." Miranda was surprised to hear herself pleading.

Khabir looked a bit startled himself, but he tried to cover it with a quick smile and turned to Fae again. "I don't get paid for reopening solved cases, but if you're that keen on mysteries, you're free to bring back anything from my office that you think Miranda might find useful."

Fae smiled at him dreamily. "I've always loved mysteries."

Things unfolded so smoothly and naturally that Miranda hardly noticed she was being managed. Khabir humored her, and Fae assisted, both of them glad to give her a task that could be a distraction or even a bribe. One morning when Miranda was refusing to do her physiotherapy and Nurse Benet was at the end of her patience, Fae turned up with a thick folder, took one look at what was happening, and said to the nurse, "She's not ready for these yet. Call me when you're done."

Miranda yelled at her as she left, but Fae only turned around once to give her a disappointed frown. Miranda spent the rest of the day in wordless brooding, but the following day she completed all her exercises with a grim precision that made the nurse look at her in silent worry, forgoing the encouraging platitudes that she usually employed to urge Miranda on.

"Call Fae," Miranda ordered as soon as the last exercise was done, and Nurse Benet hastened to obey.

Fae came that very evening. She stood warily in the doorway of the atrium, expecting a quarrel, but Miranda was past that. "What have you got for me?" she asked her cousin bluntly.

Fae relaxed slightly and came closer. "Lists. Volunteer rosters, guest registers, and invitation lists for events at the City Shelter over a six-month period."

They divided the work. Fae kept to one side of the atrium, maintaining a peaceful distance between them. Miranda quickly found herself scratching little tally marks into a notebook indicating how often a particular name came up and in which settings. As she ticked and tallied, she wondered which of the unfamiliar names might belong to the Mermaid.

The guest registers held the names of the truly unfortunate of the City, like Xandre Lacalle and, in the earlier pages, Danil Skalnis showed up briefly as well. Niko Tsavian had used the shelter once or twice, perhaps for a nearby bed and a quick nap between two close work shifts. A step up, and there were the volunteers: Danil again, returning the favor to the shelter that had assisted him when he had been a newcomer to the City. Galina Arnaud, a woman who by rights should have had little to do with the shelter, save to donate from a distance. She had been particularly active in helping to organize the shelter's social events, events that she rarely attended.

Finally there were the events where the top tier came in at last, the gentleman benefactors and the ladies bountiful. Professor Malveaux, Dr. Boadu, and Julian Outis all made appearances. Nobody in the top tier was a victim, which was no surprise to Miranda.

The knowledge, the answers . . . it's all in your head, an inner voice murmured.

If that was true, why was she wasting time poring over lists and lists to prove—to prove what? That the City Shelter was a popular place?

Can you feel anything? A certain similarity?

Khabir and Fernando were very, very good at what they did, picking apart the fine, jumbled details of everyday life and finding threads and patterns of unusual activity. Miranda's forte lay elsewhere, not with facts but with people, intuitively and ruthlessly uncovering their motives and motivations.

She suddenly realized that she was twitching her fingers in the motions the Trickster had taught her for weaving a barrier against the pain. She was not yet sure that the Trickster was real, but the barrier worked regardless.

She smiled and announced to Fae, "I think I need to sleep on this."

Preparing for bed took time. Miranda endured Nurse Benet's assistance meekly, feeling as if she needed to make up for her previous behavior. When at last she was alone in the bedroom, she spoke aloud into the empty darkness. "Can you teach me to spin a maze?"

There was no answer, but she was so tired that before she had time to feel fretful about the lack of response, she had already fallen asleep.

CHAPTER FOURTEEN

Miranda had not dreamed since the accident, not properly. It might have been the drugs. It might have been stress or pain, the unfamiliar bed in the hospital or the unfamiliar bed in the guest room of Khabir's country villa. Whatever the reason, she could recall only dim, strange, unconnected scenes, scant of meaning or substance. It could be said, then, that her half-serious, half-whimsical request about spinning a maze was granted when sleep took her wandering to bear witness to a strange confrontation.

"I offer the usual for the usual price."

It was a dream, and dreams had their own rules, which allowed for the possibility of conversations between the seen and the unseen. The first speaker was only a voice, but the other person was visible and familiar, very familiar. It was Professor Malveaux.

"Wealth?" he queried, looking into the distance with his arms folded. He did not look as if he had lost his sanity. He was merely engaged in monologue. "I have more than I need.

I am too old and comfortable in my solitude to wish for a companion, however beautiful. And as for immortality . . ." His gesture encompassed the world around him and dismissed it with a quick, careless wave. "Useless! Everything changes, everything dies—peoples and worlds and suns."

"What if you could be immortal in a place where nothing dies?"

The professor turned his head slightly, betraying a hint of interest and attention. The invisible tempter paused patiently and let the silence do its work on the old man's mind.

"What could the price for that be, I wonder?" Malveaux asked eventually, shrugging off his temporary lapse into considering the unspeakable. His heavy cynicism was a little too world-weary. It begged to be convinced, and the tempter heard his cue.

"Oh, not the usual at all. You'd get to keep your soul, for one."

"Really?" The word vibrated with deep sarcasm and distrust.

"And yet the price is higher . . . but it would be paid by others."

"Indeed? Would I have to sacrifice a few innocents in some kind of disgusting and no doubt meaningless ritual? Is that how you got at poor Walther, promising him immortality?"

"No. His mind barely touches this reality. He tries to find patterns and meanings for his own urges. I am speaking about something entirely different."

Malveaux balked, shaking his head. "My soul, should you

yield it, is not enough. Immortality, could you grant it, is not enough. I want . . . I want to be able to continue my work for as long as I'm needed, here in the City or anywhere else. And I want Walther mended. He deserves a chance to redeem his soul, and he's never had a moment of clear thought to do so. I want him freed of his demons."

The other paused for a moment before answering, "Yes."

The professor's eyes opened wide in triumph and disappointment. "You lie. There *are* some things you can't do. I thought so."

"I do not lie," claimed the unknown one. "I cannot."

"No, no, of course not," Malveaux muttered. "But that does not mean that you tell the truth." He sighed deeply. "I will stay as I am. Hallucination, nightmare, or demon, whatever you may be, I have entertained your presence for far too long."

The vision flashed and disintegrated. Miranda woke up coughing loudly, her throat so dry that even swallowing was an irritant, a scratching of raw tissue rubbing together. She tried to stifle the noise, struggling till tears of exertion poured from her eyes and ran past her lips.

A shadow loomed in the doorway of her room, startling her into hiccups. "Nurse Benet!" she said hoarsely as the waking nightmare became a familiar shape in a close-tied cotton night robe.

The nurse came quickly forward, bent over the bed, and held a cool cup of water to Miranda's mouth. She drank it all in silence and gratitude.

"Why didn't you ring for me?" the nurse asked.

Miranda was silent.

"It's what I'm here for. It's what I'm *paid* for." Her tone was kind and firm but slightly exasperated.

"Of course," mumbled Miranda, feeling embarrassed and not knowing why. "I . . . forgot where I was for a moment. I thought I was at home . . . I mean, in the City."

"Oh," said Nurse Benet more gently, embarrassed in turn. "I understand." She nodded and left quietly.

Such a very little lie, but it was enough to make Miranda feel miserable. How did the undying ones avoid falsehood? Was reality too present for them to even pretend or imagine the existence of anything not real? That thought allowed her to drift away from thinking about her discomfort and return to contemplating her vivid dream.

The senseless crime now had an impossible motive—immortality—and she could hardly tell anyone *that* without being thought insane. The dream appeared to confirm what she had already decided: that Malveaux was not the type to attempt murder for gain. *I have more than I need . . .* and so he spent the excess on those who had nothing. *Everything dies . . .* and so he worked with fatherless sons at the shelter, passing on something of himself in those moments of care and guidance, making an undying legacy of a thoroughly human kind.

From his quick assessment and rejection of the impossible offer, it seemed that he knew something about choosing wisely.

"A man like that—he might be worth talking to," Miranda murmured to herself, and she slipped gently into a sleep without dreams.

"Have you noticed," Fae said the following morning, "that Grey doesn't appear on any of these lists?"

Miranda fidgeted uncomfortably in her recliner, not from the topic but from a persistent itch at her side, which was inconveniently covered by the brace. "The lists are recent, and by then the most he did was go to the dining hall for a bite to eat. Grey had a much closer association with the shelter further back. He lived there as one of the child soldiers who came to the City fifteen years ago."

Fae's face went somber as she thought this over.

"No," said Miranda, knowing which version of the story Fae had heard. "It's not that the assimilation program failed. The children *did* change. But the City never changes. When they grew up and their special status expired, most of them left for other places rather than remain permanently foreign in a city of Freeman privilege."

"Some even went back to war," said Fae with a small, twisted smile. "We used that to mock the City. Even war is preferable to City life."

"Don't tell me you envied me for living here," Miranda said, eyebrows raised.

"Maybe, a bit. Not so much now I'm here. It's like balancing on a fast-turning barrel, isn't it? No one stops to help you if you slip; you just get run over. No, I wouldn't want to live here for long."

Miranda shifted uncomfortably again, but before she could

respond, she saw the housekeeper approaching. "Yes, Madam Emlin?"

"Mr. Lucknor is here with a guest," Emlin warned her in a low voice, reaching out to quickly tidy Miranda's files and papers into neat stacks.

Miranda eyed the housekeeper's slender, busy hands with distress, but she said nothing. At the end of the day, they were both Khabir's employees, and Emlin was tasked with catering to her needs, not her whims. "Very well," she said. She shifted again, smoothed her hands wearily over her face, and straightened the blanket over her legs. Most of her friends had visited by now, so perhaps this was to do with the case. She looked up as Khabir and another man entered the atrium.

She was right, in a way. It was Professor Malveaux. For a moment she could not speak. She stared. She knew his face only by distant acquaintance, one among many in the crowd of a courtroom audience. Before she had anything resembling a clear thought, the blood was draining dizzily from her head.

"Dr. Ecouvo. I'm . . . I . . . thank you for seeing me."

She snapped out of it. "Of course. Sit down. Please, don't distress yourself. I—I don't remember a thing."

"But . . . but I do. You see . . . I was traveling on that bus. Sitting near the front . . ." He trailed off into a painful silence.

My God, she thought, astonished. *What can I possibly say to that?* She had a sudden image of herself, sprawled in the road without dignity, lying in a pool of blood and heaven knows what else while bystanders gawked and pointed. That was the image he remembered. She could not speak.

He looked at her for a moment in dismay and concern, then fumbled his way to a chair, giving a distracted, almost apologetic nod to Fae. Khabir gave the scene a quick glance and headed straight to the drinks trolley.

Fae jumped in. "I understand you knew Grey, Professor. Did you meet at the shelter?"

It was blunt, it was gauche, it was discourteous, and it was still a thousand times better than the way the conversation had opened. Malveaux seized the diversion eagerly. "Yes and no. I spent some time in Vyerland doing historical research decades ago, so when the opportunity came up to assist with the child soldier rehabilitation program I had the language and the cultural experience to be useful as a volunteer."

"If you know Vyer culture, perhaps you can guess whether there was any rhyme or reason to Grey's choice of victims?" Fae asked. "Because from all reports, no one's been able to find any proper motive."

Professor Malveaux bowed his head, and the worried look returned. "He . . . I have no proof, of course, but I fear Grey imagined himself as a vigilante of sorts."

"What?" said Miranda, interested at last. She didn't even glance at Khabir as he gently, even submissively, placed a drink at her elbow.

"I understand that each of his victims had committed some sort of crime—legal, social, or religious. He was not exactly *devout*, but he had a very strong need for boundaries, both for himself and for others. People who transgressed boundaries upset him."

"But the Mermaid—what did she do wrong?"

"Dancing," said Malveaux gravely. He refused Khabir's silent offer of a drink with an equally silent shake of his head.

"What's wrong with dancing?" Fae began.

"Dancing at private parties," he clarified quickly, with a certain emphasis on the word *private*.

"You *knew* her?" Khabir sounded vexed.

"I knew *of* her, or someone like her. I never saw her. I didn't want to say anything in case I was wrong and inadvertently maligned some poor young innocent who could no longer speak in her own defense. It is best to keep one's reputation unsullied in this city."

"She's dead now," Khabir pointed out. "I'm sure she's beyond worrying about her reputation."

Malveaux acknowledged the truth with a little nod but replied, "Let sleeping rumors lie. After all, her murderer has been captured and will soon face the ultimate justice. What more needs to be said?"

"What do Grey's moral codes say about punishing transgressors?" Miranda asked. "Perhaps he thinks he'll be rewarded for his actions after death."

Malveaux paused, thinking hard and clearly not liking his thoughts. He clapped his hands together and rubbed them briskly as if feeling a sudden chill. "Dr. Ecouvo, I believe I'll take my leave now. It would be very unkind of me to tire you, and all I have done is talk about your work . . . hardly a cheering topic for a casual visit."

"Not at all, Professor. This is my bread and butter in more ways than one. But I think you understand that, what it's like when your work is your passion."

"I do. But passion or no, there comes a time when a man must retire and leave the work to others to complete." He got up, nodded courteously to Miranda, Fae, and Khabir, and began to make his way to the door.

"A pity we cannot work as long as we wish without age slowing us down, especially if our work is in doing good for others. It almost makes you want to live forever," Miranda said, smiling with every part of her face but her eyes.

Malveaux did not quite stumble, but something in his gait suggested that his legs had lost their strength for a moment. He turned and stood still in the doorway, considering her, then spoke in a near whisper. "Not me."

"You were on the bus. What happened? What did you see?"

He stared at her, looked down, smiled, shook his head, and met her eyes again with such regret that Miranda faltered. "Dr. Ecouvo, one word from you could have me committed to the psychiatric wards. I'll keep the fullness of that nightmare to myself."

He walked away. Miranda waited until there was the distant sound of a car's motor starting up and moving away, and then she sagged and turned to Khabir. "Tell me, what was the point of that visit?"

He shrugged, but uneasily. "I ran into him at the Club, and he was extremely upset about your injuries. You said that there might be a motive attached to your accident, so I thought if you spoke to Malveaux directly . . ."

Miranda was already nodding along mockingly. ". . . I'd see how far-fetched the idea was. Or something. Khabir, you have to stop taking my words so literally."

"Rail at me all you want," he said. "We know something about the Mermaid that we didn't know before, and *that* case isn't closed. Not yet."

"Dancer at private parties?" Miranda said doubtfully. "There's not much in that."

Khabir grimaced. "I think I know the parties he's talking about. Some of the Club members have smaller, more exclusive gatherings . . ."

She stared at him. "I see. Khabir, when you're investigating that lead, there's something I want you to think about. Imagine, in a completely not-taking-my-words-too-seriously way, *imagine* that the Mermaid did not commit suicide but was killed by a Freeman. Do you think you could adjust your approach to your fraternal colleagues accordingly?"

He was appalled. "Miranda! I've been working in this City almost as long as you've been alive. I *know* they're most of them a bunch of crooks. There's no need to warn me how to handle myself."

"Of course," Fae interrupted cheerfully, "according to the best crime stories, the murderer-mastermind would most likely be *you*."

Khabir gave her a tired look. "Like I said, I've worked in this City a long time. I've encountered the petty, the clichéd, and the arbitrary, but in all that time I assure you that I've never seen 'the perfect murder.' Anything that *can* happen *will* happen. The most successful murderers do what they do simply and directly. It's when they add frills like insane executioners and arcane rituals that they get caught. Having a mastermind behind Grey wouldn't make this a perfect crime but a perfect crime *story*. It wouldn't stand up to the vagaries of real life. *I* certainly wouldn't try to kill anyone in such a convoluted way."

But a storyteller might, Miranda thought, a new idea slowly dawning.

CHAPTER FIFTEEN

"This is inconvenient," Miranda mused aloud, looking at her reflection in the water of the atrium pond. Her couch was in a different position today to spare her from enduring the sun's path, which was changing with the season.

Days had passed, and during that time Miranda had learned that it was impossible to dream on demand. The glimpse into Malveaux's mind had clearly been a coincidence of some sort, because there had been no corresponding vision about Julian Outis, that rumpled caricature of a novelist in decline. Now she was trying to investigate a man who did not even feature in the case files.

"I have no idea why you suspect him," Fae complained. "He's completely peripheral to the case. He's not even a Freeman or a Club member, and he can't go anywhere without being recognized."

Miranda had no reply. Apart from the weak link to the City Shelter and that remark by Khabir that had struck her so oddly, there was really absolutely no reason to consider Julian

Outis. A dream would have been so helpful. As for any hope of seeing the Trickster, she admitted that with her new narcotics-reduced lifestyle, talking to spiders was unlikely to happen anytime soon.

"Any word from Fernando or Khabir on the Mermaid?" she asked instead.

"Nothing yet," Fae said, "but Khabir seems preoccupied—which is good, right?"

"Could be," Miranda said vaguely. "He wants the Mermaid's name. He's taking *that* seriously at least."

"And not the rest of it?"

"Not for the right reasons. I wonder sometimes if he's hoping that if I keep busy, I'll forget to ask him whether I'll still be his employee when all this is over." *This*. She did not detail what *this* might be, but the meaning was implicit in the way she glanced around the atrium nervously. *This cannot be the rest of my life.*

"There's also Dr. Boadu," Fae noted, changing the subject.

"Hmm?"

"Well, he has a link to the shelter, he's a Freeman and a Club member, and even if he *is* the City's chief pathologist, that might simply make it easier for him to find allies for a cover-up."

You can't hurt me. Miranda shook her head at the echo of a nightmare. "Yes. Why not? Dr. Boadu it is. At least his name actually features in some of the case materials."

"Why don't you see if you can get an appointment with him? You'll be starting hydrotherapy sessions at the pool soon."

Miranda was unenthused. "Yes."

"Poor you," said Fae. "It's not like you ever took to swimming, not even when you were able."

Miranda felt her teeth grinding. Fae's unsentimental, cool manner, which had been so attractive in earlier days when everything was still raw and painful, was becoming a simple irritant, like constant grit against the skin. The words were bad enough, but what really grated on her nerves was the mildly amused tone Fae used, as if she were commenting on an ironic situation that had happened to a stranger far away and long ago.

Miranda wished she could say that she had almost drowned as a child or been terrorized by storm waves while sailing, but the truth was that she simply hated being immersed. She hated the lack of solidity under her feet, the slowed reaction of her limbs when she tried to move, the stinging of her eyes, and the hollow warble of water in her ears. She especially hated the stabbing sensation of water flooding up her nose and into her sinuses, which would *always* happen, no matter how careful she was with her breathing.

Nurse Benet told her not to worry. She would be kept at the shallow end, there would be someone with her at all times, and she would be fitted with a special vest that would not only prevent her from accidentally overextending her legs and spine but would also make it impossible for her to sink. She should have no fear whatsoever that the water would go over her head.

Instead, hydrotherapy proved to be frightening in a completely different way. Miranda had not realized how much her muscles had weakened. She was accustomed to having the brace removed briefly each morning for a sponge bath and change of clothing, but that was all accomplished while she was lying down. When the therapist took off the brace this time, she was seated, and she had to seize the arms of the chair to keep upright. Then, to her surprise and dismay, she was given an inflatable vest that stopped above her waist and a broad, belt-like brace to strap around her hips. Her waist was unprotected, unsupported.

The therapist saw her concern. "It will be easier to hold yourself upright when you're in the water," she assured her.

It wasn't the same pool, the large, deep pool where she had spoken to the Mermaid, the pool where the Mermaid had died. It was smaller and warmer. She should have felt safe. She gripped the edge with both hands and moved her feet cautiously, going deeper while the therapist walked alongside her. She felt her body lift as the water closed around her. The lightness was disconcerting, the buoyancy gently stretching joints and vertebrae that had been compressed for a long time. It was almost pleasant, but then she understood that what she was experiencing was not pleasure but a lessening of the constant pain that had become a part of her very self, an extra layer of being over sense and sensation.

She smiled tentatively at the therapist, who smiled back. "It's not so bad," she admitted.

Dangerous words. A slicing, shattering pain seized her. She cried out and reached desperately for the side, falling slowly through the water, her ankles suddenly too weak to bear her up. *It's not the same pool!* her mind protested as she tried and failed to banish the image of the Mermaid sinking gently into oblivion. *But injustice haunts people, not places.*

Behind her closed eyes, the darkness flickered and became dominated entirely by a flat stone path that coiled haphazardly over hard-packed earth for as far as she could see.

She found and gripped the edge just as the therapist took hold of her arm. "Sorry," she said, her voice hoarse and shaking. "I lost my footing."

"Open your eyes," the therapist said gently.

She did so, blinking and glancing around at the walls and ceiling.

"What are you looking for?" the therapist asked.

"Spiders," Miranda whispered without thought, then tried to backtrack. "Sparkles. I mean . . . you know how your vision gets those funny sparkles just before you faint?"

"Let's get you out of the water," was the immediate reply.

With the hydrotherapy session cut short, there was nothing for her to do except wait in the main reception area for a half hour more until Khabir's driver came to take her back to the villa. She was particularly surprised, then, to see Khabir appear at the entrance of the hospital. Her first thought was that the therapist had, counter to her request, contacted Khabir at work, but then his eyes met hers with a look of equal surprise. He wavered visibly, then came over to her.

"I thought you'd still be in therapy," he began.

"Yes," she said quickly, cutting him off before he could proceed to the logical *How did it go*, a question that she did not want to hear, much less answer. "But what are *you* doing here?"

"I'm meeting with Dr. Boadu," he replied, lowering his voice and looking away from her.

"This is in connection with the Mermaid?" she asked. "May I come?"

"No. I mean . . . it's a fraternal matter . . ." Unable to explain himself, he let his words trail off into a mumble.

She frowned, debating whether to believe him. "You told me you could handle yourself."

"And I can. But that doesn't mean I'm going to commit social suicide. Certain things have to stay within walls, Miranda."

Her eyebrows went right up at that one. He flinched. "There's no palatable way to say this, Miranda. There are things that he may tell me that he will certainly not say in front of you."

"Then do what you have to do," she said. "You're the boss."

He held her stare, not fooled for a moment by her pretended surrender. "You have to trust me, Miranda."

She watched him walk away, feeling helpless again. *If only I could be a fly on that wall.*

Or a spider.

She glanced down at the unspoken words and caught the eye of a small spider that was climbing the edge of her chair's arm. He waved two of his legs lazily at her in greeting.

"Why are you wasting time on Boadu? Trust me, he's not the one we're looking for. He's a liar with unclean hands, but he isn't important."

"Don't tell me what's important," Miranda muttered through clenched teeth. "If you're not going to be helpful, go away, or I'll stop believing in you again."

He laughed at her and vanished.

"Dr. Ecouvo?" the receptionist called. "Your car is here."

She barely responded to the driver's queries about her well-being, forcing herself to answer for the sake of courtesy and out of the increasingly painful sense of obligation that she felt toward Khabir and his domestic staff. He noted her mood and soon returned his focus to the City traffic, leaving her to brood in silence.

Did she really need the Trickster's help? She could imagine it: Khabir and Dr. Boadu exchanging their special twisted handshake while grinning like two neighborhood boys with the password to the tree house club. They would probably inquire about each other's work, perhaps discuss some shared responsibility for the latest fundraiser or social event, and then Khabir would manage to come around to the meat of the matter. Would he grow serious, speaking in a low voice that invited confidence? Would he be embarrassed and apologetic, trying to hide it with a nervous laugh and a shrug?

"You did the autopsy. You saw her dead on a slab. Did you ever see her alive? Did she dance for you at a special-invite party? Did you notice who she smiled at? Do you know how she got home? Did you find out her name?

"Don't take this the wrong way, but . . . was she familiar to you, that drowning case? There's a hint, a rumor, that she might have been a dancer. Perhaps at the Club, one of those closed-door events. You know I'm not into that sort of thing, but maybe you saw something? Or heard something?"

She settled herself against the warm, comfortable upholstery of the back seat and closed her eyes to better see the view in her imagination.

The chair behind the huge desk with its stacks of sloping files would be unoccupied. Instead they would both sit on the fat leather couch before the large bay window that looked out onto busy streets and beige brick buildings and, far beyond those, the blue-gray harbor. Khabir would be slumped, hands laced over his belly, fingertips lightly tapping. His eyes would be lazy in an effort to convey the impression that nothing about the situation was remarkable. Dr. Boadu's posture would be slightly tense and a little too upright.

"Drownings are difficult," Dr. Boadu would make haste to explain, his hands in nervous motion. "The features are so disfigured, you see."

Perhaps Khabir would use the shrug then. "Please, Allen, don't think you're being accused. It's been niggling at me, that's all . . . the last unraveled thread of a knotty case."

Dr. Boadu . . . would he lean back and sigh regretfully? Or would it be a forward lean, seeking sympathy and understanding? "I may have seen her, or a woman like her. She was a dancer at a forenight I attended."

Ah, the forenight. The final fling of a soon-to-be-married man. Of course they'd have such parties in abundance at the Club.

"What was her name?"

A pause, then, "I don't remember."

"Did she stay till the end of the party?"

"I don't know, Khabir. I *was* very drunk by then."

The little play in Miranda's head stuttered for a moment, then disintegrated. She opened her eyes and sighed. "I want her name. Patience, I'm still walking; I haven't given up yet. Let me walk her labyrinth—only a little way, only far enough to know her name."

Later it would be easy to say that tiredness and stress and the leisurely drive homeward had lulled her to sleep and that her speculations about the conversation between Khabir and Boadu created the content of her dreams. In that moment, she was only aware of a fierce pain—not the pain of being broken past repair, but the pain of muscles and ligaments stretched to the limits of their training, a pain that was almost unbearable and nearly pleasurable all at the same time, mingled as it was with a strong shot of adrenaline.

She leaps high in the air, disguising strength with grace, and lands gently. She is sure the judges will miss the tremor of feet wearied by constant walking on uneven roads in bad shoes as long as she keeps moving lightly, swiftly, free of care and pain. After the last pirouette, she holds her posture with consummate control, then comes back to first position and stares bravely at the emotionless faces behind the long desk. They look back with blank, almost cruel gazes, giving nothing away. One of them glances down and pencils a mark on the sheet before her.

"Your file is incomplete," the head of the review panel notes.

"Yes," she admits. "The work permit is being processed. You can see the—"

"—temporary permit, yes. But we require all necessary documentation to be in order before we can finalize your contract."

Her breathing, which was running quick and strong after her activity, halts, then resumes unevenly, shaken by the suddenly increased pulse of her heart. "I . . . I will try my best to expedite the matter."

"Do so. We will be waiting to welcome you into the Corps."

Faces relax; there is even a faint smile or two and one odd look, nearer to pity than kindness. She feels her heart change beat again, this time singing, but she admits to feeling a slight irritation at their lack of reaction. She chides herself for expecting . . . what? Congratulations? They will see hundreds like her during audition season. It is hard to win admission to the Corps, harder yet to stay in. But first she needs to get in. She needs that permit.

As she walks home on the hard roads in her ruined shoes—dancing shoes cost money that should not be wasted on ordinary footwear—she thinks about the official bribe that the Employment Bureau calls the facilitation fee. Of course she cannot afford it. It is not priced for ordinary people to afford. There are semiprofessional, barely legal lenders everywhere in the City, but she refuses to sell her future to them. It will be a risk, but she may have to work a private party again.

She was careful. She *is* careful, and she will be careful again. She did private parties when she first came to the City and everything cost money, from securing the small room that she shares with three other women to obtaining the temporary permit. She made up another persona for those parties, a woman with bold makeup, wild hair, and six centimeters of added height from ridiculous secondhand heels. That persona could never be associated with the clean-scrubbed face and pulled-back hair that is the mask of a sober shopgirl and aspiring Corps dancer. She knows that. She served the wife of a Club member once; he stood bored beside her at the register, and he did not once blink or show the hesitation of uncertain recognition.

The night of the party is unremarkable. She fears for an irrational moment that she might see a member of the Corps panel who would easily recognize her—not her face, but her movement. Dance is the only language in which she has never learned to lie. She manages to make enough—more than enough, even though the stupid heels turn the small bones of her feet into a piercing mass of pins and needles. She is happy because now she can throw it all away—shoes, clothes, makeup, and character—into the anonymous bin at the City Shelter. She takes her pay, changes into something more suitable for the night air, and slips out of a back door, wondering if she can hope to find a taxi at this hour.

Then a car pulls up. The driver looks at her. She is covered modestly from top to toe, and a brimmed hat hides her face. Only the shoes betray her. She recognizes him as one of the quiet, embarrassed ones from the party.

"It's very late," he says. "Would you like a ride home?"

She ponders, then accepts. She slides gracefully into the car and, not yet abandoning caution, gives him the address of a friend who lives near her lodgings. Her heart is still singing. Besides, he looks harmless.

"No!" Miranda cried out, trying to lift herself out of the dream, to become more than an unheeded voice struggling to scream a warning. "I can't believe it. Not *him.*"

He is harmless. He is surprised at her reaction. Why should she become abusive merely because he decides to park the car for a moment? It is a clear avenue with lanterns and trees alternating light and shade. It is only for a moment. Surely she is used to this, working as she does. But instead she slashes at him, nails out like a cat. He catches her wrist and grips it tightly—purely in self-defense, of course. She winces, but then she lashes out at him again.

"You can't hurt me. I'm a dancer with the City Corps."

He gives a short, cynical laugh. "City Corps dancers don't do private parties. Please, just—"

Dancers, whether they are members of the City Corps or not, have strong legs. She plants her heels in his chest to shove him back, lands a kick in his belly, then pushes open the door at her back, tumbling onto the road. He curls over and wheezes, trying to find his breath, as she scrambles to her feet and runs off. The clatter of her shoes on the paving stones gradually fades away.

He straightens slowly and looks out of the door, but she has disappeared, no doubt already halfway down one of the small, dim side streets. He feels scared for a moment, then ashamed, and finally furious.

"She thinks I'll follow her. Forget that. She can find her own way home."

He slams the door, starts the car, and screeches away from

the curbside, his only thought to get away from the moment and place of his humiliation as quickly as possible.

No. Not him. And yet . . .

And yet who else? It must have been weeks before he saw her at the hospital and realized that his nemesis had found him. Was it by accident or design that they came to be in the same room? Did he see her first? Or did their eyes meet, did they both freeze in mutual fear, did he act on impulse and push her under, or did she . . . ?

"She threatened me, of course. She was trying to get out of the pool, and she slipped and hit her head. She went under so quickly. I was embarrassed. I rushed out of the place. I thought the hydrotherapist was in the adjoining room. She shouldn't have been there alone. Unscheduled, unsupervised—it was an accident that could have happened even if I hadn't been there." *Most regrettable*, was the message in the heavy, sorrowful tone of his voice. *Most regrettable, but surely not my fault.*

Khabir sat, nodding and nodding, his face a mask. What does one say in such circumstances to a man who has the power to erase rosters, silence junior staff, and, most of all, who signs the pathologist's report at the end of the day?

Miranda woke up with a jump, her mind still coated in the grimy scum of Dr. Boadu's fear and shame. The car had stopped, the door beside her was open. Nurse Benet was leaning in, looking at her with an expression of concern. Miranda only shook her head tiredly and submitted to being helped out of the car, into the wheelchair, and taken inside.

CHAPTER SIXTEEN

"There has to be an end to this," Miranda muttered to herself.

"Beg pardon?" Fae asked, looking attentive.

Fae had been unusually gentle and courteous toward her recently. Miranda realized that she must have scared the household with her bout of mute depression after the crisis at the hospital pool.

"Nothing." She was silent for a while, then sighed. "Fae, I want you to start packing up my things at the town house. Everything."

"What? Why?" Fae straightened with a nervous movement that was almost a jump.

"I'm never going back to live there!" Miranda cried. "I can't. Not like this."

"What will you do with the place?" Fae asked, her voice nearly monotone with shock.

"Sell it." The words were dropped bluntly, no softening possible. "Give it away. I don't care."

Still staring, Fae sat back a little, bracing herself against the back of her chair. "You don't have to decide that now. Perhaps—"

"If you want, you can have it," Miranda interrupted.

Fae shook her head. Of course she would not take the town house. She had scoffed when it had been willed to Miranda, but in cynicism, not envy. "Where will you go?" she asked.

"Fernando has suggested a rehabilitation center in Delma. It's only two hours' drive from the City, but everything would be on-site, with none of this driving back and forth to the hospital. I can afford it if I sell the town house. After that . . . Khabir's recommending me for a place at the Law Academy."

The blankness on her cousin's face finally gave way to an expression: guarded, distrustful, and mildly accusing.

"It is not a bribe, Fae," Miranda said patiently. "Believe me. Besides, I think you'd be happier if I left here."

Fae's slow acceptance of Khabir had taken several giant steps back. There was no overlooking his sudden reluctance to continue with the investigation after his chat with Dr. Boadu. To Fae, this was conspiracy, obstruction of justice, and typical City Freeman behavior. Miranda agreed, though with far less vehemence, because she knew that at least Dr. Boadu wasn't guilty of murder, only of being an unethical doctor and an unprincipled beast.

But Khabir *had* disappointed her, not only because he wouldn't tell her what the chief pathologist had said but because he had responded to her request to check the auditions records of the City Corps with a startled look and a brusque change of subject. When she challenged him, telling him she expected better of him, he had responded with a counterchallenge that was more weary than wounded.

"You think I can do better? You think *you* could do better?" Then he made his offer—he would sponsor and support her application to the Law Academy. She could gain the kind of qualifications needed for the highest positions in the legal profession. "*You* change the City, but don't accuse me of not having tried," he finished.

Not a bribe, but a burden, a weight of responsibility that would be hypocritical to turn down. If only Miranda could turn her back on the place and make it one of the forgotten failures of her life. With that charge, Khabir had made her his accomplice. Reject the offer, and she was as much or more of a coward as he was.

She had made one concession to her own pride. She would accept his recommendation but not his money.

She called Priya the following day. Priya had been one of her first visitors, and she still called occasionally. When Miranda considered the friends and acquaintances who hadn't yet worked up the courage to do more than send a get-well card, she felt guilty for not appreciating Priya's efforts more. At least she could get her a big fat commission on the town house sale.

Priya sounded somewhat stunned at the news, then definitely sad, but she soon returned to charming professional courtesy. "I must warn you, it's a big step to let City property go."

"I know, but I don't want to be an absentee landlady," Miranda told her.

"Fair enough. So why not long-lease the town house to a tenant? To *your* tenant, in fact? It would be an amazing opportunity for him."

"Oh." Miranda paused and thought. *If I'm going to make a grand gesture, why not make it a meaningful one?*

It was time to go into the City again for another hospital visit and another attempt at the pool. After that she could visit Priya, then go through the town house with Fae and point out what could stay and what should go. She could stop in at her workplace to pick up some files and even pass by the City Corps, just in case someone there remembered auditioning a dancer who was all but perfect except for the small matter of a work permit.

Then she shook her head, angry at herself. She was still planning her days as if she could walk the boardwalks and sidewalks wherever she pleased. It would make more sense to meet Priya at the town house, invite her colleagues to come in for a quick visit, and make a phone call to the City Corps.

And then, somehow, she had to find Julian Outis. She knew she was putting it off—almost but not quite as if the world would end when they met at last. Maybe in a way it would. Maybe she would return to find herself at the end of a labyrinth, with the so-called real world nothing but a dream. Maybe she would not, which was world-ending in a different but no less drastic way. Denial was a powerful thing, according to her physiotherapist; perhaps it was powerful enough to invent talking spiders, guardian angels, blue-skinned men, and silver-haired women.

Miranda said nothing to the physiotherapist about all that. She simply pushed her way through her exercises with her jaw clenched against the simmering fear that still burned in her gut as the water pushed and pulled at her. It was supposed to be relaxing, she was told. It was supposed to make her feel supported and immune to falling. She smiled tightly and lied her agreement, yearning for the sensation of solid weight to anchor the universe.

Fae called a taxi to bring her from the hospital to the town house. They could have had Khabir's car and driver, but they were both feeling the desire to avoid Khabir's largesse. Briefly dependent on the arms of a stranger, Miranda let herself be half carried up the steep, uneven stairs and over the threshold and put into a wheelchair—not the ample one she used at the villa, but a smaller flimsy folding thing on loan from the hospital. She slowly wheeled herself farther in and looked around at her once tidy home, now dusty with neglect and littered with scattered books and papers. Fae's expression was sheepish.

"I didn't have a lot of time to clean up, but I got the kitchen done at least," she said, pushing some of the books under a table with her foot. "I made lunch; do you want some?"

"Not yet," Miranda said briefly, biting back criticism. "I'm not hungry, and Priya and Kieran will be here soon."

She tried to move around. Fae hustled to clear obstacles from the wheelchair's path, but even without the additional debris it felt like the doorways were too narrow, the turns too sharp, the corners too angular, and the furniture completely in the way. It made Miranda irritable, but she eventually parked herself at the table in the center of the living room, forced herself to keep quiet, and accepted the conciliatory cup of hot chocolate Fae made for her.

She sighed and looked around again, wondering how long it would take to catalog everything, pack what she wanted, dispose of the rest. Something tickled her ankle, and when she drew back to look, she saw a fat, comfortable spider sitting undisturbed in a well-established network of webs under the table. She snapped.

"How can you not see this? What have you been doing that leaves you so little time to dust?"

Fae snapped back, "I've been writing and researching—and taking care of *you*."

Miranda's breath stopped. Fae stared at her, looking as if she wished she could take back the angry words, but they were there, tainting the air.

The doorbell rang. Fae escaped the room. Miranda exhaled. She managed to smile brilliantly at Priya and Kieran as they came in and greeted her, and her voice did not shake as she invited them to sit and be comfortable.

"Is everything fine with your apartment, Kieran?" she asked her tenant.

He nodded vigorously. "Fantastic. Don't worry about a thing. Priya's been taking good care of me."

"And she told you what this meeting is about?"

He nodded again. "To arrange about the rent when you leave the City."

"Yes," Miranda said slowly, tilting her head at Priya, who shrugged innocently. "More or less. We were talking about a long-lease. In fact, if you wanted to, you could rent out the part you're not living in and pay your way to full ownership in about twenty years."

She looked at him, smiling with the satisfaction of a good deed done well, and then she faltered. The surprise on his face was genuine, but as she continued to watch him she caught sight of quickly hidden dismay and then mild resignation.

He doesn't want it, she realized. *He was looking forward to leaving the City.*

"But only if you want it," she added, fumbling the words in her haste. "You mustn't feel obligated."

He blinked as he shook his head. "No, no, don't be silly. This is an amazing opportunity. Thank you. Really. Thank you."

A gift, a responsibility, a burden. You don't want it, but you're scared to refuse it. Am I turning into Khabir?

"Only if you're sure," she insisted, desperate to give him one last chance to back out. Perhaps he was like her mother, quietly despising the City and its elite even as he earned his living and returned a tithe of it to the City's hungry urchins. Perhaps he was like Fae, content with a temporary stay but wanting no ownership of the City's tainted dust. Why did she ever think this would be a favor?

"I'm sure." Too late. He had convinced himself.

She retrieved her smile, though the cheer was harder to recapture. "I'm glad you're the one who'll have it."

Priya caught her eye, reassuring her with a firm nod, and then the doorbell rang.

Fae frowned. "Are you expecting anyone else right now?"

"It might be someone from work. I told them I'd be here," Miranda replied. She struggled to wheel her chair between the low table and an armchair.

Priya put a gentle hand on the frame of the wheelchair,

guiding her out and forward. "Go ahead. We can take care of the paperwork downstairs."

This meant the newcomer was faced with a contingent of four when the front door opened. He blinked at them, momentarily startled, and then quickly regained control of himself. Indeed, he gave the impression of being a very controlled individual. His dark hair lay flat, neat and shining; his eyes were a deep black that heightened the intensity of his gaze; and his sober, almost formal attire gleamed at the buckles, cuff links, buttons, and clasps. It was difficult to guess his age. The smoothness of his skin hinted at youth, but the smoothness of his expression spoke of maturity. He nodded courteously as Priya and Kieran excused themselves and went past him to the apartment below, and then he fixed his gaze upon Miranda. She was relieved to find curiosity there, not pity.

"Do I have the honor of addressing Dr. Miranda Ecouvo?" His voice suited him. It was only a shade deeper than the average male voice, but more remarkable for its resonance which, though perhaps unusual coming from such a slight frame, matched his authority and self-possession.

"Yes," said Miranda. She glanced to the side, about to ask Fae silently if she knew the person, but to her astonishment, the small hallway was empty. Muffled noises behind her suggested Fae had fled to the kitchen. She frowned in puzzlement and continued, "And you are . . . ?"

He paused for a beat before saying calmly, "I am Julian Outis."

CHAPTER SEVENTEEN

She stared at him. There could be no greater contrast between the pictures she had seen of the round-faced, disheveled, pale, and balding author and this slender, angular man with every thread and hair in place and skin like that of the gilded angels painted on the walls and ceiling of the City Basilica.

He smiled very gently, as if understanding her confusion. "I am the *real* Julian Outis."

Miranda still stared, not knowing how to respond to this. There was a false Julian Outis? His expression grew apologetic at her obvious bewilderment.

"I am the real Julian Outis in the sense of what he is thought to be: an author of some successful works of fiction. I am *not* the public face of Julian Outis, an actor hired to carry out the duties of promotion and publicity. In other circles, I am called—"

"—Anrheis Do-silva Moreira, son of the Jaguar Emperor, fifth prince of Gurya of the Hill Kingdoms," Fae said softly, appearing quietly behind Miranda.

The prince looked at her, once more giving that split-second blink of shock. He recovered, exhaled, and smiled rue-fully. "In the City, most people call me Reis. Please, I would prefer if you did the same."

Miranda found her tongue. "I—I think you'd better come inside."

Fae dashed back to the kitchen, leaving Miranda with the strange prince. He came in, closed the door, and took Miranda back into the living room in a manner that was far more "es-corting a lady" than "wheeling a patient". She realized from the familiar noises that Fae was exerting herself to make tea and arrange sweetmeats. The prince settled himself into a chair and looked around, neither curious nor assessing, but as if creating his own comfort by rapidly absorbing his surround-ings and making them familiar. It did not take him very long. He reached absently for a cigarette, realized in an instant that this would be injurious to Miranda, and began to apologize. But then somehow, between their apologies and acceptances and counterapologies, he ended up in the broad window seat with his feet up and his arm hanging loosely over the sill, hold-ing the evidence of his offending habit out of sight. At intervals he lifted his arm and brought the cigarette to his lips for a shallow draw, almost a taste, before dropping it hastily below the sill once more and sharply exhaling the smoke up and out of the window.

Fae approached with his tea and a laden plate, resting it on a small side table within arm's reach. He looked at her, nodded his thanks, and said, "*You* knew me. How is that possible?"

Fae clasped her hands in front of her, almost comically

deferential. "I've read a lot about the monarchies of the south-western continent . . . for my book."

He relaxed—notoriety for his lineage was clearly of little concern to him—but then twitched at her final words. "You are a writer?"

She stammered. "I . . . not yet. Trying to be."

He smiled. "And are you writing about far-off lands rather than your own backyard? No—that wasn't a criticism," he added quickly when she looked stricken. "I've done the same, after all. Tales of intrigue, romance, and adventure in every place except the Hill Kingdoms. And do you know, my books hardly sell in my own land? Fortunately I have a good agent who knows where the markets are to be found."

"Was it your agent who suggested the pseudonym and the public face?" asked Miranda.

His smile slipped. "A necessity, I fear, which was imple-mented by mutual agreement. Already I must live with one kind of celebrity; to cultivate another type might prove too challenging a balancing act. I am a prince, but also a priest, diplomat, representative, and role model. My books are pure invention, but readers are apt to believe there is no smoke without fire. I would rather not have any international inci-dents caused by some hopeful theorist reading intricate con-spiracies into the plots of my novels."

He straightened and became even more serious. "Which, ironically, brings me to the reason for my visit. I am sorry, Dr. Ecouvo, but I believe you are in danger."

Miranda's hand paused in the middle of reaching for her teacup. "From Julian Outis, I take it?"

The prince nodded, his eyes half-shut but still intent on her face. "I recently discovered that he was making use of my resources in ways that did not relate to the work for which he was hired. I have corrected that oversight. He has been cut off. Soon the sudden death of Julian Outis will be announced, and apart from the publication of one or two posthumous manuscripts, that will be the last the world hears of him."

"You're going to kill him?" Fae exclaimed.

The man who preferred to be known as Reis looked astonished, then amused at being accused of such incivility. "Only the persona, I assure you. It will be a simple thing, as the man himself went underground some time ago. Missing, presumed dead, likely the last victim of the City's notorious serial killer . . . though we may need a few banknotes here and there to paper over the cracks in the story. Witnesses, positive identification of some conveniently discovered remains—it all adds up." He focused on Miranda again. "But as I said, he vanished a while ago, and I believe he is seeking you."

"I am not hard to find," said Miranda. "And although I have never met him personally, he is a frequent enough visitor to the City that I have friends and colleagues who have seen him. Why should I be in danger now?"

Reis relaxed his posture, drew a little more deeply than usual on his cigarette, and took his time answering. "I think you have been in danger for a while. The man we call Julian Outis . . . we discovered that he has been writing notes, rather like the notes an author might make about characters, locations, and events in a book. He has a file that appears to consist entirely of different ways to kill you."

"What?" Miranda said, too bemused for fear.

"Oh, he never wrote down your real name, but from the location, the events, and the character's appearance and occupation, it was clear that he meant you: Dr. Miranda Ecouvo, forensic therapist of the City."

"How do you explain the bus accident, then?" Miranda asked. "Hardly the sort of weapon a murderer can arrange." She did not like his body language; he was almost aggressively peaceful, reminding her of how her doctors would begin to speak slowly and calmly when about to do something that would cause incredible pain.

He shrugged. "Perhaps the driver was startled. Perhaps he saw something that he had never seen before."

"Or had seen once in a nightmare and never expected to see in waking light," she murmured, thinking aloud.

His eyes met hers, communicating the intensity his voice lacked. "Something like that."

He took a final taste of the cigarette, exhaled, and in one quick motion crushed the lit end with his bare fingertips and placed the remnant delicately on the edge of his plate. Then he took up his cup and sipped the steaming tea.

"What will you do after you've put an end to Julian Outis?" asked Fae.

He sighed. "I won't stop writing, if that's what you mean. Giving that name up is very freeing for me, do you realize? People had come to expect a certain style from the Outis pen.

I was getting bored. Perhaps I could indulge in poetry for a change. Listen."

He set down his cup and took a self-mocking pose, back upright, hand on breast.

> *"The sons of patience steal shadows from the dead,*
> *rule as kings and gods from age to age,*
> *breaking one habit of power with another,*
>
> *but chance is born of will and not misfortune.*
> *He will provoke envy among many;*
> *angels covet his death, men his immortality."*

He stopped declaiming and looked at Miranda expectantly as he returned to his tea. She stared back, stunned at the realization that this too was an undying in human form, sitting placidly in her house and talking serious matters in verse. *And undying seek his life,* she completed the poem in her head, remembering how viciously they had been attacked, how close they had come to annihilation before Patience had saved them.

Fae shook her head, but her face still showed admiration. "I have no ear for poetry. It sounds like it's good, but I don't understand it."

"That's the key, at least in these lands. Good poetry must never be easily understood. Now, in my own country I could never get away with that. At least two or three meanings are required per stanza, all set in the traditional meter and framed by appropriate art. It is a very serious business to be a poet in my country. I wouldn't risk it, personally."

Fae smiled sadly. "More of a risk than being a writer in this country?"

"To the reputation, certainly. To the pocket, both are hazardous. For example, I wish to write a novel set in the City. I breathe the air, speak to the people, eat the food. Then I write my book, you see. But those who have not the wherewithal to visit the places they would write of, how authentic can they be? The discerning reader will sniff you out, or worse yet, they may simply not be interested in any other story but the familiar. No readers, no money. I at least have no need of money. If *you* do, I would advise another line of employment, or at the very least a rich husband."

The twinkle in his eye and the twitch of his lip were far too teasing. Fae became suddenly flustered. She gathered up the cups and plates and retreated to the kitchen. Miranda watched her go, then eyed him sternly and spoke softly.

"You remind me of someone—someone charming, witty, and accustomed to always having his own way."

He smiled and replied just as quietly. "The habit of power. It's very hard to break. The most one can hope to do is divert it into harmless activities."

"What do you expect me to do? If you can't find Outis with your *resources*, how do you expect me to manage?"

He raised an eyebrow. "Are you sure that you understand who I am? The problem is not finding the man. The problem is that the man will know he is found. I cannot approach him. He has too deep a knowledge of me."

"Does he have an amulet?" Miranda guessed boldly. "They can both summon and banish your kind, can't they?"

He stiffened. "There is good reason those are no longer permitted to be made."

"You could send people—"

He waved his hand. "I have sent people. He is more than a match for them. You . . . now you are something else."

"What do you expect me to do?"

For a moment, the urbane mask was laid aside; for a moment, he looked at her as one would look at an equal. "Live. At all costs, Miranda, live."

He stood up abruptly, raising his voice to be heard beyond the room. "I wish you well."

Fae rushed out from the kitchen, but before she could begin to frame an appropriate farewell, he stepped forward, took her hand, and kissed it warmly, leaving her speechless.

"Allow me to see you out, Mr. Reis," Miranda said loudly. She pushed herself after him into the foyer with as much haste as she could muster, and when he opened the door and stepped out, she followed him up to the very threshold to block any thought or possibility of reentry.

"I'd like you to stay away from my cousin," she told him.

"You don't approve? That's highly ironic, Miranda. If only you knew how much."

"But I thank you for warning me."

He bowed his head, sober and contrite again. "I wish I

could do more. I am partly to blame for the fact that he knows so much about these temptations. Good day, Dr. Ecouvo."

With that, he closed the door.

The Trickster seized him and yanked him from the labyrinth before he had time to turn around fully. "Stop! You're not Patience, and you're not an echo. Who are you?"

Reis was so shocked that he blurred slightly at the margins, but he collected himself quickly and set his lines, details, and neatness into even sharper precision. "I should ask that of you. I know all the undying who chose rebirth—such a big, rambunctious family we are—but *you* are a new one. An opportunist, perhaps, spurred by a moment's curiosity? We do gain a few that way. But you could only have been reborn with the help of someone stronger . . . see?" With a contemptuous flick, he brushed the Trickster's hands down and away with abrupt yet controlled force. "You don't have the power to manage this by yourself."

"Children," Patience said firmly. "Do not fight in my house." She was sitting on the ground again, absently running a narrow length of gold-and-red silk through her fingers.

Reis bowed deeply. "My apologies, Eldest. But why allow one sent by angels to be manhandled like a thief sneaking in unwanted?"

Patience nodded, admitting the misdemeanor. "He is not usually this suspicious, but he has had a stressful time of late. Do not judge him."

"Who *is* he?" Reis demanded with an intensity that was beyond mere query.

Patience ignored his question. "Farewell, dear Prince. It is good that you came and very good that Uriel sent you, but it is not safe to linger here. We are yet in the midst of battle."

He shrugged, disappointed yet resigned in the face of the implacable. "Understood. I am glad I was of some use. Good hunting, Eldest."

Before he vanished, one long look went to the Trickster.

"I will remember you," he murmured.

To the Trickster it sounded more like curiosity than threat, but it was worrying nonetheless.

Patience spoke briskly. "It is time to find the elusive Mr. Outis and bring him into my labyrinth."

"Bring him?" the Trickster exclaimed. "How? What happened to free will?"

She glared at him. "It is your task to persuade him. Make his life so uncomfortable that he will gladly consent to be elsewhere, even here." She smiled coldly and beckoned him closer. "We have his thread."

In an unexpected moment of whimsy, or perhaps in teasing acceptance of the human need for tangible symbols, she looped the ribbon of red-and-gold silk around his fingers. There was a translucent, cloudy-white stone tied to the ribbon, and it pressed against his wrist, hot from long holding in her hand.

"There," she said. "Now bring him to me."

CHAPTER EIGHTEEN

"For now you may call me Ajit," said the Trickster.

The transition away from Patience had been quick but rich with information. The amulet pulled directly and sharply, like snagging a thread, and there were other tensions present. He could sense that Chance's labyrinth was growing deeper and more complex, drawing in like a living web to entrap their adversary. The knowledge gladdened and strengthened him, bringing insouciance to his tongue and daring to his actions. He was going to enjoy himself.

Julian Outis grimaced as he raised his head and squinted at the large spider sitting on the rumpled sheet bunched over his hip. "I know this nightmare. I fall asleep after too much alcohol and lobster; I wake up to a bonehead and a furry tongue. And in between, this." He frowned and looked around the room curiously with sharper eyes. "But usually there are more of you."

"Today is the day you are going to kill Miranda," the Trickster continued, unmoved. "I thought I'd come with you, see what you're thinking, what your motive is, that kind of thing."

Wincing, Julian put his head down again. "You're crass. Talking about murder like breakfast. Have a little sense of the occasion, please."

"What an interesting creature you are," the Trickster said cheerfully. "You almost remind me of me . . . if I were more obnoxious. Now get up and get ready. You can tell me your plans along the way."

Slowly Julian sat up; slowly he shrugged with the indifference of a man accustomed to strange dreams and even stranger happenings. "Could I even stop you? I suppose you're some strange psychological manifestation of my conscience. Poor thing hasn't had a lot to do recently. I shouldn't be surprised it decided to act out in some other way."

The man was changed. The famous paunch was vastly decreased, taking with it enough body fat that the scaffolding of his face was revealed as surprisingly angular, even under the sag of skin that was wrinkled with worry and more. The Trickster examined him, wondering for a brief, mad moment whether to feel any sympathy. Julian spoke calmly, but his eyes were sunken, the skin around them was shadowed gray, and there was a tremor in his fingers as he pulled aside the bed linens, evidence of more than one night of drunken oblivion. The Trickster laughed. No, there was no need for sympathy here. It would be easy to push him to the point of breaking, and it would be so satisfying to be able to make sport of someone who was so very deserving of it.

Julian got out of bed slowly, holding his torso carefully still and upright as if afraid his head would fall off otherwise, and went into the bathroom. The Trickster unfolded into his human form and lay back on the rumpled sheets. He heard the sound of water running, a few sulky groans that suggested Julian had moved his head too quickly, and the noisier splashing of half-hearted, half-asleep bathing. Finally there was a short silence, then water gurgled down a drain, a long musical sound that so lulled the Trickster that Julian's sudden yell shocked him wide-eyed.

"What the hell?" Julian sputtered, clutching the waistband of his unfastened trousers with one hand and the open neck of his tunic with the other. "Who are you? Get the hell out of my room!"

The Trickster laughed. "I told you, I'm Ajit. You prefer the spiders?"

In a blink he let his body transform—not neatly and abruptly into a single arachnid, but into a dark pile that resolved itself with a gradual, crawling, scuttling disintegration into myriad many-sized creatures, all with that bright, wicked glitter in the eyes and the nervous energy in the limbs. Those limbs trampled the untidy bed linens in a feverish, malicious dance while a thousand eyes watched from every angle as Julian huddled down to the floor under the windowsill and screamed and screamed.

Eventually the Trickster grew bored, pulled himself together, and yawned. "That's enough. Let's go."

Julian glared at him, panting a little with receding fear. "I know another of your kind," he threatened vaguely.

"I know you do. I notice he's not here. Why is that? Does it have anything to do with the lack of an amulet around your neck?"

Julian looked blank for a moment. "That's just a game, a mind trick," he said.

"It is, but it works. It captures human attention and leaves a good, thick trail of conscious intent for an undying one to trace. But it's a strong tie, a rope that pulls both ways. You wouldn't want that, would you? Better find someone disposable for that."

"*He* brought Walther into this," Julian tried to explain.

The Trickster smiled. "Ah, I must have truly frightened you. Already we come to naming names."

Shaking slightly, Julian got to his feet and pressed his hands hard against the wall behind him. "I know you can't harm me. You can scare me or harass or persuade until I do what you want, but you can't hurt me."

"Why, I never said a thing about hurting you. I only wish to observe. Today is an important day for you. Walther Grey is in jail, and there's one more person to kill. Today you commit a murder, and I get to watch. So please proceed. Don't mind me."

And with that, he faded from mortal view.

Julian kept his hands against the wall until his breathing calmed. Slowly he straightened, slowly he walked to the bed and stirred the sheets with a cautious hand. "I can't let this get to me," he muttered.

Still smiling, the Trickster looked on, silent and unseen, and stepped backward through the closed door of the room. That was enough play to satisfy him for now. Eventually, when his prey emerged, the real work would begin.

When Julian finally got himself outdoors, he went straight

to a side-street café and ordered lunch, most of it liquid and strongly alcoholic. The Trickster let him relax and begin to feel comfortable. That too was part of the game.

"Really, you've been working too hard," he murmured sweetly into Julian's ear. "The mind plays such tricks. As soon as this is over, you owe yourself a vacation." Julian nodded to himself. He deserved a vacation as a reward for not going mad when the rest of the world was clearly already in the asylum.

"How *did* you manage to get yourself into this?" the Trickster wondered. Julian sighed. He'd had it so good. Paid to do nothing but show up and smile. But then he'd started believing in the part he was playing. Naturally writers have odd research interests, and a serial murderer preying on the overlooked underclass of the City made for an excellent topic. No one would guess how close he had been to the action. He could put it out under another name, his own work this time . . . though he'd be unable to claim it. He chuckled at the intricate irony of the layered deception.

"Who are you?" a voice whispered in his head. Existential musings: proof of his growing insanity. An actor, a masked man, a hand puppet. That's what he'd always been. He did it very well, and in his earlier years a change of location had always solved his problems whenever he had made a mistake. Unless he was in a city. There was never any need to run from a city. Cities were full of stress and haste, a beautiful blurring cocktail of humanity and heat that made it easy to dip in and out of the fractured viewpoint of a hundred thousand heads. You could be many people in the City, and no one would notice.

"Why Miranda?" It was a mere breath, a tiny tickle from the remnants of his sense of decency. He pushed it away. No regrets. Miranda Ecouvo had researched Walther Grey, and that meant she was close to finding out some uncomfortable truths about *him*. Besides, there had to be one more death, and now Grey was in jail. That meant *he* had to do it.

"No, really, why *Miranda*?"

His thoughts choked off in confusion. He frowned at himself. He shook his head. He had a good reason. Wasn't she already doomed, a crippling accident waiting in her future? It was meant to be a mercy, better than leaving her to suffer. A quick death. That's what *he'd* want if he were in a wheelchair and in constant pain, if he ever had the choice.

No. Not true. He didn't want death at all.

I'm not a superstitious man, he told himself. *I don't need rituals and trinkets.* Part of him thought that to kill Miranda would be best for her comfort and his, but another part said that this was an act of pure intent, that last bit of ritual needed to blur the boundary between living and undying.

Someone tut-tutted at him. "Tricksters should never trick themselves."

What did it matter if he had vivid waking dreams? He knew the difference between fantasy and reality, and oaths sworn to imaginary beings did not count. He would kill Miranda quietly, steal her briefcase discreetly, and make his own immortal name in another city. That was it. He needed the information in her briefcase to complete the story of Walther Grey, the greatest serial killer in history. And to remove evidence of any connection to him. Yes. That was why he was killing her.

"You poor thing. You really have been used. You aren't even sure why you're doing this."

He moved his neck and shoulders uneasily, trying to force his body to relax. This was too much introspection. Everything was perfect: the time, the means, the escape plan. To falter now would only give the game away.

An old clock tower, obscured by the taller modern buildings of the City's center, chimed a few brief bells. Julian settled his bill and left to begin a leisurely walk to meet Miranda, moving slowly in order to keep himself calm and resolute. Everything must be casual. There was a small square opposite her office; he could easily linger there until she came out. He would plan his trajectory to cross her path as she joined the crowd on the busy boardwalk. Until then, it was a shoulder-jostling jaunt through the inner city, dodging people and vehicles. He kept a hand in his pocket, fingering a capped fountain pen, and waited to cross yet another street.

Miranda! Here? Now? There she was, crowded with a few other intrepid souls on a small brick island in the middle of the traffic.

He moved to the curb, nudging his way through the other pedestrians, keeping his gaze on where she stood. There was a moment when she vanished from his view, but she soon appeared again, looking unusually grim. She must have had a bad day. She glanced quickly, misjudged, rushed out into the relentless traffic, and was narrowly missed by an omnibus driver with better judgment and reflexes. Julian was there to catch her as she nearly stumbled trying to reach the sidewalk.

"Do be careful, miss," he said, grasping her by the arms and yanking her out of the road.

The pen was uncapped in his hand. She cried out and pulled away as the nib scratched her arm. No one noticed. She was already shaken from the brush with the omnibus, and most people were already continuing on their various routes, desperate not to block the flow. Julian took the briefcase before she dropped it, slipped the pen carefully into his pocket and into its case, and let the crowd carry him away. His heartbeat accelerated. She might still have time to cry out, to point a finger at him. He refused to look back; that would be too obvious. He crossed the road, walked on for a while, waited, then glanced around.

She was down, a few people gathered about her. He looked away again, pretending not to see, trying not to show his sudden elation. It was over! He raised his face to the sky, squinted into the sunlight, and masked his grin with a grimace. Such a big thing, and now it was over!

Something firm and padded hit him in the shins; something broad and padded broke his fall. He flailed in bewilderment and snagged his empty hands in large quantities of cloth.

"Not over," said the Trickster, standing at the foot of the bed and staring down at the man strangling the bed linens. "Not yet. You can call that a dry run, if you like."

Julian tried to comfort himself. This was only one of those anxiety dreams where you sit down to do the exam you've been dreading and just when the teacher says, "Pens down!" you wake up and find you've got to do it all over again for real.

So he did. He went out to meet Miranda again, superstitiously looking for her not at her office but at the intersection he had seen in his dream. And there she was! The poison pen had been replaced with a poisoned scalpel, but it worked as brilliantly as before, and his escape was as elegant.

And yet it all came back once more to waking up aggravated and dissatisfied, facing the malicious grin and verbal barbs of the spider-man who summarized and assessed each unconsummated killing with inappropriate delight.

On the fifth try, he openly stabbed at her in utter frustration, desperate to change the dream into something of his own shaping. Instead he woke to find himself pounding ineffectually at his pillow. The time after that, instead of pulling Miranda to safety, he gave her a little shove, just enough to make her stumble from the sidewalk and fall in front of an omnibus. He changed the timing of the encounter, yet he always found her. Once he even stabbed himself, but the poison only took his consciousness for a few brief moments before he woke up alive and furious in bed.

He decided that his only option was to refuse to get up. Three days of moping behind closed drapes passed, but eventually, having eaten the few snacks he kept in his lodgings and drunk two bottles of wine, he dragged himself up and went out to a restaurant on the other side of town, far from Miranda's offices. He ate, he drank, he relaxed at last. A party of three businessmen got up from a table nearby, leaving behind a newspaper in plain view on one of the seats. He craned his neck to scan the headlines. Thus Julian discovered, with a feeling like petulance, that Miranda had managed to get killed in a traffic accident without his assistance hardly a day after he had been scheduled to murder her.

Waking up from that scenario left him with a strong desire to murder someone, anyone.

At that point he grew crafty. Whatever was happening to him, he would get well out of its way. He rented a small cruiser boat, went on a three-month carouse up and down the islands of the bay, and docked again at the City, certain that all the old newspapers would have been burned or pulped, taking any untoward news with them.

On returning to his lodgings, he made the mistake of lounging to gossip with a pretty chambermaid. He had been wrong to fear the old news. She had fresh news instead, straight from a respected source of scuttlebutt, her cousin's friend's sister who worked as a nurse. A noted professional of the legal community had been found dead in a suspected suicide by drowning after a long and difficult struggle to recover after a terrible accident.

Julian woke up chewing at his torn sheets and crying in vexation.

After his tantrum subsided, he got up, bathed, and dressed, but he found himself unable to go further. He sat on the bed instead and stared at the pattern on the curtains until he stopped thinking.

A tingling chill crept up his skin, forcing him to snap out of his depression. Brushing at his arms quickly became panicked clawing as he hauled up his sleeves. Cold darkness was unfurling around his wrists and arms like ribbons, deceptively gentle shackles that represented a compliance born of a shattered will. Grim-faced, implacable, the Trickster materialized before him, holding the other ends of the ribbons—no, drawing them into himself like pliable extensions of his being. Julian gazed up at him in total exhaustion.

"Now you're ready to meet the real Miranda," the Trickster said. "And after that, there's only one more thing left for you to do."

CHAPTER NINETEEN

It was evening at the villa. The majority of Miranda's belongings had already been taken to her new residence. She walked out to the front patio—she was finally walking with the help of two canes. She had hired a cab over Khabir's protests, and it was nearly time for it to arrive.

Khabir adjusted a chair for her so she could sit facing the driveway, then took a seat himself. He was very quiet.

"You're getting your villa back," Miranda teased. "Look happier."

A small smile twitched at the corner of his mouth. "I'm glad you're getting on with your life, but I'm still concerned about you."

"Why? You tell me the case is wrapped up, you're sending me off to a grand future as a defender of justice, and I've finally learned to take care of myself. Why the concern?"

Khabir paused, then shook his head.

"Still suspicious about the Outis death?" she asked with a sly smile. She had told him nothing about the mysterious Mr. Reis, the prince who had created Outis and also, as promised, uncreated him, but Khabir had clearly been vexed by the news of the author's death. Fae might have said something, but she was home once more. She had left after Miranda assured her (without rancor, without resentment) that she had learned and healed enough to take care of herself, that the town house was safe in Kieran's hands, and that the mystery had been solved as much as possible.

Lying to Fae had been too easy, just as saying goodbye to Khabir now was too easy, but Miranda had found herself surprisingly tired of being grateful.

"Coincidences happen," said Khabir. "He didn't live what you might call a healthy life, and heart failure isn't that unusual an end."

"Well, then," said Miranda, her words meaningless but her tone final.

He gave that small smile again. "I suppose you don't need the distraction anymore. I'm glad you've let go of your obsession with that case."

Miranda sniffed. "As if you weren't as intrigued. You still are, I think."

He shrugged. "Loose ends. I'm accustomed to that, but still . . ."

He sighed a little sadly, and Miranda recognized the sound. It was that depression he got after a big case or project until the next big thing turned up, a depression that had trained him to know all the wine bars and rum shops within walking distance of his office and the law courts. The thought brought an unexpected wave of envy. She was still not allowed alcohol. She picked up one of her canes and absently prodded the low hedge of bright pink flowers that bordered the patio, trying to ignore her own melancholy.

They both heard the sound but were slow to react, expecting any noise and shadow in the twilight to be the scheduled cab. It was indeed a cab, but instead of drawing up to the patio, it paused halfway down the long drive, deposited a sole passenger, and departed again with an unusual haste that raised white clouds of dust from the unpaved edges of the road.

Unfazed by this strange behavior, the passenger turned his back on the cab and began to walk toward them. He wore a long, draping coat and a hat pulled low—appropriate garb for late-year fogs in the City, but terribly out of place on the dry, warm plateau where the villa was located. By the time he was ten meters away, there was no longer any need to guess who he was. Miranda clutched her cane, the flowers forgotten, and wondered what in the world she was going to do.

Khabir moved first. He got to his feet, stepped forward far enough to stop the passenger from approaching any farther, and spoke, admirably calm and almost humorous. "Haven't you heard that you're dead, Mr. Outis?"

The passenger raised his head only slightly. "I have. Oh, I have. I am well acquainted with death."

Forget melancholy, thought Miranda, *that's despair.* In an instant she went from being afraid of Outis to being afraid *for* him. Whatever paths he had been walking, they had brought him no peace.

He tipped up the brim of his hat with one finger, a slight motion that could have been done with flair if the hand had not been trembling. His face, his eyes . . . he looked like an addict with one foot in delirium and the other in the agony of withdrawal and no clear idea of which way he intended to step. He turned away from Khabir and faced Miranda. She was unable to move or look away, transfixed by his pain.

"I killed you once," he muttered. "It was in a busy street. You hardly even looked at me. I pushed a scalpel tipped with poison between your ribs. You were startled at the sharp elbows of the people in the crowd, but you kept on. Only a few more steps, and you fell. Another time, I stood on the sidewalk with my blade unused and watched you die, struck by an omnibus, scarcely three meters away from me. You died there in the road. Another time, I read in the paper that you died days later in the hospital. Another time, I heard that you had killed yourself, drowned in a pool." He peered through the entrance gate into the small atrium and pointed. "That's it there, I think."

The concluding comment jolted Miranda. She had been expecting to hear him say that she had drowned in the hospital pool.

He sighed a little. "I am so tired. I have been back and forth and back so many times."

He stretched out an arm, dragging the sleeve up for them to see. It was a dramatic gesture—overly so, thought Miranda at first—and then her eyes began to understand what she was seeing . . . or *not* seeing. His arm was no longer solid flesh. It was . . . unraveling, gaping with holes like a swatch of fabric with a thread or two pulled in the wrong place. The holes were pure darkness, shifting streaks like ink curling in clear water. Khabir began to back away.

"Behold!" Julian Outis laughed with quiet but poignant

hysteria. "I am devoured by the void, consumed by silence, made nothing . . . uncreated . . . undone."

"Undying essence," Miranda murmured.

The words cut short his moment of melodrama. He glared at her. "Of course. You should know."

"Why are you so desperate to kill me?" Miranda asked him.

He covered his arm again, shivered, and turned his face away. "I am not a murderer. He . . . it . . . he insisted. Grey had taken care of all the rest."

"Why *them*?" Khabir demanded.

Julian looked at him in surprise. "For the ritual."

Khabir remained baffled. "What ritual?"

"The ritual for the amulet. It binds him to that undying one. Am I right, Mr. Outis? Grey was the hand, but you were the intent, so *you* became bound, not him," Miranda said. "And now Grey is in jail and you have no amulet, so why me?"

Julian began to laugh again, a weary, cynical sound. "Is that what you think? It was a ritual for nothing; a nothing for a nothing. *He* told Grey, 'The amulet requires you to sacrifice a certain number of people in a certain order by a certain day. Only then you will receive its protection.' That's all Grey knew, or wanted to know, to calm his nightmares. Convenient lies. I didn't need any children's tales. He told me the truth—you are worse than any amulet. I had to remove you to be certain."

"Certain of what?" Khabir shouted. Miranda wanted to shout too. The more Julian spoke, the less sense he made, and it was terrifying to hear.

"Of my immortality," Julian said with a simplicity that was almost innocent.

Khabir inhaled and drew closer to Miranda, curling his fingers around the second cane in preparation.

"I am not a murderer!" Julian insisted. "He showed me. You were destined to die in so many times, and those times when you did not die, you lived in pain and misery. It would have been a kindness to kill you. It *was* a kindness."

"And now?" asked Miranda.

She stood up, shaking, with one cane, leaning only slightly on Khabir's shoulder. She got herself firmly settled, unsupported, then dropped her cane into the blossoming hedge with a flick of her hand.

"And now?" she dared him.

He bowed his head, the slight tremors in his body becoming stronger, more visible.

"Make up your mind, Julian," came a new voice.

It was Ajit, the Trickster as human. He stood behind Khabir and Miranda, feet planted a little apart in a relaxed and ready stance, stationed in front of the gate to the atrium. Khabir swung around with the cane, but at the sight of such an ordinary, harmless figure, he hesitated, glaring from one to the other in an attempt to determine where the threat lay.

"I've been showing Julian our version of immortality. I don't think he likes it—do you, Julian? Time doesn't run straight for the undying, and a human mind wasn't made for that kind of existence. And what do you think of our Miranda, Julian? Are you killing her this time or not? It's time to go, man. Make a choice."

There was a flash, a blink, and Julian suddenly loomed close, but before he could touch Miranda, the Trickster leaped the short distance of time and space to block him. She stumbled back against the chair and was immediately seized and dragged away by Khabir to the far corner of the patio. They crouched and watched the pair as they grappled for the small, thin blade in Julian's hand.

Julian shook the Trickster off and backed away, laughing as he lowered the scalpel. "I knew you wouldn't let me do it. This isn't like the other times; this is real, isn't it? This isn't one of your damned webs?"

"No. Not real, but not one of mine," replied the Trickster.

Miranda must have missed something in the Trickster's expression, because Julian's eyes widened in fear as if he had realized that he had been about to step into an abyss.

"It's true, then." He absently put away his blade, looking utterly lost. "What a foolish thing I've been doing. You can't fight *her*, can you?" He paused, contemplated the shifting patterns on the back of his hand, and breathed as slowly as a dying man savoring the last of his oxygen.

"Now go do what you have to do," said the Trickster sadly.

Julian stood still for a moment; then his lips twisted, and he nodded. He walked down the driveway, and although there was neither fog nor dust, his image vanished into the deepening dusk far sooner than human vision should allow.

"Why?" cried Miranda, facing the Trickster. It was an all-purpose cry. Why was he here? Why had he put her through all that? Why had Julian simply walked away? She yanked her cane out of Khabir's weak grip and pushed herself to her feet. "Is this it? Is this the end?"

The Trickster opened his mouth, caught himself, gave a half laugh of amusement and resignation, and was silent.

"Oh look," he said suddenly. "I believe that's your cab."

"No, wait, don't go—"

It was too late. The air was empty, the night silent. The cab drew up and stopped; the driver got out and looked quizzically at the two who stood silently on the patio.

Khabir came alert, eager to be able to do something ordinary. He waved, signaling for the cab driver to wait a moment, then turned to Miranda. "I'm coming with you. I'm going to see you safely to Delma, and then I'm going home."

"Khabir," she began gently.

"My City home," he continued, almost babbling. "I'm going to sleep in Club lodgings. Lots of people around. Lots of ordinary people. I feel the need to be surrounded by ordinary people making mundane noises about mundane matters. Please."

"Of course," she replied even more gently, understanding his plea. He would not, could not protect her from the things beyond this world, things that paid no mind to money, status, and Freeman privilege. He could only protect himself from what his mind could not comprehend.

The driver loaded Miranda's bags, and off they went, driving into the night. The journey was no more than twenty minutes, but it felt far longer with the silence between them. Once Khabir started to speak, but he glanced at the back of the driver's head, frowned, and said nothing. Miranda looked at him, concerned and apologetic, but similarly held her tongue.

The gates to the residence at Delma were designed to look affluent rather than institutional, but when they came to the front of the reception area, the illusion faded. There was a nurse waiting with a wheelchair, much to Miranda's gratitude. She was too tired to pretend to be brave and independent.

Khabir turned to her with a look of utter bemusement, and she gazed back helplessly. What could be said after the events of that evening? She touched his hand and tried to make her voice warm and reassuring. "You've been a good friend to me, Khabir, a very good friend. I'm sure . . . I'm sure everything will work out."

He nodded, at first avoiding her gaze, then giving her a glance that was quick and almost suspicious, as if he expected that she too would vanish. He patted her hand and gave it a strong squeeze before letting go and staring out of the window into the darkness.

Someone opened the door for her. She looked up, reaching automatically for her canes.

"It is time," said the Trickster. "Leave those. You no longer need them."

She got out of the cab unassisted and found herself standing in the center of the labyrinth. Khabir, the cab, and her new residence were . . . gone. She felt light, almost happy, and could not guess why at first, but then she recognized the distinctive euphoria of the absence of pain.

The Trickster looked around at the intricate coils of the labyrinth with an admiring expression. "This is truly a work of art. Rituals like these are key to binding humans, but few of us can manage this level of subtlety on such a large scale."

"Don't rituals bind the undying as well?" Miranda asked, grateful for the small talk. It helped with the disorientation she was feeling as she tried to remember her state of mind and her state of being when she had first begun to walk the labyrinth what felt like almost a year ago.

He looked surprised. "Oh, no. They may gain our attention, but they have no real effect on us. We see too clearly for that. Humans, now—they fool each other, they fool themselves. It's practically impossible to influence them without putting in some element of foolery, benign or otherwise."

"And you *are* the Trickster," she noted. "Did you try to fool me?"

"Why should I, when I don't want to influence you? None of us wants to influence you. That's why you get truth— perhaps more than you can handle." The sudden concern in his look said what his voice did not. *Was it too much?*

She raised her hands and let them drop limply. "I'm here."

"Thank you," he said, looking directly into her eyes.

His gaze shifted to a silent figure sitting quietly nearby on the ground. "Here's Patience. I'll leave you to it."

He walked away.

Still cool, still removed, Patience observed Miranda for a moment. "Take a little time," she suggested. "If you have questions, I will try my best to answer them."

"Who is Chance?"

Patience actually smiled. "An experiment. Which makes his offshoot . . . an oversight. To make Chance fully human, I had to remove from him some aspects of his undying nature."

"That sounds painful."

Patience shook her head. "It happens all the time. When the undying ones have traced all their paths, they return to me, their source, and go out from me anew, reformed, with different selves. Or sometimes they send out their own fragments of Being to trace separate paths, becoming sources themselves."

"And what you removed . . . has chosen to become a killer."

"I am not omniscient. I did not anticipate envy. No undying in the world has ever been fully human. Chance is the first. The other is trying to become the second, but on his own terms."

"But what about Ajit?"

Patience shook her head. "Ajit is the ultimate trick. Paama would not have had two sons born alive without my interference, and Ajit is not precisely the same as the son who would have died."

Miranda showed her confusion. Patience smiled and spoke more plainly. "He's like Mr. Reis—a changeling, using the shadow of a stillborn child."

Miranda hunted for a question with an answer she might be able to understand. "Why did Outis say I'm worse than an amulet?"

"You are bound to Chance's future."

"To him? Not Ajit? But when we met, Chance treated me like he barely knew me."

Patience looked at her with amused eyes. "Of course. He knows you as you will be, not as you are now. And yet he made a world for you. What more do you want? But I have not finished answering your question."

Miranda nodded slowly, waiting, sensing that Patience was hesitating.

"I may also have something to do with what you will become, but ultimately it depends on the choice you make," she said.

Miranda began to pace. "You're asking me to live this ordeal again. I don't know if I can. I can say *yes*, say it as many times as I like and even mean it, but when I'm in it, right in the middle of it, it might be too much. I might give up."

"I understand," said Patience. "I am not merely asking you to say *yes* at this moment. I am asking you to say it every day for the rest of your life."

"That other undying one—I know he has to be stopped. He's used up Julian. He's too strong for Chance and Ajit. He'll keep on until he gets what he wants. He'll find some other human who wants to live forever and feed them warped promises."

"That is what I fear," Patience acknowledged.

"Then yes. Yes. Do it now, before I get accustomed to this body again, before I forget how to bear pain," Miranda said.

Patience came to her quickly and embraced her, once more the comforting mother. "I will help you bear the pain. I can do that much."

It was a hosting, not a possession, and Patience did what was necessary with the ease and courtesy of a familiar and welcome guest. The gift was accepted. Events began to unfold as anticipated.

Patience stepped out into sunlight. She breathed warm air tinged with the scent of the sea and tainted with the reek of too many automobile engines. A busy City intersection was the best place to watch humanity ignoring each other, closed in on themselves, trying not to be overwhelmed by too much proximity. She had only a little time. There was Miranda, shoulders braced high with tension, briefcase in hand, waiting to cross . . . and there was Chance, clearly visible to the un-clouded mind, stretching out his hand to seize hold of her.

Patience began to run.

She passed close to them, brushed by Miranda's shock, Chance's confusion. There was only time for a quick, reassuring smile before they disappeared behind her and she continued on.

Already she could see Malveaux behind the windscreen of the looming omnibus, his eyes wide, looking not at her, not yet, but at something else in the road before him. Malveaux, alas, had long suffered the blessing and curse of an unclouded mind.

She moved, placing Miranda's fragile body squarely in the path of the omnibus.

"It begins here," she declared as she accepted the impact.

And Miranda will end it, she thought as silence fell.

BOOK III

METANOIA

CHAPTER TWENTY

He had always been slightly wary of mirrors. As he pondered memories of before and after, of his undying existence and his human life, of Patience and of Paama, he remembered the mirror. It had been a terrible way to remind him of himself. When a beautiful, ageless, and strangely familiar woman appears in an adolescent boy's mirror, he should be allowed some time to enjoy the experience before he starts screaming, but his childhood had been too mundane to prepare him for such unusual events. The screaming had begun almost instantly.

"Yao? Are you all right?"

At the sound of his mother's voice, he choked on his breath. He meant to reply in the negative, but before he did, he beat the flat of his hand against the mirror in the hope that it would banish the ghost that had replaced his reflection. He stared at his hand, and the words choked deep down in his chest along with the rest of his breath. Like white blotting paper under a tipped-over ink bottle, his skin was turning blue.

"Yao?"

"I'm all right, Maa!" he answered loudly. Constancy, his occasional cat, jumped down from his bed, sat on the floor, and eyed him with amusement.

"*Yao?*" The actual sound of his name never changed, but something in the resonance of the tone spoke of power and danger. He responded to the challenge instinctively.

"Paama, I said *I'm all right!*"

In the shocked silence that followed, the face in the mirror gave him a very slight smile and disappeared. The cat rolled over, still keeping her eyes fixed on him, and gave the impression that she might be stretching or silently laughing very, very hard. The blue tint faded swiftly, or perhaps it simply went under, seeping into flesh and bone and marrow.

As the mind of the boy called Yao struggled with the awareness of the being known as Chance, one thought was clear: the hope that he would be allowed to forget what had just happened.

To give Patience credit, most days he *did* forget, a small but necessary precaution to preserve his human sanity. Other times, like this night, he found himself wandering, mind expanding and growing clearer, vision enriched to a broader spectrum, his very skin becoming an organ of all senses that sifted reality for information with each habitual and unnecessary inhalation. The world was no longer a smooth track but a gathering of perilous cracks in which a mind could lose itself playing hopscotch.

Not perilous to him.

With such journeys, it was always best to orient oneself

with a glance in the mirror, if only as a warning of what kind of behavior to expect from others. Chance crossed the threshold and stood still for a second before looking to his left and his right. There were mirrors everywhere. Each wall was a wide, glass-paneled window showing several aspects of the same scene. Then he blinked, and the otherworldly strangeness became merely human. It was only a dance studio.

"They told me that mirrors would confuse you."

"They?" he inquired politely, turning with slow calm to face the person behind him.

She was seated on the wooden floor, back against a mirrored wall, legs stretched straight in front of her. Her right hand held a pair of dancing shoes by their knotted ribbons. He did not have to look twice to realize she had no feet.

"They warned me not to come," she said.

"I made it a compulsion, not a coercion," Chance said, explaining, not excusing, "but either way, mirrors wouldn't have made a difference."

"Oh yes, they did. You didn't see me." She sounded bitterly triumphant, as if not being seen was no new miracle in her experience.

"That wasn't the mirrors. That was you." The best labyrinths were all about choice, and he had kept to tradition when making this one.

"They also said you'd be a monster. That you'd kill me just by looking at me."

He glanced once more at his reflection. Monsters were also part of the labyrinth tradition, but he doubted his powers in that regard. The mirror showed a small, old man, white-haired, dark and weathered as aged wood, wiry from hard work and meager nourishment, and still dressed in peasant cotton—clear evidence of the Trickster gift in action. His brother had been known to disguise himself as an old man, particularly when on the road where he might be taken for a beggar or an itinerant craftsman.

"I do not look very dangerous, no," he admitted. "I am sorry to disappoint you."

She sighed with impatience. "You'll have to carry me."

He crouched beside her, drew her arms around his neck, and pulled her up. She was heavier than she looked. When he put her on his back, she gripped his waist desperately with strong knees. "I will not drop you," he protested.

She did not seem reassured. The ballet shoes whipped into his ribs as she clutched his shoulders. He was about to suggest that she leave them behind, but he looked a little more closely and saw how they appeared empty one moment, and the next moment . . . they filled out, pointed and flexed.

The ribbons pressed flat against his throat, more warning than threat. "I suppose I can't kill you?"

"Why, then I might drop you after all," Chance replied gently. "But no, I think you cannot kill me. Now, which way do you wish to go?"

She tapped him lightly on the right side with her shoes like a rider guiding her mount with a touch of the reins. He went obediently. The mirrored studio fell behind, and the path led once more into the cold air of the silent desert, but the woman on his back kept her substance and her weight. He kept walking, carrying her as penance and compass.

"I'm sorry," she mumbled.

"Eh?" he replied. "What for?"

"I mistook you—"

"—for the one I am seeking. I gathered that. Don't dwell on it. You're allowed a little suspicion and uncertainty when you're dreaming. Still . . . don't listen to *them* next time."

"What if they're angels?"

He almost staggered, but he quickly caught and composed himself. "Angels . . . it's worth it to listen to angels . . . some of them. What have the angels been telling you?"

"They said it wasn't my time to die." She relaxed a little as she spoke, dropping her head close enough to tuck lightly between his shoulder and ear. Was it the beginning of trust? He hoped so.

The ground changed to paving stones below his feet, and the wind blew alternately fresh with salt spray and rank with rotting seaweed. Night was turning to dawn. It was a familiar district. The town houses of the City lined the low seawall, the mossy bricks of the wall topped the wave-weathered boulders above the beach, and the boulders edged the thin strip of coarse sand that was all the sea had to offer at low tide.

"Danil's here," she said.

Chance stared around him as the light grew, but there was only unpeopled land and empty sea. One of the boulders shifted slightly, gray-brown against gray-brown, and the shape of a man emerged to the eye like a chameleon breaking free of camouflage. He was naked, sitting hunched and hollow-eyed with his limbs and body curled around his lap in what appeared at first to be an attempt at modesty. He turned his head and his head only to stare at Chance with anger and accusation.

"Give me something to wear," he demanded.

"It's your dream," Chance countered. "Craft a garment for yourself."

Danil looked away, grieved. "I tried," he said. "Nothing changes."

He stood up carefully, keeping his back to them. He held a simple length of fabric gripped in his left hand, which he quickly wrapped and knotted about his waist. For a while he stood there, gazing out to sea, looking more like a village fisherman than a resident of the City. Chance was about to voice his confusion when Danil sighed and turned around. A neat oval pierced him through so that where there should have been cloth, skin, flesh, bone, organs, genitals, there was only a small window showing the motion of the waves behind him.

"An ancient punishment for adultery," he explained. "I prefer other ancient punishments. Shunning. Conscription. Death. But you're a man. Surely you agree?"

"I am not, strictly speaking, a man," said Chance.

"He had no right," Danil went on querulously, blinking back tears. "He had no right to judge. I would have married her. I would have been a better father to her son."

Chance shook his head very slightly. "I believe that you think so . . . in hindsight, at least."

"That's another ancient punishment for fornication. Forced

marriage. Impossible when one party is already married," he said morosely.

There was a small silence.

"I hate morality," he added with sudden harshness.

"You were young," the woman said. "You thought there was no rush. Few young men are moral. They wait till they are old for that, and even then . . ." She too concluded on a sharp, resentful note.

Danil slid from the boulder and tentatively climbed up and over the seawall as if favoring a body wracked with phantom pain. When he finally stood before them, it was with hands clasped in front of him, screening his lack, flesh and bone managing what mere clothing could not.

"Two guides, and four or five more to follow, I take it?" Chance asked him directly. "Is Galina next? I don't know her story. Why was she killed? And the child—the case notes never said if the child was living or dead."

"Don't be in such a rush," Danil warned him. "It's not pleasant."

"I thought *you* would know who lives and who dies," the woman said in surprise. "Don't you know how many of us there are?"

Chance shook his head. "I don't know everything."

"And?" she pressed, a little hardness coming into her voice.

"And I pay little attention to those who cannot make choices," he admitted. "Choosing is what makes a difference to probabilities; choosing is what makes a human stand out. Millions of infants die before they can make a definitive choice. They barely make a mark on the tapestry."

She sniffed. "You write off many, old man. Many people cannot choose, not only babies."

"Perhaps," he demurred, "but still fewer than you think."

Her body stiffened, reversing the gradual relaxation of their journey together. "Danil can carry me."

"If you wish," Chance said, bewildered by her withdrawal.

He handed her over with care; Danil took her and held her across his arms like a bride. The drape of her dancer's skirt gave him the screen he coveted, and he knew it well, for he stood taller and looked happier, once more a handsome, well-proportioned man. The woman glanced at him, bit her lip to mask an instinctive smile, lowered her eyes, and muttered, "Better the monster you know."

"Lead the way, Danil," Chance told him.

Danil took a step, the light changed, the ground shifted, and they walked once more in the desert.

"So, how *did* you die?" asked the woman.

"Carelessly," was Danil's brief reply. "I was sleeping. I woke up to pain and death."

"Grey used a narcotic on you. Probably didn't want to risk a fight," Chance said, recalling the contents of the file.

"Grey," Danil snarled. "Everyone knew Grey. He seemed harmless. Pathetic, but harmless."

"Pathetic?" The woman raised an eyebrow.

"Shy, stammering. You know."

"He always sounded perfectly eloquent to *me*," she insisted.

"He sounds very changeable, very accommodating," Chance said quietly, hoping they would keep talking.

"He certainly knew how to make people feel superior to him. *That's* why he stammered around you, Danil— not because he was shy, but because he knew you wouldn't see him as a threat."

"Oh, I see. Very well, then—what did he do to make *you* feel safe around him?"

She dropped her head to avoid his scornful look. "Not safe, never safe . . . but he did manipulate my feelings. He told me about his life during the war. He was just a child then. I couldn't blame him if he was a little strange given such a nightmarish childhood. I couldn't be unkind to him."

Chance listened with growing depression. Was that all it was, the sum and total of the murderer's plan? To kill those who were careless or caring enough to allow him to get close? Some little sin of theirs to justify the deed would be easy to find or imagine, or perhaps the one who directed him had also fed him a reason for righteous execution of punishment. It was foolish for someone of his ilk to be irritated by a set of random acts, and yet Chance was irritated and disquieted. He wanted a solved mystery, the end to this evil.

The ground beneath him changed from the soundless drag of sand to the cheerful bounce and ring of a sprung wooden floor. The stars assembled themselves in a precise pattern that became a network of lights in the high, spangled ceiling of a ballroom. That dim sparkle grew to a bright blaze, revealing the players in the room. Members of an orchestra sat onstage at the end of the room, silently poised with their instruments, waiting for a signal. Dancers filled the floor, standing still, looking around expectantly. Diners sat at the tables positioned in two broad corridors bracketing the dance floor, also quietly anticipating some event.

"Galina's place," Danil confirmed, leading the way to an unoccupied table. He gently settled the Mermaid into one chair and sat beside her, crossing his legs self-consciously.

Chance remained standing so he could turn and look all around him, but he still missed the moment when she appeared.

"And . . . *begin.*"

As the unseen speaker gave the cue, the diners began to chatter and laugh over the clink of glasses and cutlery. The dancers swept off to the swelling music, exchanging the tension of the hiatus for an effortless intensity of graceful movement. Never before had so many people striven with such passion to enjoy themselves.

Their director surveyed them from her position at the entrance to the ballroom. She too was effortless yet intense. Her pale dress was simple, draping in long folds to her ankles in the style of a priestess or a femme fatale. Her hair was pulled back in a tight looped braid that left her neck bare and her face coldly exposed. Her eyes and her mouth dominated her features—large, wide, and generous, but hungry instead of giving. When she finally moved, her steps were slow, and the side split in her dress opened and closed to give a glimpse of legs drawn in lines of tight, toned muscle. The Mermaid shifted, leaning forward with professional interest. Dancer recognized dancer.

She walked to the center of the dance floor where the lights shone brightest. The dancers acknowledged her by adjusting their orbits to accommodate her passage, but not with their eyes. The music did not change pace, but when she stopped, the entire room hushed for just a moment.

"Once I was beautiful, and my life was like a play."

CHAPTER TWENTY-ONE

Chance sat down.

There was no denying this woman. She was utterly spellbinding, her performance of the highest art. Whatever urgency he felt for his own mission turned to a compulsion to hear her story, be the audience for her play. He suspected she had lived her offstage life in similar fashion.

A man approached her, inviting her with an outstretched hand to join him in the dance. She accepted, and they danced in that studied yet wistful manner in which both look off to the side, apparently expecting something better to happen any moment.

It was easy to guess what would—what *should* come next. The newcomer's entrance was subtle. He timed his steps to the dance, finding the right pace and direction to go straight to his goal without disrupting anyone else on the floor. It made his interruption even bolder when he smoothly detained the woman's partner with an out-turned palm to the shoulder (more block than blow), took her hand (still raised and open in her confusion), and matched the flow of the dancers.

Chance noted the indignant blink of the dismissed partner, the swift recognition that erased his anger from view, and his dignified but prompt withdrawal. It was indeed a play, but if his assessment of the newcomer was correct, it would likely be a tragedy.

A disembodied narration continued in her voice as she and her leading man proceeded in their wordless conquest of center stage.

"He was new to me, but the regulars accorded him an old deference rather like that given to those of royal lineage. In time I discovered he was indeed a prince, but a barbarian prince of blood feuds, street warfare, gaudy wealth, and brute power. Suavity was a cloak he wore in cold blood when things were going his way. I mistook it for integrity and found out too late how different he could be when in a passion."

The lights dimmed, and a single spotlight tricked the eye into keeping focus on her while the dancers flitted into new positions as if filing into pews. The music changed to something majestic but somber as the man stood behind her and solemnly draped a white veil over her head. The sternness of his expression and his movement did not suggest a groom doting on his bride but a man putting a collar on a highly bred, highly prized, temperamental bitch.

"Persuasion amused him but did not move him. Tantrums vexed him and did not move him. I began by admiring him for having a strength of purpose that matched my own; I ended by hating him for having a strength of purpose that matched my own. My life was a play, but I was not the director nor the lead. I was not even a supporting character. I was a prop."

By now the lights were so dim that her face, covered in gauzy white, looked like it was drowning in fog. There was an awful pause.

"But it improved . . . or perhaps we matured."

Music and lighting both brightened. She moved across the now empty floor. The dining tables behind her had been stripped bare of their white cloths, revealing heavy business desks. Some of the supporting cast sat, others stood, still others moved briskly from desk to desk, and in the center was the largest desk of all with her husband behind it.

"We carved out our own spheres, ruled our separate kingdoms."

Two men swiftly brought in a chaise lounge and placed it behind her. Without giving them a backward glance, she reclined on it and watched various people assemble and disperse before her: small tea parties, media interviews, and a constant swirl of household staff, decorators, designers, musicians, and artists.

"Of course," the narration intoned, "ruling is not the only duty of a queen. Heirs are required for the kingdom, and in that I was deficient. He was supportive, reassuring me with fresh honeymoons and undivided attention, but I tried to glimpse the truth behind the effort. It was there in the caution and concern of the doctors I consulted. I caught hints of it in the side glances of some of the staff. They were assessing the likelihood that I might be set aside . . . gently, of course, but still, needs must. He loved me after his own fashion, but he had long ago learned to be ruthless about his own desires.

"Years passed. In my desperation, I let some things slide.

They had said I did too much, drank too much, stayed up too late, ate too little—so I changed. Sacrifices had to be made."

The light faded from brightly artificial to dim daylight. The population of her salon dwindled as the mass of cultured urbanites departed gradually, gracefully, and permanently. A smaller household staff remained to tend to her as she brooded on her chaise, and the shift in light made her clothes look dowdier and her figure less trim.

She sprang up from the chaise with unexpected energy and walked toward the audience as a frenzy of scene-changing commenced behind her. The chaise was bundled out and a crib trundled in. Her husband came to stand beside it, smiling proudly as the chorus gathered and cooed around the new arrival under the crib's blankets.

Standing in front of the domestic tableau, stationed at the edge of the action, the woman took up the narration once more from her unseen avatar. "At last, in time, I was rewarded for my self-restraint. I provided my husband with a child to carry on his line. The congratulations bore an inappropriate amount of relief, but I took them without complaint."

The chorus moved again, drawing slowly away from the center of the stage until the last admiring well-wisher was left to wave with shy fondness from the very fringes of the spotlight.

"But there were some . . . doubts." There was bitter emphasis in the woman's words as the last person turned away and her husband abruptly let fall the mask of paternal satisfaction to frown in perplexity at the crib, caught somewhere between vexation and pity.

A lone clarinet warbled a forlorn melodic line as she paused and looked back over her shoulder at the tableau, displaying her own vexation and regret for a moment before facing forward once more to continue the tale.

"In time I learned the truth. Many years before, doctors had said that my husband would never father children. The family had kept it quiet for political as well as personal reasons, and that silence only encouraged my husband's denial. After all, people have certain expectations of a king. My child was to me a surprise and a pleasure but to him a surprise and a problem. I thought I could solve it. I did and said everything I could to reassure him, to convince him of the miracle."

As she spoke, he reached into the crib hesitantly and picked up the tiny, blanket-swaddled shape, holding it almost at arm's length in a parody of the unpracticed new father faced with a wet diaper. Still with that expression of confused emotion, he handed it over to a nursemaid with unseemly speed, and while crib, maid, and child receded in their own fading circle of light, he strode forward in a blaze of spotlights and trumpets to grip his wife by the arm and yank her back to center stage.

Their argument unfolded as a tango, a violent push and pull with each demanding control.

"It did not suffice," she cried out over the quarreling music. "He became cruel, accusing me of lies, questioning my loyalty. Then, most terrifying of all, he grew silent."

She spun away from him, spurned by a flick and release of his hand. He walked away in quiet, suppressed fury, returned to his desk, and sat behind it like a man finding a fortress and determined to stay there. His face slowly relaxed and became calm; he took up the papers before him and began to read.

"In the end, he found my greatest weakness. I could endure his possessiveness, his controlling manner, and even his hatred, but I could not abide his indifference."

The room went dark, and the music hushed; then the lone clarinet once more began to lament. A pool of muted light formed and widened around a solitary figure holding a small child covered and close in her arms.

"I left," she stated. "I left him, I left my home, and I made myself a new one. I left to find another stage, another play, another role in which I could direct myself again. It is never too late to start again."

She walked offstage as the well-known silhouette of the City's towers and town houses slowly appeared on the curtains behind her and the trumpets sounded a last soft farewell.

"The end," whispered a familiar voice in his ear.

Chance turned. "Galina," he murmured.

She was seated beside him as if she had been part of the audience all along. To some, she would be barely recognizable as the woman who had been on the stage. Her face and attire were devoid of glamour and her voice stripped of drama. To one with some experience in the art of crafting shadows, she was easy to identify. Frankly, he preferred her this way. She still sat with poise, but her body curved a little, released from the severe mastery of the performer's will. Her mouth was softer and her eyes more vulnerable. She was human.

"My latest work," she explained with a self-deprecating smile. "It needs a little refining, but I think I've pulled together the best elements. Don't you agree?"

The last sentence came in a rush, a flutter of uncertainty

abruptly modulating her tone, betraying her sudden fear that she had been too presumptuous in her self-assessment. Chance wavered. Even though she showed herself as a woman of ordinary appearance, the old pull was there, the power to persuade, seduce, mesmerize. He found himself leaning toward her in instinctive anxiety, wanting to please her, to make her happy, but then he caught himself and smiled at her with an admonishing shake of his head.

"Madame, you are good, but I have been a man for only a fraction of my existence. I have retained a certain amount of immunity."

She ducked her head and smiled, both pleased and embarrassed that he had been able to catch her out. "I see you do not even pretend to lie. How fortunate your friends are! Very well, then. Tell me what you truly think."

"I could not help but give your play my attention, my sympathy even, but the lead female was at times too present."

"What do you mean?" she demanded, not offended but intrigued.

"She might have said more by speaking less. I think she communicated most clearly when dancing."

She frowned and nodded. "Yes, yes, of course. The narration is superfluous, no?"

"It is hard to blend your history and your dreams," he offered. "Emotional attachment is natural, but it will rob you of objectivity."

She continued to frown and nod as she stood up and allowed her imagined world to dissolve into desert. "Fyodor doesn't like masked autobiographies. He says that an author building on the subject of his own life will write the truth too large to be credible as fiction." She sighed. "As for my part in his life, I wonder how small he will have it written to suit his comfort. Ah, well. Let us be off."

Chance felt the awkwardness of knowing that there was no delicate way to press for the information he needed. "Ah . . . before we go, are you the only one here?" He looked at her discreetly, his gaze lingering at her waist, where a simple sarong was wrapped and tied over a tucked-in tunic. Her figure was lacking in no area—no void, no bloody bandages, nothing to hint at her loss. *Accustomed, perhaps, to feigning wholeness,* he thought.

She gave a little shake of the head, part puzzlement, part irritation. "Who else should be here?"

He was too baffled for courtesy. "But . . . your performance . . . the child? *Your* child?"

Her expression was unreadable. It was both artfulness and sincerity, with her eyebrows quizzical but her eyes blank. "*My* child? I have no child."

There were several counterquestions to that, but Chance faltered into silence. The performance was more than mere play; it was tragedy at a safe distance. It appeared there were sorrows beyond her capacity after all.

She turned and walked away, and for all that Chance had claimed immunity, he took a moment or two before following, a moment to watch the curve of her leg as it showed briefly through the folds of her sarong at the farthest stretch of her stride.

CHAPTER TWENTY-TWO

As he followed his guides deeper into the labyrinth, Chance found himself set slightly apart. Galina seemed to know Danil well, for she walked beside him and chatted without artifice. The Mermaid occasionally joined in the conversation, but mostly she was silent, content to be carried by the untiring Danil.

Chance was not fooled by his own crafting. They were neither alive nor dead. They were not real. Were they memories, dreams, or solid projections created by his own ruminations on this bizarre, angel-assigned case? All of the above, or none, or simply fragments of possibility. Labyrinths could do that, hypnotize the human mind to break free of time-bound perception and remember precisely, see clearly, foretell accurately. His labyrinth was made of his own mind coiling back on itself and examining itself, and these walking ghosts were all connected to him by a ritual that was only myth, but a myth powerful enough to acquire a kind of shared reality.

And yet . . . it was hard not to care about them. Whatever his actions as an undying one, the uncertainties of his human life had taught him to bear the weight of the mystery of death. To want to die well, with meaning, as more than an unlucky accident or the victim of a murderous whim—this was a desire he could understand. That was what made ritual, and even the rumor of ritual, so powerful. It gave meaning, however ill-founded, to death. Humans would look for a pattern in anything—a face in the clouds, a voice in the wind, and a reason in chaos. The problem was not that patterns did not exist but that people were better at fabricating them than discovering them.

He saw clearly. He knew what was of his own making. They were not real, but even the shadow of their existence deserved his respect.

He walked unseeing from dim starlight into dim twilight, from sharp, dry cold to damp coolness, and into the next place. It was a walled garden, but not a neat and overgroomed patch of boredom. Here were crumbling bricks fallen in a pile to breed thick moss under a dripping cast-iron downspout; there were straggly nests of dry grass and scraps of wild cotton poking out of the uneven holes left in the wall. The birds that flew unerringly in and out of those close-quartered nests were in constant song, lilting a teasing tune and then chuckling at the joke. The very weeds bloomed obligingly, bright yellow-gold and emerald-green treasures that made marvelous alchemy of the mud and gravel caught in the long, narrow gutters alongside the paths.

The trees were small and appropriate to the spot. A cherry tree was the centerpiece of the tableau, with fruit too high to reach, branches too thin to climb, and beneath them all a thick blur of fruit flies gorging on the half-fermented pulp of fallen fruit amid the grass. The hot, sweet scent of frangipani dominated, wafting from white- and pink-crested trees with dark, glossy leaves and dark, glossy trails of black ants following lines of sticky sap.

Xandre was sitting on a stone bench under a white frangipani tree, trying and mostly failing to pick up small bits of broken masonry with his toes. He noticed them and instantly adopted a poised, meditative posture.

"I wasn't always a street rat," he said in a tone that was too heavy with pathos to be taken seriously.

"Liar," said Galina, her voice deep with amusement and admiration at his showmanship. "This is the courtyard garden beside the City Basilica. I suppose you've broken in here many a time to steal fruit and throw stones at the birds."

He relaxed into a more natural slump and shrugged. "Maybe. Anyway, it's my favorite place. So I get to keep it."

"A thief to the last," said Danil with dry approval.

The boy grinned at that, but then he saw Chance, and his grin became a gape of shock. "You!"

"Yes and no," Chance replied. He was not surprised to be recognized in spite of his new shadow. After all, Xandre was the only one of them who had actually met him.

Astonishment became confusion. "But . . . don't I know you?"

"A lot has happened to both of us since then," Chance explained. "Are you willing to guide me?"

Xandre hesitated, still unsure whether or not to be scared, then nodded. The Mermaid watched with a small, knowing smile. Chance did not have to face her directly to see that the smile held no kindness.

Xandre walked ahead, leading them down the path and through an open gate of black-painted cast iron, which hung askew from the stone wall on rusty hinges. His gait was off. He moved like one accustomed to speaking with his hands even in silence, and the lack of them unbalanced both body and mind to halting midflow. Whenever he stumbled, physically or verbally, he soon drew himself together with extreme control and self-possession, but it was a temporary measure, impossible to sustain for long.

Chance let himself drift to the rear of the group again. The Mermaid peeped over Danil's shoulder, watching him.

"Brace yourself," she warned.

The ground dissolved into ocean, and the group broke into a cacophony of yells, screams, and laughter. The Mermaid swam free of Danil, who was well occupied with Galina clinging to his arm in panic.

"Ahoy! Ahoy!" shrieked Xandre, bobbing up and down as he splashed the water with his blunted arms.

Chance shook water out of his ears and eyes and finally saw it: a small sailboat moving lazily in the light wind, and a familiar face below a sailor's cap.

"Hello!" Niko answered. "Xandre, is that you? Ship's boy, what are you doing overboard?"

He drew closer, secured the lines and rudder, and tossed a lifesaver toward the boy.

"I wasn't always a street rat, you know," Xandre said, laughing and spluttering as he splashed toward the boat with one arm hooked through the lifesaver.

"Well, I know you were a piss-poor cabin boy," said Niko cheerfully as he hauled him into the boat.

Xandre panted out an explanation as he scrambled over the side. "You can't quit mid-ocean. There's nowhere to run to. Cities always have places to run to."

"You were lazy." Niko tossed a casual, smiling glance at the rest of the group, no doubt assessing whom to help next, and saw Danil. Their stares clashed with neither man giving an inch, but Galina was clearly in distress, and Niko was too professional to let a woman drown, even if it was for a moment's indulgent vengeance.

"Hand her over," he ordered Danil.

Danil obeyed, but he maintained a steady, suspicious glare as Niko coaxed Galina to let go and climb into the boat. Niko smiled at the Mermaid, who was visibly happy in her element, frowned at Chance, and began to settle himself once more near the tiller.

"Wait!" said Danil. "You can't expect us all to keep up."

"Well, *you* should float fairly easily, *she* swims better than anyone I ever knew, and for some reason I don't think that old man is human enough to drown. I'll keep with the passengers I have, thank you."

Final words spoken, he moved the small craft off with a briskness that had little to do with the prevailing winds.

"Follow them!" cried the Mermaid, and she curved her body gracefully into the boat's wake.

Danil cursed, put his head down, and swam like a professional at a competition. Chance gave him a favorable current and paid him no further mind. The horizon was too close and impenetrable for the swimmers to see any destination. What he needed was a crow's-nest view. Keeping his eye on the boat, he lifted himself out of the water and into the air.

Niko saw him. "Cheater!" he yelled, but it sounded more teasing than accusing. Chance ignored him and looked ahead.

A flat, seamless ring of white sand sloped gently into the ocean. The shoreline's blue was delicately pale where water met sand and sunlight; farther out there was the deep, heart-stopping blue of many fathoms of ocean, the blue of falling in endless space. There were no trees or shrubs along the sandy barrier, but beyond it in the sheltered lagoon, tiny islands poked sharply out of the water like small green monsters, shaggy and craggy, sitting hunched in cool water and hot sun.

He spent so long staring at it that by the time he looked down, the Mermaid was stretched out on the sand, half-in, half-out of water. Danil was struggling a short distance behind her, and the boat was several lengths off, keeping from running aground in the shallows. Xandre was already in the water, beckoning to Galina, who was leaning over the side of the boat, nervously gripping the lifesaver. At last she held her breath and tumbled over with a clumsy splash. Xandre slipped a loop of rope into the crook of his elbow and began to pull her to shore.

Chance descended to the boat. "Aren't you coming?" he asked Niko.

Niko jumped slightly, startled at the sudden appearance near his mast. "Oh, it's you. No, this is as far as I can go."

Frowning, Chance descended all the way to sit near Niko.

"I need you to guide me all the way. Leave the boat and come with us."

Niko shook his head, and his crooked smile was a little smug. "I'm not saying I don't feel like coming. I'm saying I *can't*. There's nothing you or I can do about it, old man."

He pointed down at his left foot. There was a heaped-up length of chain at the bottom of the boat, one end attached to a ring in the bow, the other to a shackle around his ankle. There was no other anchor.

"Ah," said Chance with an understanding nod, resting his right hand on Niko's shoulder in apparent sympathy.

He then thrust his left hand up into Niko's chest, right under the sternum to the place where his heart used to be. The man was too shocked to scream. He stared at Chance, appalled, unblinking, and more frightened by what he saw before him than by the invading hand.

"The part of me that is a man is not yet old, and the part of me that is old is not a man," Chance said quietly.

Niko tried to squirm away from the iron hold on his shoulder and the alien probing beneath his rib cage. Chance pulled out his hand, now bloodied, and held a large key before Niko's horrified eyes. "Both parts are getting impatient, so kindly use this now, and let us be on our way."

Niko was shaking so hard that it took him two attempts to take his key from Chance's fingers and many more tries to get it into the lock of the shackle. Chance leaned over the side of the boat and rinsed the stickiness from his hand, taking his time until he heard the shackle click open. Niko dived over the opposite side in haste. Chance paused to pick up the blood-stained key, glanced once at the shackle, and skimmed the key far away into deep ocean, out of temptation's reach.

He looked toward the beach again and made an effort to calm himself. The Trickster veneer had cracked and strained in the heat of his frustration, but with a few deep breaths it cooled, coalesced, and once more encompassed him smoothly. He could have walked on water—it was his labyrinth, after all—but he dived fully into the waves and made himself struggle the last few meters like any other human.

At last he grasped the sand with fingers and toes; at last he stood slowly while his guides looked back at him, some fearful, some only curious, and the Mermaid, as always, judging his very presence with her steady gaze.

"We're all here," Xandre prompted, impatient.

"Now what?" asked Galina, as anxious as any actor with a changing script.

Chance shook his head, sending saltwater droplets flying, and carefully wiped his eyes and brow with his fingertips. He was so deep within himself that he could be excused for being oblivious to the rest of existence, but from the moment he had read the files in Miranda's briefcase, he had kept his fingers on certain threads, waiting for the signal that their weaving was finished and their patterning done. One key thread remained, and it was no accident that his coming to the center of his labyrinth should coincide with that thread's completion.

"Now we wait for the last guide, the man who really caused your deaths."

He did not tell them that it was a statement of hope, not fact.

CHAPTER TWENTY-THREE

"Now go do what you have to do," said the Trickster sadly. Julian stood still for a moment. There was no more room for self-deception now, not with the humming and tugging of undying essence coiling around his wrists and hands and fingers. He turned in the direction he was to go and walked until the hard surface of the driveway became the fine, ankle-turning sand of the desert. He cringed under a bright sky, suddenly naked and exposed.

"I didn't hurt her—I never touched her," he babbled, keeping his head down and hands raised protectively.

"Of course you didn't," Chance said, reaching out to Julian's warding hands and stripping the Trickster's mark from him like a man ripping a label from a package. "But you would have. Oh, by the way, everyone? I think most of you know Julian. Julian, these are the victims of Walther Grey, the ones you chose."

Julian straightened slightly from his crouch and looked around at the unfriendly faces gathering around him. "That's not true," he pleaded. "I never said—"

Chance wound the mark around his hand, an action that had no other purpose than to keep his hands occupied with something harmless. "Perhaps you never said it exactly, but you shared gossip, you hinted at who deserved to die, and you gave him that old legend—that you could summon a spirit by assembling a body for it."

"You think you know everything," Julian sneered.

"No, I'm only guessing. You've kept us guessing for a good while. Do you know how hard it is to track down a man who barely believes in the reality of what he's doing?"

"This isn't real either!" Julian shrieked, trembling badly. "This is another one of those damned dreams!"

"He's half-mad," murmured Galina contemptuously.

"No. Entirely sane, but not very bright," Niko remarked.

Xandre made a noise of disgust and turned away, but Danil stepped closer and rested a calming hand on Julian's shoulder. "We used to talk about the old folk tales, the legends, the things our parents and grandparents passed on. And yes, we used to laugh and say they were all just stories. But seriously, man, when things started happening to you, where was your respect? Your caution? Why did you keep fooling yourself? Why play with things you don't understand and pretend it's a game of make-believe?"

"I don't want to die." Julian whimpered. "I don't . . . I don't want to die."

"Old man," whispered the Mermaid.

Chance turned around. She was sitting comfortably, still half-in, half-out of the water. She was looking at him with a strange mixture of resentment and triumph.

"Old man, do you really think this is the end? Do you think this is all of us?"

Chance looked back at the rest of his guides. Danil was still reasoning as if desperate to understand what kind of mind had caused his situation. Galina stood with her arms folded and watched them with exasperation. Xandre was arguing with Niko about whether it was even possible to kill Julian in this place, and shouldn't they at least try, in the spirit of experimentation if nothing else?

He sat beside her on the wet sand. "Go on."

"You've forgotten the child."

"I can't . . . I don't know how to find him, not while Galina refuses to remember what happened."

She looked at him for a long moment. "I can take you to where he is."

Chance did not misunderstand her. "But will you?" he inquired.

She squeezed a handful of wet sand, hesitating. "Show me who you really are."

He was taken aback at first, but then he slowly nodded.

First he became the human Yao: a young man, pale-skinned with yellow-white locs, inheritor of his mother's smooth skin and his father's fine bones, bearing a clouded, careful look in his violet eyes. Next he revealed the indigo lord: cold, proud, and terrifying, marked by unearthly beauty and the deep hue of moonlit midnight. For the last, as the world came to life around them once more, he showed her his undying essence infusing every grain of sand and drop of ocean and breath of air in the labyrinth he had made from and for himself.

Everything stopped—the waves, the sound of the ocean, the breeze, Julian's sobbing, and the voices of the others as they debated over him. The only movement was the startled blink of the Mermaid's eyelashes, and the only sound her faint gasp.

"Is that enough?" he asked her.

She was crying. He thought—he *hoped* it meant that she understood him just a little, but she began to speak, and he realized her tears were for herself.

"I wished for so much from life. I told myself not to be greedy, to focus on one thing. Skill wasn't enough, so I asked for fame. Well, I got it. No one knows my name, but everyone talks about me. I'm . . . a *thing* made up by people craving something memorable. I didn't know I'd get tragedy wrapped up in my wish. If I could wish again, I'd be content with just skill— not genius, but just the honest, ordinary skill of someone who loves each and every small miracle of order created from chaos."

She was silent, the waiting silence of a woman who has shared much and is hoping for a similar gift. Chance cleared his throat and made an effort.

"I was never allowed wishes."

She touched his hand. He rushed on to avoid her unexpected, unwanted pity.

"But I am in children's rhymes and grandmothers' tales. I understand what it is like to be made into a *thing* by the power of words."

She nodded as if it was enough. "Come with me." She pushed off the soft sand into the water.

He wavered, fearful at last of what lay ahead. "I . . ."

Her look was implacable, tears and all. "You *must* see this." She softened. "Please."

Already cold and sick with dread, he followed her into the sea. She swam to the edge of the reef and quickly ducked under a craggy lip of old coral fringed with frond-draped sea creatures and quivering plants. The cold rock scraped hot over his skin as he kept close behind her, down and down into darkness, then up once more toward the pale blue-green light above. They both surfaced, still under rock, to his surprise, but in a cozy underground sphere where the water was faintly illuminated by light from some other unseen opening.

"This was the safest place to keep him," she explained.

Then Chance saw him, folded and curled up comfortably in the center of the dim light, a tiny specimen in an invisible jar. He looked barely a year old, an age at which it was still easier and more instinctive to swim than to walk. Walking now would be out of the question. The soles of his small feet were as red and raw as the rest of him, and yet no blood tainted the water. Tears ran from Chance's eyes into his mouth, indistinguishable from the taste of saltwater or blood, but he knew the child was in no pain. Eyes closed, limbs tucked in, the child stirred occasionally in half sleep. A small fist rose for a moment above the surface, coated with a pink, clinging sheen of water that did service in place of the skin that had been taken from him.

Chance inhaled and exhaled painfully. Something in his chest felt broken. He could not forget that this was the kind of thing that had driven him to the false ease of cynicism and contempt and the colder, more dangerous ease of indifference. Witnessing human cruelty had helped make him inhumanly cruel, forget his duty, and rebel against Patience.

The Mermaid watched him as he struggled with the human, unnecessary task of breathing. "Is it only choice that matters? Is power the only thing that makes someone real to you? Is that the only way you can see them?"

"No," Chance whispered. "He mattered to Galina . . . to you. I can see that."

"*Love* matters," she said with a bitterness that complicated her words, as if the fact did not bring her pleasure but pain.

He did not contradict her; he did not dare. He was not sure what lesson she thought she was teaching him, but he was terribly afraid of appearing to fail.

She stayed stern a few moments longer, sighed, and spoke further. "A friend of mine was hired to be his nurse. She was with him so much that some people thought she was his mother, and I believe Galina preferred it that way. I don't understand why. Did she hate him because he was her husband's son or because he wasn't? But she called him by her husband's name. She called him Fyodor."

"Fyodor," Chance repeated in acknowledgment. He spoke silently to the child. *You are my last guide. Will you come with me?*

He waited, straining to sense the reply. There was the bewilderment of one who had been in the world too briefly to understand it, but also relief and acceptance that what had been done was done and nothing worse could follow. There was curiosity too, that after a life of knowing nothing but the whims and demands of others, a single, simple choice was finally being offered.

I will.

Chance reached out his hands, his human hands, but when he came close to the child he dissolved and dispersed them into indigo ink that surrounded and swaddled the small body in a coat of imperial hue. He carefully gathered the bundle to himself.

"Let us go back," he told the Mermaid.

Not much had changed on the narrow ring of beach. Julian had paused his breakdown long enough to sit up, hugging his knees and gazing with pathetic eyes at his former victims, who huddled together, still arguing over his fate.

"Come," Chance interrupted them. "It's time to go forward."

Baffled faces turned to him.

"Into the water," he clarified. "The inner waters." He waved a hand at the lagoon, cool blue and still except for the occasional stir from a gust of ocean breeze.

Their expressions turned from confusion to the vague regret of those who must leave an enjoyable but somewhat formal party.

"Well," said Danil. "It's been a kindness—no, really," he protested in answer to the puzzled rise of Chance's eyebrows. "What you've done here . . . you've helped us too."

"No one wants a walk-on role," Galina said. "Now we know why we died—it restores a little pride, a bit of self-esteem."

"Oh," Chance said. For a moment he could not think what to say. "I . . . thank you for allowing me to meet you and pay my respects. Thank you for guiding me."

He stepped forward abruptly and placed the bundle of indigo into Galina's arms; she took it in bemusement, instinctively holding it with motherly care.

"Take this with you," he said. "The water won't be so frightening when you're holding it."

She gave him a nod of gratitude, still uncertain but trusting.

Niko and Danil both approached the Mermaid to carry her over the sand to the other shore. They paused and looked at each other with hesitation, challenge, and hurt, but the Mermaid simply lowered her head and held out her hands to both of them. Her arms went around their necks, and their arms went around her back, one above the other in truce for the few steps to the waterline. They put her in the water gently, and she quickly pushed off with her hands and swam away. With one quick farewell glance to Chance, they too waded in and let the water take them. Xandre looked over his shoulder once and followed, and Galina went last, stepping carefully in with the bundle held safe against her heart.

The sky was as clear as the water and the completing curve of the ring reef girdled the lagoon well before the horizon's bounds, and yet the six faded from sight like dreams, shades, and memories.

Julian started forward. Chance let his hand fall heavy on the man's shoulder. "Not you."

"B-but I have to finish it," he stuttered.

Chance gave him a long, steady look. "Finish what?"

For a moment Julian forgot his fear and disorientation. "There's a logic to this. It's from a lovely little ritual from Vyerland concerning a list of special gifts for life rituals. A blanket at birth. A belt and breeches when a boy becomes a man. Guild bands on the wrists mark your apprenticeship; boots are made for the first journey. A heart-shaped pendant is a first-love token; a wife is given a carrying sling for her firstborn. And finally an ivy wreath crowns your corpse when you're dead."

A coldness grew and spread as he spoke; the waves hushed, the sun dimmed, the sands changed once more to desert and the skies to night and starlight. Chance let go of his labyrinth and its dear echoes as he listened to the other man relate his bungled attempts at pattern-weaving. When Julian's words ran out, he stood staring hopefully, peering through the faint dawn light glowing like distant fire on the edge of the eastern horizon.

"Elegant," Chance said, breaking the deep, dreadful silence. "Mere body parts have no meaning, but work, passion, love, and loss—those mean a great deal. How powerful to take a dancer's feet, a thief's hands, a lover's manhood, a husband's heart, a mother's womb, and a child's skin. How appropriate to build a life rather than a mere body. A well-crafted ritual, if accidental, and now you want to finish it. How?"

Julian spoke in a frantic, panting whisper, as if he feared he might give way to gibbering panic at any moment. "The crown. It lacks only the crown. That's how it will happen. The—the other one will enter through my mind, inhabit my body, and make it immortal. I have to—I have to give up my head."

Chance regarded the man with amazement. "And how do you propose to do that?"

Julian's hands twitched toward him in a helpless motion. He tried to say something but kept silent.

"You expect me to kill you?" Chance guessed.

"Send me where the rest went," Julian pleaded. "That should do it."

"The rest died long before you came here. Those you met in my labyrinth were shadows and echoes. *This*," said Chance, digging his heel into the soft desert sand, "is real."

"Then—then kill me! Yes! That should do it! I should die before becoming immortal. It makes perfect sense!"

Chance shook his head in pity. "More than you realize, and yet not so. I do not have the authority to kill you, as much as I would like to."

He turned away and started walking toward the slowly growing light at the line of land and sky.

"Wait! Wait! If this is real . . . you can't leave me to die in the desert!"

"Why not?" Chance asked calmly without turning back or slowing down.

"It has to be done properly!"

"Not by me." He stopped short and looked more closely at the dawn. "Not by me," he said again, turning around to face Julian.

They moved like slow lightning or a groundling star, the sword plowing a line of flame in the sand behind them. Julian barely had time to realize that the stunned expression on Chance's face was not for him, barely had time to start to turn around, and then the blade and flame were at his neck and all was asunder, dry bones and tattered clothes flung to the sand. It was quick, carried out with the skill of an executioner accustomed to taking life with Time instead of edged metal.

"It is done," they declared without sorrow, without anger. "It is accomplished."

"You killed him," Chance said, voice hushed in wonder. "I didn't—"

The angel looked at him. It was a look that promised no explanation, no apology. Chance met the look and nodded with all the deference of a junior to a senior.

"Thank you, Uriel," was all he said.

Uriel inclined their head. All around, the horizon blazed with a light that no longer resembled dawn. The angel stooped, took up the smooth, empty skull that had belonged to a living man, and held it out to Chance. "Are you ready?"

Somber, Chance replied, "Now I am."

He knew where to go. He did not take the hollow skull with him. He did not have to.

CHAPTER TWENTY-FOUR

Chance hesitated at the fringes, made cautious by experience, but he shrugged the Trickster essence around him like a cloak and proceeded.

The roof was vaulted timber with winged creatures—angels—carved into the beams that arched overhead. The floor was cold stone, dark and light, but on this occasion a labyrinth coiled thereon like a sleeping serpent. There were pillars, also of stone, which were like yet another maze, deceptively straightforward but bewildering in the quantity and sameness of arches and columns. The stone of the pillars glittered faintly; starlight from some other universe was shining through them.

There was a throne. The throne was . . .

. . . occupied.

Chance walked slowly to stand before the throne, taking it all in with a slow, sweeping glance that ended with a calm, forthright look into the eyes of his nemesis. "I see."

He had never liked the practice of having a junior. It was

common enough with the Lords of Misrule, who liked nothing better than to pinch off bits of their essence and send them, sentient and eager, to make fresh mischief with their new-bright imaginations. It was expected of the more senior of their kind, a way to diversify the tapestry of possibilities with a slight change of thread color here and there. Chance had not wanted it, and he had not done it, but it had been done to him. There he was, wearing that old, familiar shadow, robed in regal white linen—and yet . . . so different. It was not simply the fact that Chance was still clad in the Trickster's shadow, the old man's peasant form. It was in the other's frown, the slight curl of his lip, the cold pride in his eyes. It was fascinating, like looking at a picture of a former time. The superior sneer faltered as the other detected Chance's thoughts, which were filled with the quiet assurance of primacy and dominance.

"I, *your* junior?" he spat.

"Who came from whom?" Chance replied.

There could be no truthful rebuttal to that. He, Chance, was the core, the origin, the one who remembered what it had felt like when Patience had picked out a portion of his being, raveled it up, and sent him off without it to be born. The lesser one knew it even if he would not admit it, even if he wore the same shadow and crafted the same hall and sat on the throne that Chance had never liked. It showed in his bluster, his shallow villainy, his limited and two-dimensional view.

Chance had never thought to ask what had become of what had been taken out of him. He could not come up with a reason for his obliviousness, but he felt, perhaps selfishly, that ignorance had been preferable.

"Why?" he asked, raising his voice in anger. "Why this behavior, this unnecessary evil?"

His junior grimaced. "Evil? You insult me. Mere evil is tedious, but the missteps that lead to tragedy—*those* are worthy of note. It's the unconscious villainy of well-meaning people that interests me. But I don't need to tell you about that, do I, Chance? Or should I call you Yao?"

Chance blinked, incredulous. "Are you actually blaming Patience?"

"Who else but she, who made me as I am?"

"She made us all as we are," Chance stated, unmoved. "Why this conscious villainy on your part? What is your reason?"

"Why bother to ask? You know how it felt, being me not so long ago. The trials of humanity do not matter to such as you and I. I wanted to get your attention. I believe I have succeeded in that. It is true that I might have gotten some use out of the man, but he was a poor alternative for what would have been best—what *is* best."

The rogue undying one stood and took a swift single step from the throne's dais to stand before Chance. "So much was taken from you, kept from you for so long. Accept me again. Imagine it: fully human, fully undying, unfettered by duty. We could conquer worlds beyond both space and time. Nothing could stop us."

"Accept you? After all this?"

"*All this* is nothing more than what you could have done," the other said.

"Could is not would. I will not accept you. You are something beyond me now. What good or ill you have done is yours, not mine. You have made your own path."

"Be careful, Yao," said the junior, and he smiled with satisfaction when Chance winced slightly at the second use of his human name. "Terrible things happen when parents reject their offspring."

Chance recovered and smiled. "Really? Shouldn't you be saying that to Patience?"

It was the other's turn to twitch.

"You are afraid of her," Chance stated with satisfaction. "You have been trying to hide from her from the beginning."

A feeling of excitement began to build in him like the tingle in the air before a lightning strike. Stripping away his disguise, he gathered the Trickster's substance and collected it in cupped palms. When he clenched his fists, it squeezed through his fingers like a living shadow, flowing over and around his hands and stopping at his wrists like thin, close-fitting gloves. They stood facing each other, mirrored twins save for the white peasant cotton and the white chief's linen, and between them Chance's outstretched hands as black as if dipped in ink.

"Come see her now," he said and seized his doppelgänger.

There was no time for elegance, only brute force, raw instinct, and speed. He tore a hole in the crafted world and tumbled through. The other had frozen, shocked by the impossibility of being seized by one of near-identical essence, but soon he was desperately striving to pull free. Chance kept his grip strong, knowing the transition would take no more than a millisecond.

They flashed into sight midair above a busy street in the City. As they struggled, they shifted in a glitter of prismatic light, too fast for most human eyes to notice. One or two, blinking and shaking their heads, surely convinced themselves that they saw the sparkle of an impending migraine. There were two, however, who saw them clearly. Professor Malveaux reacted with fear and shock, unable to understand, much less believe, what was before him. The woman who wore Miranda's face knew well what she was seeing. The sound of the impact came soon after.

No need to look, Chance thought. There was nothing in him, human or undying, that wanted to see Miranda lying in the road, lifeless. It was done, it was over; he had failed to protect her.

No. It begins here.

With the searing roar of igniting air, Patience manifested, invisible to human sight, overwhelming to undying senses, and terrifying beyond anything Chance had ever experienced. He saw a glimpse of her before he was forced to look away, reminded of a time when he was a small human boy and had done something that had driven his mother beyond mere anger to fury.

This was far worse. Patience blasted them both out of the City and into high open air with a speed and force beyond nature. She was silver cloud and sheet lightning wrapped around them and carrying them to the limit of the sky. She could not be appeased or reasoned with. Submission was the only possible response. Chance opened his hands and let go, unable to do more than try to protect his own integrity as he spun helplessly. He felt the other one disintegrate all around him, felt Patience whirl around and through him like a fine net filtering glass fragments from clear water. The awful buffeting gradually eased as he fell into the eye of her hurricane.

Daring another glimpse, he saw her towering above him, a massive, intimidating figure coldly assessing the debris in her hands. She took the shattered bits and ground them to fine, colorless sand between her fingers until they were nothing more than tiny sparks of translucent fire. Then she threw a handful at Chance. He flinched, a human reflex, but the undying matter only swirled around him, coalesced, and disappeared into his body. The other handful she flung into the wind, where it was carried to earth and to water.

"Dust to dust," she said. "And I am air and dust and water. I am Earth, the Eldest and Firstborn of all that walks here. I make my children, I destroy them, and I remake them again."

CHAPTER TWENTY-FIVE

The tumult subsided, and Patience sighed, but the moment of regret, if regret it was, was brief. "There is more to do, Chance. Miranda—"

"—is dead," Chance concluded, deciding to accept it as quickly as possible. He did not feel shocked or grief-stricken but reproachful that Patience had failed him.

Patience shook her head and smiled. "This pain that I bear for her tells me otherwise. Go to her. The angels are with her."

Too stunned to think, he turned away in automatic obedience, but something—perhaps jealousy, perhaps pride—made him turn back. "Miranda's pain—give it to me."

For the first time in his existence, he saw Patience surprised. "Why? Still seeking punishment after all this?"

"You should know better," he chided her. "You're right. What she's seen and endured is all because of us, but if someone is to bear her pain, let it be another human. Anything else would be cheating."

Patience stared at him. "My child," she murmured. "This

grand gesture is more than a mere token. Would you take her pain? Would you take her death?"

"Yes," Chance replied.

They had drifted from upper air to the gray between worlds, a transition as smooth as only Patience could accomplish. She faced him, eye to eye, of equal stature. She pressed her lips together in an almost-smile and nodded approvingly. "It is your right." She extended her hand. "Take."

He touched her hand and nearly screamed. It had that same electric surge and flow as undying essence, but instead of life, it was a burn of consuming agony creeping over and into his skin.

He knew what it was to be human. He had endured stomachaches, experienced the discomfort of a full bladder, heard the creak and crack of overworked joints, and felt the skitter of a heart surprised by fear or love. And yet inhabiting his undying form made all those things mere memory, the memory of bits of bone and meat strung inelegantly together. The only thing that never faded was the sensation of skin. Skin touched the outside world and maintained the inner being. It was the boundary that defined the self. It was the only place where Chance, human and undying, could keep the pain.

His hand fell away from hers, but not before he noted that there was more pain in her reservoirs, an ocean's worth to the small handful he had drawn.

"Be careful," she told him. She was drifting away from him, trailing tatters of fog. The solid gray was turning to shreds under the weight of a new reality that was full of harsh light and hard edges. It was disorienting and frightening, enough to make him close his eyes. He had never encountered anything stronger than Patience.

Except the angels.

Some angels. Sometimes. He had never truly understood them, and they had never felt the need to explain themselves. It had not been Patience who had called him out of the depths of his human dreams at midnight to walk as undying through a changeable past. It had been the angels, and he still did not know why.

He opened his eyes.

A sphere of unnatural stillness centered on a motionless figure in a bed—Miranda. Uriel was there, bending their imposing presence to the limits of the small, surgically white room. There was another angel facing Uriel, identical in their terrifying utter reality, identical in the sword held drawn but at rest.

"You?" Chance gasped. He kept cautiously still, knowing himself overmatched.

"Yes. Us," the angel said simply. "Uriel could keep her safe while she was in your world. Beyond that, the usual rules apply."

"What rules?" Chance demanded. "Why should you want her to die? There have been more than enough deaths. What use is she to you?"

"The question is what use she will be to *you*. You were given the potential for immortality, and she may help you reach that potential, as Patience well knows."

"They fear being supplanted so very much," Uriel murmured to Chance, glancing briefly at the other angel.

"We have reason. It is unprecedented. Unplanned," the

276 • KAREN LORD

adversary replied to Uriel with a frown so mild they might have been disagreeing on the likelihood of rain. "We have had enough trouble with humans without encouraging more of this experimental behavior."

"They speak as if Heaven's borders were finite," Uriel said with a sigh, "and as if its hierarchies were set in stone."

"Or as if we had a place and a role and a reason for being," came the adversary's cool rebuttal. "We will not let anyone usurp us."

The debate was delivered with the boredom of familiarity, age-old positions casually stated and no resolution in sight. Chance shut them out. He could not oppose them—he had no power for that—but he would do what he could. He came close to the bed and looked at Miranda, rested his hand lightly against her bruised cheek and listened with all his senses for her breathing. He began to speak, not as witness before the angels nor even to convince himself, but for any part of Miranda that might still be awake and able to understand.

"Did the angels tell you that it is your destiny to die? Perhaps, but you died once already today, didn't you? Miranda, what they won't tell you is that humans are not only permitted but encouraged to change destiny."

He moved his thumb gently along her scraped chin and rested it below the curve of her bloodied lower lip. The half-clotted blood sparked in mute, instinctive reaction to his touch. He did not dare smile before the angels—he could not hope for triumph from such a fragile sign—but he let light tendrils of deepest blue leak forth from his fingers to tease and stir the sparks to a stronger kindling. He continued to speak idly, communicating with and without words.

"You said yes to Patience, but I must warn you: when we say yes to her, we agree to more than we realize. Look at yourself. You are human . . . and more. We began on opposite banks, and here we meet."

A tiny drop of fluid coalesced from the traces on her blood-smeared skin, and stretched thin and translucent like vapor. Chance gazed at it in delight as it moved toward him in vague, curious yearning, but he quickly hid it under the shadow of his hand. Patience had left no careless debris, no accidental trace to seed a new undying. She would always follow the rules. This was a new awakening. Perhaps it was a virtue of the flesh, that same stardust from which Patience had first gathered her sentience, but it was neither a subordinate nor a distributary of the Eldest. It was entirely its own . . . and yet was it not inevitable to expect some powerful effect when one considered how often humans became irrevocably dream-touched by the mere shadow-borrowing of a junior undying?

"Say yes again. If you choose to live, I choose to be with you in life and in death. What that means for such as us, what dangerous precedents will be set, only Patience and the angels can guess."

He could think of nothing more to say or do, so he withdrew his hand and turned to face the angels again. The walls and ceiling of the room had vanished, and both stood to their full height, swords ready and faces inscrutable, regarding the rise and fall of Miranda's shallow breathing.

"It is finished," declared Uriel once more.

"Indeed?" the other questioned, fixing Chance with a stare that was as dangerous as any flame-edged blade. "We will see."

They both departed with a speed and power that twisted perception and reality. Chance struggled reflexively against the current of their wake, but he eventually caught himself and relaxed into the flow, letting it pull him from Miranda's side. He had done all that he could in that place and time, and the present—the bright, alive, solid present, now certain as any completed duty—was waiting for him to return.

When he arrived in the village, he was not surprised to find that the first angel had reappeared to meet him once again at the well.

"Well?" he demanded. He was not exactly angry, but he felt a greater energy and a stronger emotion that he could not identify.

The angel ignored his belligerence and greeted him with courtesy. "Hail to thee, begotten son of Earth. I see you are more awake than previously."

Chance inclined his head, acknowledging both the salutation and the observation. "Are you satisfied? Have events unfolded as you anticipated?"

Cryptic as ever, the angel gave him truth rather than explanations. "So be it," they confirmed. "So it was, so it is, so it will be."

They vanished. Chance mused that it was the closest thing to a proper farewell that he had ever heard from any angel.

CHAPTER TWENTY-SIX

"I'm here too," said a quiet, amused voice.

It was the Trickster. In the darkness his typically sardonic look appeared softer, closer to something like pride. Chance gave him a small smile. Raising his hands, he cupped them into a bowl and prepared to collect the Trickster essence that had served him so well in his task. "Let me—"

The Trickster shook his head. "No. Keep it. I don't miss it now."

Chance looked at him and realized argument would be useless. "Very well, but you can at least accept *this*."

He did what he had never done willingly before and pulled a thread of himself from the core of his being. He did not have the spider's skill to spin it as neatly as the Trickster could, but he remembered the blaze of a fire-star and the power of a lightning strike, and he wove his brother a banner of blue light and pale fire.

"Take it," he said, extending it to the Trickster. "If a trace of you is to remain with me, then take this trace of me into yourself. Now, if you wish, you can move freely among the undying without depending on your humanity as mask and shield. No undying one other than Patience will ever be able to recognize you as what you once were."

The Trickster captured the stream as it flowed out of Chance and tangled his hands in it, not so much holding it as allowing it to hold him. He glanced up once, the glitter in his eyes more liquid than usual, and returned to staring at the gift.

Now we are brothers in truth, Chance meant to say, but he too stayed silent and merely watched as the Trickster breathed in deeply, absorbing the colors. When he moved, the starlight glanced off his skin with a new muted iridescence, blue over black.

At last he spoke with warm affection in his tone. "Go home, Chance."

Chance went down the road to the old family house, the place his grandfather had built, the place where his mother had grown up. The village was deep asleep at this hour with only the occasional barking dog or restless yard-fowl to punctuate the relentless chirp of the tree frogs and crickets. He could look ahead with undying senses and be certain of his welcome, but instead he chose to let the indigo tint slowly leach from his skin with each step closer to his gate. It was the man Yao who lifted the latch on the gate with a light *clack* and pushed it open. It was with human eyes that he saw that the three steps of the veranda were occupied. Paama was sitting there, her form relaxed and unworried, propping her chin sleepily on her fist.

She looked up as he approached and shifted aside so he could pass, but instead he sat beside her and gazed up at the stars shining in the spaces between the leaves of the trees. The details of what had happened at midnight and beyond were already beginning to fade and blur, but he kept the emotions: relief, gratitude, and a strong appreciation for his family.

"I love you, Maa," he said.

Unexpectedly, Paama laughed. "What does love feel like to you?" she wondered.

Yao sighed, but he was smiling too. "This will be hard to explain."

"You can tell me anything," she reminded him.

He eyed her in the dim light. Her face, as always, gave nothing away. "Very well. I can feel the spaces where the threads will go, the threads that will weave your life and mine together. If I haven't lived it yet, it feels like a lack, as if I'm missing something very important, missing someone who's very close. Every encounter we have takes away the space that makes me miss you and replaces it with a cord that links me to you and you to me. Loving you when I haven't yet lived our times together feels yearning and unfinished. Loving you with all our moments accomplished feels sweet, strong, and complete."

"When you put it like that," said Paama, her eyes shining with tears and pride, "why would anyone fear death?"

"Certainly not I, Mother," he whispered fondly, nudging her shoulder with his.

She sighed as she patted him on the arm. "I was worried about you. I should have known better. Now go to bed. It's late."

He squeezed a quick hug around her shoulders, got up, and

went inside. Just past the threshold he paused, shook his head, and laughed a little at his own forgetfulness. He spoke over his shoulder.

"We'll talk in the morning, Maa. I have a journey in mind for you. The last thread has been woven, and it's time you met Miranda."

She turned her head suddenly to face him, eyes wide in mock excitement. "No more vagueness? I will find out who she is? You will tell me how you first met?"

Chance nodded. "I will tell you how I first met her: years ago, in the City, sitting on a bench in the shade. And after that, since you know me so well, I will tell you the *other* story . . . about how she first met me."

I n the years that followed her return from the labyrinth and from death, Miranda recovered and readjusted. Life in the real world did not mirror the labyrinth experience, but Patience had known or guessed well enough for the final outcome to be quite similar. With Khabir's support, Miranda studied and worked hard to meet and surpass his challenge to change the City. She became an advocate for the rights of non-Freemen and gained such a reputation that two benevolent trusts appointed her as their special counsel. Her mother was proud of her at last, and though it did not fully mend their relationship, it allowed her to visit home without the bitter sense of being seen as an apostate.

Kieran came to terms with his new responsibilities and, with Miranda's blessing and Priya's help, turned the upper floors of the town house into a hostel for transient youth. Fae was distant, always traveling, often studying, and Miranda might easily have lost track of her except for family gossip . . . and that memory of a flirtatious prince with far too much worldly and otherworldly power. If he approached her cousin, if he abused his power, Miranda promised she would find her own way to deal with him.

Throughout it all, Miranda remembered. She remembered the Mermaid . . . no . . . the Dancer. She remembered the wrenching grief of watching Niko and Marinel, and the searing shame when she silently stood by as Chance and Ajit interrogated Xandre's grandmother. Miranda could do nothing for the dead and departed, but she wondered about the grandmother. She investigated and eventually found out where the old woman lived. A few more months passed before she found the courage to visit her. The woman's relatives, though absent, were taking care of her well. The town house apartment was comfortable with a housekeeper to keep things in order and a lovely sea view from the back rooms. She was installed on an upper floor, something Miranda at first found strange, but there *was* a stair lift for emergencies that was kept firmly locked into position on the lower floor because, as the housekeeper cheerfully put it, sometimes Mistress Joy's wandering mind set her feet to wandering as well.

Perhaps it was one of her good days, but she was far more alert than Miranda had dared hope. She almost recognized Miranda in spite of the scars and the cane, even though they had never been formally introduced.

"It is hard, not remembering," she confided. "Anything

might have happened to me. Perhaps I had a hard life. Perhaps someone was cruel to me yesterday. A good memory is the only thing that keeps the past where it is, and without that, anything might have happened. But I think it might not have been so bad. I think I was happy. I feel it. You know I had a son?"

Miranda nodded.

"I am sure he is dead. Do you know . . . is it possible . . . that someone killed him?"

Miranda swallowed but could not find the will to open her mouth and speak the words.

"You would imagine that having a murdered son in one's past would be distressing, but I do not remember. In a way that makes my son still alive, potentially alive. Memory is the only thing that makes it so, and I do not remember him dying. Anyway, we all die eventually."

Miranda murmured a polite agreement.

"But then I wonder if I had a son. You know what they say in my country? They say that if a willful woman cannot control herself, she must take that rebel self and birth a boy out of it. Then she must raise him and tame him before he destroys her life. Did I have a son, or was I a willful woman birthing excuses for my actions? I do not remember. Did my son die because of me? Was that the reason he was born? Heh . . . hear me talk foolishness. We are all born to die."

Miranda noted that this was indeed the case.

"I can see the blue of the sea and the sky through the window. I can feel the breeze on my face and smell the salt it brings. Sometimes, when it is a very good day, they will put a little honey liquor in my tea, strong enough and sweet enough to wake up my taste buds. There is little to complain about. Soon I will be dead. I dream of it. One day I will dream myself awake again. It scares me—you are shocked? You think an old thing like myself should embrace death? It is not the thought of death that troubles me. It's remembering. If I dream myself awake into a place where my memory never fails me and my past is nailed down firm with all its twists and turns, how will I be able to escape it? It will be finished. No maybes. Everyone dead, everything finished and nailed down."

She was silent for a while. Slowly she began to frown, then laugh. "Heh-heh. I had *two* sons. Two, not one. But *someone* died." She looked worried. "Who was it?"

Miranda left the town house with slow steps, deep in her own thoughts. She absently declined the housekeeper's help and immediately embarrassed herself by stumbling on the threshold. Gripping the doorframe with her free hand, she righted herself before the housekeeper had time to become solicitous, and gave her a firm farewell. Once the door closed, she walked a few steps away from the eye of the nearest window and its twitching, curtained lid and sat down on a tree-shaded bench with a grateful sigh, resting her forehead on the smooth handle of her cane.

After a little while she raised her head and saw him standing on the sidewalk across the road, distinctive in his country clothes of pale cotton and his sandaled feet. Immediately she smiled. She had been wondering for a long time how and when she would meet Chance as human, and although a shaded avenue in one of the City's better districts was a far more mundane location than her imagination had dreamed, there was still a kind of magic to how he stood there, looking out of place and at home all at once.

He crossed the street and came toward her. The leaves overhead shifted in the breeze and dappled his skin with shadow and sun . . . but then she blinked and saw instead indigo chasing ivory with an excitement and nervousness that contrasted with the calmness of his features. By the time he sat beside her, resting his hands neatly over the curves of his knees, he had regained control and was uniformly pale of skin, squinting as a patch of sunlight touched his eyes, entirely human.

She skipped greeting and courtesy. "I thought I would have an advantage over you, meeting you in my world and time, but it seems that you know me still."

He turned to her and smiled, his face familiar and yet new in its unexpected youthfulness. "Time and space are never strange for us, and you are one of us now. Let us say . . . we have always known each other."

She raised her right hand slightly, keeping it sheltered from broader view between their bodies. With a slight exhale like a faint sigh of relief, she stretched her fingers and strummed the empty air. A faint smoke of coiling umber trickled from her fingertips and played shyly in the space between them. Chance watched with a proud, polite smile.

"That's it," Miranda said. "That's all. I thought there would be more. What can I do with this? What am I meant to do?"

He took a moment to be silent, respectful of her query and her confusion, before replying, "Perhaps you are not meant to do anything. Perhaps your only task is to be."

She said nothing, but her gaze swept in an arc that encompassed the tyranny of the cane and the dancing freedom of her spirit's essence.

Chance nodded. "Both. Power and vulnerability. Both." He uncurled a hand and extended wisps of dark blue, weaving them expertly among her wavering threads of dark, dusty gold. "This is true for everyone. None of us is alone in this."

"Patience—isn't she alone? Who can match her? She *must* be lonely."

"She might have been a little at first, but now less and less, I believe," he said. "She has created many threads to weave a larger and more colorful tapestry, and now she includes borrowed lines."

"Is that what I am? New yarn, sourced from beyond to improve the weft?"

"Or a new instrument for an old song, or a path to a different destination?" he countered almost jovially. "There is no certainty; there are no answers. And I suspect there will also be no risk of boredom."

In spite of his attempt to speak lightly, her face grew more solemn. "What of—what about the other one? That part of you . . . ?"

"Resolved." he replied. "Resolved in my future so that in this present I may at last be fully myself. *You* know."

A part of her, that new part that saw time and existence very differently, did know, but there were still no words in her human brain to begin to explain it. "And the angels?" she asked instead.

"They watch, as always," he said.

If both the query and the reply were spoken softly with a hint of fear, who could blame them? Immortal Chance and Miranda might be, experimental without doubt, but invulnerable? Never.

She looked away and said with gentle reproach, "I expected to see you and Ajit sooner. What kept you?"

He tried to answer, but she began to laugh. The floating trails of amber thinned and vanished as her focus and control disintegrated. He smiled, realizing he was being teased. "It wasn't time. You had a lot to do."

"I did," she said proudly. "Perhaps I don't know yet how to be anything more than human, but I'm being the best human I can be. Would you like to see what I've been doing?"

His eyes widened. He was still young, still awakening, still human, and he could still be surprised. "Yes."

Miranda took him to her office and residence at Midhaven, a place located three hours' drive from the City. The journey was comfortable—Khabir in his stubborn generosity kept a car and driver at her disposal—and there was plenty of time to explain on the way.

"When I was in the rehabilitation center in Delma, I had a lot of time to think about people and cities and brokenness. Badly broken bones never heal perfectly, and neither do broken societies. Many people have tried so hard to heal the City, to change it. I wanted to do something different. I work with groups who want to build a community without external walls and internal barriers, a community that can do everything the City will not."

"Is this an attempt at a heavenly city?" Chance inquired with gentle skepticism.

Miranda blinked, not expecting what felt like a sneer from Chance, but in the pause she considered swiftly, acknowledged the point, and smiled. "We are not angels. Competition. Choice. Some people want walls, and that's part of their strength and their vulnerability. In Midhaven we offer another way."

"This is ambitious," he said, still cautious.

She nodded. "It is. Fortunately, according to some, I may have plenty of time to see it unfold."

The landscape began to change from dry, open land to clusters of dwellings and pools of unexpectedly green parkland. Miranda continued her commentary. "There is an underground lake beneath all this. We have wells feeding the oases, and only temporary houses are allowed out here. We still have to improve transportation, but that's coming."

Chance was looking ahead. "The skyline is very low," he noted.

"Early days," Miranda said. "Besides, we build below more than above. It's best to be out of the noonday sun. Khabir says I'm making a crepuscular community—by which he means we're active around dawn and dusk with two sleeps in between. But the nights are pretty vibrant too."

The road dipped into a tunnel as Miranda explained that the rudimentary grid of city streets for central Midhaven was, like so many working spaces, mostly underground. Minutes later they were at her door. The large room inside was illuminated by sunlight from light tubes and skylights, pale stone walls curved to a high, domed ceiling, and the air felt cool and dry. Miranda brought Chance to a chair in front of her desk and tried to play hostess, but as she spoke more about the agencies that had designed Midhaven and arranged for the first settlers, Chance kept her free of distraction by playing host himself. Still listening, he wandered around the place, unhindered by the flimsy and haphazard room dividers—cloth screens with more artistic than functional use. He found the tea, biscuits, cups, and saucers, and when he went to answer a ring at the door, it was with kettle in hand and an air of being familiar with the place.

"Hello, Miranda—oh. Good day."

Khabir stood on the threshold, briefcase in one hand and a bundle of envelopes in the other. He spoke his greeting politely enough, but there was a shadow of worry, a hint of puzzlement. It might have been mere suspicion, but his expression could also pass for the face of a man disturbed by the echo of a memory of a dream that had never happened. "Who's this? New secretary?"

"This is my . . ." Miranda paused in reflection, then grinned. "My companion."

"Companion?" Khabir repeated in a tone that asked a thousand silent inappropriate questions. He settled on the most innocent query. "So his job is to . . . ?"

"Accompany me," Miranda replied sweetly, not giving him any satisfaction.

"Good," Khabir said, cheerfully surrendering. He put the envelopes into Chance's free hand and took the seat in front of Miranda's desk. Chance placed the correspondence in Miranda's in tray, silently served them, and went to get another cup.

"You know, Miranda, I asked you to change the City, and instead you ran away to another place."

Miranda's laugh was both amused and slightly cynical. "Jealous? You could always move here. Plenty of room."

"What, and give up Freeman status?"

"See?" she said sadly. "You're taken in by the mystique of that title, even you. Let it go, Khabir. It's meaningless."

He shrugged, unoffended. "It's useful to both me and you for now. Anyway, joking aside, did you know that the transient population of the City has dropped by 45 percent at last estimate?"

"And you thought I wasn't changing the City," Miranda said with a smug look.

Khabir sputtered at her impertinence, then grimaced in surrender and laughed at himself. And then, with an unconsciousness that made Miranda frown and wince, he raised his half-empty cup toward Chance for a refill without even a glance in his direction. Chance quietly set down his cup, took up the teapot, and poured.

"This is excellent tea," Khabir complimented Miranda.

"I learned from my mother, who is a professional chef," Chance said.

Khabir looked startled at being addressed. Miranda smiled.

Chance took the tray with the empty teapot and his cup and went through the maze of room dividers to the kitchen.

Later, after the sound of conversation had moved to the entrance and was concluded by the sound of the closing door, Chance looked up from his newspaper to find Miranda hovering over him, her face tragic with remorse.

"I am so sorry for his behavior."

Chance stood up, folded the paper, and rested it on the kitchen table next to his teacup. "His behavior is his responsibility, not yours."

"But I didn't say anything to him."

"Well, he is a typical Freeman. A few words to him about me aren't going to change his attitude toward the next servant he sees," Chance reasoned.

Miranda flinched. "You are not a servant."

"I'm your companion, aren't I? To most Freemen that's a servant."

"Yes, but you are—"

"—meant to be here as your companion, and what people choose to think about that is not relevant." He lowered his voice and spoke with more seriousness. "We are not more or less than they are. We are different and rare, human and undying. Their expectations should not, *cannot* limit us."

She smiled and said, "Years from now, when sun and stress have weathered your human skin to a wiser mask, you will meet my younger self in another place. In memory of that younger Miranda and the patience you showed in dealing with her, I will not quarrel with you now. Stay under whatever name and on whatever terms please you."

Chance picked up his cup and raised it in toast. "Good. Let us observe and experiment and see what we are made of. To a hundred years, or a thousand, or whatever may be given."

Miranda curved her hand around an imaginary glass and touched it to his cup. "To us."